Twilight

Twilight
Dance with the Devil 7
By Megan Derr

Edited by Samantha M. Derr
Cover designed by Natasha Snow

Second Edition November 2019
Copyright © 2019 by Megan Derr
Printed in the United States of America

The Banished Knight

Desperate Times

"Damn it all, I just bought these."

"You mean *I* just bought them," Devlin said in the snotty tone he only used when he was in a truly foul mood and wanted company for his misery.

Neirin looked up from his charred and blood-spattered trousers, casting Devlin a look that held every bit of the ire he was feeling. "Shove off, Winterbourne, or I'll toss you right into that pile of ash and stomp on you. The trousers were bought with your coin because the pair they replaced was set on fire. *By you. While I was wearing them.* I think I'll throw you in that ash anyway."

"Someone is getting tetchy," Devlin drawled. "Lack of food? Lack of sleep?"

Refusing to dignify that by acknowledging it was said, Neirin bent to retrieve his poor sword, which looked the worse for wear after their fight with rogue wolves and a handful of particularly nasty trolls. Standing, he pulled a piece of cloth from an inner pocket of his jacket and tried to clean the worst of the mess from the blade. He frowned at the nicks and a scratch that no amount of buffing was going to save. Damn it.

He shoved the sword back in its sheath and tried to think of something else. Troyes growled sleepily beside him and rubbed his head along Neirin's thigh. Neirin stroked his scales, silently soothing him. "Food soon, I promise." He looked at Devlin. "Are we done here?"

"One should hope." Devlin threw out a hand to recall his runes, kissing the last as he dropped them into the bag in his jacket. "Let's be on our way. The sun is rising faster than any of us wants." He strode off across the yard, looping around the house rather than choosing to cut through it.

Once had certainly been enough. Neirin dragged himself after Devlin, fighting the exhaustion that washed over him but not quite managing to stifle a yawn. The carriage was where they'd left it, the horses waiting patiently... but there was no Barra or Midnight.

"Would it be so difficult for people to stay where I tell them just once?" Devlin grumbled.

"Oh, yes, because *you* did such a bang-up job of staying where you were told last month when we were dealing with that demon," Neirin said.

Devlin didn't bother to look at him as he replied with a few choice words regarding Neirin's parentage.

"You two are in fine form tonight," said a smooth, cheerful voice.

Neirin could practically see the unhappiness drain from Devlin's body as he turned and held fast to the figure that practically threw himself into Devlin's arms. Devlin kissed him softly and then drew back with a stern frown. "Where did you go?"

Midnight rolled his eyes. "We made one last sweep of the house and two more of the little terrors bolted into the woods. They're gone now. Barra stopped at a creek to wash the blood from his hands."

"Fat lot of good that did," Barra grumbled as he came out of the woods, clothes a bit askew and a leaf in his hair. He smiled when he saw them, laughing softly as he reached Neirin. He pulled a kerchief from his jacket pocket and reached up to wipe at Neirin's cheek. "Ash."

Neirin captured his chin and leaned down to kiss him, enjoying the smell of fresh leaves that clung to him and a faint tang that belonged wholly to his werewolf blood. He smiled as he drew back. "Shall we be on our way now that this little side trip is at an end?"

"Yes, we shall," Devlin groused and climbed into the carriage.

Barra lifted his eyes to the sky then slipped away to mount the driver's seat. Next to Neirin, Troyes shifted into his human form. He smoothed down his clothes then lifted his head in silent demand. Neirin gladly acquiesced and kissed him, the hot, metallic scent and taste of dragon surrounding him, mingling in his mouth with the lingering taste of Barra. If there was anything better than his dragon and his wolf, Neirin never wanted to know it.

Troyes nuzzled against him and slipped away to join Barra. "Wolf-elf kiss."

"Stop trying to be bossy." But even as he issued the reprimand Barra was leaning in to kiss him.

Smiling, Neirin unbuckled his sword and followed Midnight into the carriage and settled across from him and Devlin, setting his sword next to him on the seat. "Well that is certainly enough of that. I suppose there is little chance of dinner now."

"We'll muster up something," Midnight said with a smile. "I do not want the two of you cranky on through morning."

Devlin grumbled, but Neirin let the words wash over him, leaning back against the plush cushion of the carriage and closing his eyes. He was *tired.* They'd been on the road for a month, going here and there as they tracked down the rogue monsters of an alchemist who had lost his bloody mind.

And throughout the affair—actually starting a few days before it—he'd been plagued by a constant feeling of being watched. The prickle on the back of his neck had been there so long, he was almost growing used to it. Even now his fingers itched to try and rub it away.

He ignored it. Whatever was wrong would present itself eventually, and going out to find trouble was not something he cared to do. Well, not anymore. His days of guarding the border of Clan Pendragon territory were seventy-three years in the past.

Seventy-three years... yet he had scarcely aged a handful according to the mirror. Free of Pendragon lands, which always slowed aging a slight bit given how heavily steeped in magic it was, he should have begun to age more like a normal human. He still would have lived longer, but he was no sorcerer or witch to conceivably live hundreds of years. He had initially marked it down to proximity to Devlin and other nightwalkers. Barra's longevity was partly that, the rest accounted for by his elven blood. But for Neirin and Troyes, there was little explanation save that it was a residual effect from Pendragon.

It had never proven to be a problem, so he'd never pursued it and neither had the others. Tried not to think about the family that had lived and died without ever trying to contact him. The descendants who probably didn't know he existed. Did *anyone* remember him? He could think of one person, but if Avalon remembered Neirin at all, it was just as one more dusty, faded memory lost among a hundred thousand others.

"You seem particularly foul of mood this evening."

Neirin dragged his eyes open. "Yes, and you're so cheerful. We were meant to be home hours ago. I'm exhausted, hungry, and bloody damn tired of cleaning up other people's messes."

Devlin opened his mouth, and Neirin braced to hit him because that was exactly how this night was going—

"I think a good trip to the country would do all of us some good," Midnight cut in, voice as soft and sweet as ever. He was curled close against Devlin, their arms twined together, the brooding Mad Duke and his adoring draugr. They were the strangest pair Neirin had seen in all ninety-eight years of his life, but also one of the most beautiful in the strength and depth of their bond.

He would envy it, save that nothing could compare to having Troyes and Barra at his sides. Midnight and Devlin might be a beautiful pair, but Neirin was part of a beautiful three and that suited him far more.

Old memories filled his mind like faded paintings in a forgotten attic, but Neirin batted them away. Even before he had been banished, his daydreams had been only that: the foolish imaginings of a boy who fancied himself a man. His marriage had been arranged; his future laid out. Whatever he had truly wanted back then, it had already been out of his reach. He was much happier with his three than he ever would have been with four, be it daydream or arrangement.

Neirin drifted off to a tangle of memories and dreams, mouth pulled down and his brow deeply furrowed. Voices speaking in murmurs, occasionally saying his name, floated around him, comforting in their familiarity but not enough to help him escape the unhappy rest.

The jarring halt of the carriage did wake him, and Neirin jerked up and cast one hand toward his sword. Then comprehension fell and he sat back with a sigh. "Are we home?"

"Finally, yes," Devlin replied and swept out of the carriage as only a man so insufferably arrogant could. Neirin followed him, down to the dark street and up the wide steps of Devlin's townhome. Neirin's home for the past seventy-three years, when they weren't at Winterbourne Manor, anyway.

The smell of food washed over him as they entered, and he paused only long enough to discard his sword, coat, and jacket. Devlin was already seated when he arrived, and Neirin took his own seat, quickly followed by Barra on his right. Troyes, as usual, eschewed the dining room in favor of going straight to the kitchen. He'd eventually head up to the bedroom for Neirin and Barra to find him later.

"Where did the food come from?"

"I flew ahead and took care of it," Midnight said. "Not much available at this hour, but hopefully it's edible."

"It smells wonderful. Thank you." None of them said a word as they ate, not even Midnight, who merely sat there drinking from a cup made of dark green glass. When his plate was empty and his good mood nearly restored, Neirin pushed away from the table and rose. "I am to bed. I hope I do not see any of you again until late tomorrow."

Devlin grunted, not bothering to open his eyes or sit up from where he'd slumped back in his own seat.

Barra smiled and rose to follow Neirin, tangling their fingers together as they headed upstairs to their bedroom. Troyes was already fast asleep, sprawled out like a puddle of liquid metal on the floor at the foot of the bed.

Stripping, Neirin tossed the clothes in a pile with the rest of the wash and then climbed into bed. Barra followed him a moment later, and Neirin pulled him close. He mustered the energy for a kiss, murmured goodnight, and fell asleep breathing in Barra's woodsy scent.

He woke in the dark, gloomy, gray hours of earliest morning. Once upon a time, it would have been too early even for the lamp lighters.

But what had woken him? Barra was still fast asleep, warm and soft against his side. If he'd woken Neirin, there would have been no call for complaint. Sadly, that was not the case.

Thunder rumbled softly, but that wasn't likely to have been the culprit; he slept through raging storms all the time, much to the amusement and irritation of the others.

The prickling at the back of his neck was stronger than ever, an unsettled feeling strumming through him, making him want to lash out at the unknown threat. He gently extracted himself from Barra and slid near soundlessly from the bed.

A soft growl drew his attention to the window, where Troyes had pushed back the curtain to press against the glass—in dragon form, when he knew to be more careful when they were in London. Neirin joined him, pushing the curtain back further and resting his other hand on Troyes's head. "I don't see anything."

Troyes growled again, low and rolling, but beneath the displeasure was a hint of pain—anguish, in fact. Which could only mean one thing: he sensed clan. "Stay here." Troyes snarled at him. "Please," Neirin said. "I'd rather have you to protect me, you know that, but it's more important that you stay here to protect everyone else if someone from the clans has come to get rid of us once and for all. Even Devlin, as powerful as he is, won't be any match for the full weight of a knight following a kill order." Neirin moved away but turned back as Troyes whined. He knelt, hugged Troyes close, and kissed him behind one of his fanned ears. "I'll be all right, beloved. Take care of our wolf-elf and the other brats."

When Troyes growled in reluctant acquiescence, Neirin rose and went to get dressed.

He pulled on his boots, still caked with mud and gods alone knew what else after their fight the previous night. Shrugging into a coat, he headed downstairs. His sword was where he'd left it in the front hall, leaning against the table where Devlin seemed to have dropped everything in his pockets.

Buckling the sword in place, Neirin headed outside into the misty dark. The familiar, rarely pleasant smells of London washed over him, but laced through them was the unmistakable metallic tang of dragon. And the thick, spicy bite of power, heavy enough to coat his tongue and the back of his throat. Neirin's knees felt weak as the power washed over him, a familiar urge to kneel and bow his head jolting through him.

It *couldn't* be. He wasn't *allowed* to leave Pendragon lands, wasn't even capable of it for more than a few hours in a set span of time.

Neirin followed the feeling as it strengthened,

down the street and through the thickening mist to an empty lot where a building had recently burned down, the victim of gas and a careless owner. His breath caught as he reached the center of the lot, one hand falling reflexively to the hilt of his sword. The rest of the world was drowned out by a buzzing in his ears as he stared in disbelief.

More than seventy years had passed, but Prince Avalon had not changed a day. He was tall, slender, and beautiful in a way the normal world would label effeminate. His gold-toned brown skin was paler than Neirin recalled it being, and his dragon-amber eyes were dim with exhaustion, or maybe worry. The hair was longer, woven into a heavy braid that fell over his shoulder and stopped halfway down his chest. Even tired and unhappy, he remained breathtaking.

Tears fell down Neirin cheeks, and he wiped them furiously away before bowing low. "Your Highness."

"Sir Neirin," Avalon said softly, a lilt to his voice that hinted at languages and accents long lost to history. "It's been a long time. I am glad to see you doing well. Rise, please."

Neirin rose. "What are you doing here? You can't leave—"

"I can for a time, and I have a couple hours to spare yet," Avalon cut in. "I know I've no right to ask it of you, but I need help and I know not where else to turn."

"Help?" Neirin's mouth tightened. His back ached with remembered pain. Though time had worn his scars away significantly, traces of them would always be there. "I am banished, Your Highness, have been for several decades. What help could I possibly offer?"

"You've been gone," Avalon replied, bitterness and something that might have been desperation lacing his words. "There is much to say, but I will try to be as brief as possible: a Holy Pendragon has gone missing; I believe there are traitors in Pendragon and du Lac; my Steward has gone missing, likely the thief who stole away the pendragon; and he took several grimoires as well. I fear the ultimate goal is to get rid of me and shift the seat of power. I no longer know who to trust amongst my own people. You are the only person right now, in literally all of the world, to whom I felt I could turn for help. Not for me, I would never ask you to help *me.* But I am begging you to help me save a dragon."

The damnedest part of it was that Neirin would have helped Avalon. However much he tried to hate Avalon, it was because of him that Neirin had lived long enough for Devlin and the others to rescue him. Avalon was centuries old, must see Neirin as little more than a child no matter how old he grew, but he had always been kind and friendly to Neirin. Even when Neirin had broken rule after rule, defied so many of the constraints put upon him by clan life and the particularly rigid, old-fashioned mindset of Clan du Lac, Avalon had supported him as best he could.

"Maybe you and your dragons deserve to rot," said a cool, arrogant voice, and the lightning-buzz of wild witch magic jarred against the ancient power of Avalon and seemed to make the air crackle. Devlin appeared through the mist, dressed in dark blue that exactly matched Midnight's hair. "What in the buggering fuck are you doing here? Seeing you once was enough, and Neirin owes *nothing* to the likes of the bastard who saw him whipped damn near to death. If not for me, it would have been to death, and if you have come to make his life miserable again, I will show you what suffering means."

Avalon smiled, though it was tired and strained at the edges and never quite reached his eyes. "Yes, I recall your threats from our previous encounter. I have come to plead for his help because I am desperate, Your Grace. If there was anyone else to whom I could turn, I would leave him in peace." He turned back to Neirin. "I would. I know you've been happy, and that's all I ever wanted for you. If I did not fear for the dragons, I would not be here."

"Save them yourself," Devlin snapped, drawing close enough that Neirin was slightly behind him.

Neirin barely refrained from rolling his eyes. He had never been on the receiving end of Devlin's overprotective tendencies, as Devlin generally saw him as a partner in the protecting rather than a subject of fretting like he did Barra and Midnight. Neirin would like to say he was more reasonable than Devlin, but Midnight was not mistaken when he accused Neirin and Devlin of being far too alike.

Which meant he was most certainly not about to tolerate Devlin protecting him. He grabbed the sleeve of Devlin's jacket, yanked him back, and cast him a quelling look before turning back to Avalon. "I'll help for the sake of the dragons, Your Highness. But I—"

"We," Devlin snapped.

Neirin refused to acknowledge the relief that rushed through him. "We need more information—at the very least, a starting point."

He hadn't realized until Avalon abruptly relaxed just how tense he'd been. "Thank you. Words can never express my gratitude."

"Get on with it," Devlin said.

A brief smile flickered on Avalon's mouth as he

regarded Devlin, but he said only, "Two months ago Caliburn's latest mate produced three eggs. One of them is a Holy Pendragon. We were obviously quite excited."

Elation and sadness tangled in Neirin's chest. That *was* cause for excitement. Holy Pendragons were the ruling dragons. None was quite as powerful as Caliburn, Avalon's dragon and *the* Holy Pendragon, but their presence helped to strengthen the clans and share the power of Pendragon throughout the world. Only three others existed, unless things had changed in his absence, which was unlikely: in Germany, Egypt, and France. Often Holy Pendragons died not long after birth, if they managed to survive the shell, as someone strong enough to wield them must appear within the first few weeks. The clans constantly searched for a way to overcome that, to give Holy Pendragons the same leisure to match as other dragons, but thus far it had never been managed.

That a Holy Pendragon had been stolen... Someone must have devised a way to keep it alive, or thought they had, at any rate. Such experiments, and the arrogance that always came with them, had always been the provenance of a particular clan. "Do you think Mordred has anything to do with this?"

"That is certainly what everyone else thinks and the path they think we should pursue," Avalon replied, "but no, I do not. Mordred would gain nothing by it, for even if they managed to overcome the limitations of the Pendragons, their curse would prevent bonding. Why risk the wrath of the clans all over again for something they cannot overcome? Mordred was never this... crude, either. No, I think someone within Pendragon has betrayed us. Especially as my Steward vanished the same day we noticed the missing egg."

"Steward Linden?"

Avalon gave a short, sharp nod.

Neirin's mouth tightened. The worst thing about it was that he did not feel surprised. Linden was shrewd and hard-working, but he was also power-hungry and status-obsessed. The entire du Lac family was much the same, and the reason that clan had changed little over the centuries, the reason more people than Neirin had chafed and fought. "Where could they possibly go?"

"We tracked them as far as Canterbury, but after they departed from there we lost them."

"Canterbury is on the edge of old le Fay territory," Neirin replied. "Those lands have been abandoned for decades."

Avalon gave another terse nod. "But old power lingers, power that the right people could use to wrest power from Pendragon." Power that would only be taken by killing Avalon and Caliburn, but it was typical of Avalon not to mention that. He reached into the pocket of his old fashioned jacket and pulled out a small book bound in dark green leather. "All the notes I've gathered on the matter, little enough though it is. Linden and two others who vanished the same day as he, as well as their dragons, of course. Everything we know, including the last sighting of them in Canterbury."

He reached into another pocket and pulled out a larger book bound in black leather and stamped with a familiar crest: a dragon clutching a sword, surrounded by an intricate circle of braided runes. The crest of Clan Mordred. "Our notes on Mordred, from the months leading up to their exile and everything we've gleaned about them since. It may prove useful, whether they are involved or not. Last... if you will accept it, that is..." Avalon drew a deep breath and let it out slowly. "My Steward has betrayed me, which leaves me with no Steward and entirely too much power in the hands of a traitor. Until I find someone new to take up the post permanently, I need someone I trust to serve as Acting High Steward. The places you will be going, it would benefit you to have my power and authority. I would make you my Acting High Steward if you are willing."

"Go to hell," Devlin snapped before Neirin could reply, the words nearly drowned out by the thunder slowly drawing closer. "If you are trying to draw him back into the fold by asking him to play rescuing knight, you are even more pathetic than I already believed."

Neirin rested a hand on Devlin's forearm, holding it down when it was clear he was intending to reach for the runes secreted inside his jacket. He stared at Avalon, heart pounding in his ears. "You can't be serious."

"The steward is chosen by the prince and the prince alone," Avalon said, amber eyes still vibrant with color but filled with pain and fear. "All those I call friend and ally and clan are bathed in shadows of doubt. The person closest to me has stolen that which is most sacred to the clans and seeks to possess it for himself—at the cost of my life and those of many more within Pendragon, and the ramifications of those deaths will spread to all the others. How many times must I repeat that I do not ask this of you lightly?"

Neirin bowed his head, letting his hand fall from Devlin's arm. "I serve the dragons, Your Highness, and for them I will do anything."

"Thank you," Avalon replied softly. He pulled a necklace from beneath his clothes and removed it. In his palm rested a small charm in the shape of a sword. Neirin wasn't surprised to see that hadn't changed. With a whispered word and thrum of magic, the charm turned into a real sword, magic pouring off it strongly enough to make even Devlin twitchy.

The dragons were the true swords of Camelot, but there had always been an actual sword, too, a thing of magic and power not unlike Devlin's runes, the grimoires of the paranormal world, and other such talismans and tools. The Sword of the King, wielded by Avalon and whomever he declared High Steward of Clan Pendragon.

"Kneel," Avalon said softly, and when Neirin had done so, he drew the sword from its leather sheath and lightly touched the tip of the blade to each of Neirin's shoulders. "Sir Neirin du Lac, I place upon you this sacred duty and burden, to speak for the clans and act in my name until such time as the dragons dismiss you from service. The heart of the clans is your heart. The breath of the clans is your breath. The soul of the clans is your soul. As we draw upon your strength, so too shall you draw upon ours. As the clan lives, so too shall you. As the clan dies, so too shall you. Do you accept?"

"I accept this sacred duty and burden. My heart is your heart. My breath is your breath. My soul is your soul. Until the dragons declare otherwise, I vow myself to them and the will and power of the Holy Pendragon." The blade shimmered and white-hot pain seared through Neirin. He bit back a scream only by force of habit, but blood dripped down his chin where he'd bitten his lip.

The blade withdrew, and Neirin accepted the hand that Avalon offered. His touch crackled, the sensation running through Neirin like the one time he'd accidentally gotten caught in the path of one of Devlin's lightning spells. He stared at Avalon, loneliness and fear and longing rushing over him like a tide. Avalon. He could feel Avalon. "What have you done to me?"

"I am sorry," Avalon said. "The years and decades and centuries pass, and eventually times and people run together. I forget far more than I remember. You, though, I have always remembered. I have only ever wanted your happiness..." He reached up and wiped away the blood with a handkerchief and brushed the back of one hand down Neirin's cheek, smearing the tears that had resumed falling at some point. "I am sorry I must drag you into my unhappy matters and place upon you the burden of High Steward as well. I promise that I will set you free once more when I have the Holy Pendragon safely back and the traitors marked, if not dead." He leaned in and kissed Neirin's cheeks, then hesitated a moment before brushing a last, fleeting kiss to his lips. Power thrummed in his touch, a blessing as soft as a whisper and as strong as a storm. "Should you need me, simply call my name."

Neirin nodded, throat too raw and clogged with stones to work. He didn't want this. He'd left all this behind, and even if he'd stayed, so great and terrible a burden was never meant to have been his.

"I should be going, there is not much time left and I would reserve some of it should you require me," Avalon said. He sheathed his sword, then pressed it into Neirin's hands and stepped away. The memory of his touch burned, and the heavy sword seemed to burn where Neirin held it. Avalon's eyes swept the area, as though there was more to see than charred ruins and morning mist. "The world keeps changing. I wish I could see more of it. At least I get to see a little here and there. Farewell, dear Steward. Thank you again for taking up this burden. I wish you good fortune on your hunt." He faded into the mist, and the force of his presence was gone in the next breath.

"What in the buggering *fuck* is going on?" Devlin demanded. "Why the hell are you suddenly some bloody damned Steward? Is there no one else those dogmatic imbeciles can foist this task upon?"

Neirin gave a shaky laugh, his head aching with all the new power that had just been thrust upon him. "You know there isn't. You heard him just as well as I. At least I'll have you haranguing me throughout. We'll resolve the matter in no time."

Rather than looking mollified by the compliment, Devlin only looked more troubled. "I thought your precious prince never left Pendragon lands."

"Let's discuss this in the house," Neirin said, and they walked together in silence back to Devlin's townhouse. Soft rain began to fall, thunder and lightning rolling through the heavy clouds, adding an ominous note to the morning.

Once in the house, Neirin didn't get the chance to speak further as Troyes tackled him to the floor with a resounding growl.

His scales looked more silver than steel and held a rainbow shine that was definitely new. Neirin could feel the new power in him, the greater strength. It was breathtaking.

"What's going on?" Barra asked, a tremble in his

voice as he watched them stand. "Your eyes!" Barra stared."You have dragon eyes."

Neirin crossed the hall to where Barra lingered by the stairs, wrapped an arm around his waist, and hauled him in to kiss soundly, not stopping until he needed to draw proper breath. "We've been hired to solve a mystery and rescue a stolen dragon egg."

"The weight of those words is far too great for this early in the morning," Barra groused. His eyes narrowed as he stared at Neirin, something unhappy and suspicious in his eyes, but he only extracted himself from Neirin's embrace. "I'll go see about breakfast. Come on Troyes, we'll get you fed, too."

Troyes growled and after nuzzling against Neirin, followed Barra off to the kitchen.

"So tell me about your stupid prince who isn't supposed to leave clan lands."

"He *can't* leave Pendragon lands, literally," Neirin replied with a sigh. "It's a closely guarded secret, one that normally I could be killed for telling you." His mouth twisted, and he shared a look of sour amusement with Devlin before continuing. "All of the clans bear a curse, punishment for various transgressions. Once upon a time, Clan Pendragon, King Arthur himself and his descendants, let their power get the better of them. They turned greedy, reckless, began to take for granted the sacred gift bestowed upon them. King Arthur did not survive the fallout, and of his children, only the youngest, Prince Avalon, now remains. For his crimes, he is cursed with permanence. Like demons, he has power enough to control—or destroy—all the world if he so desires and is immortal, or near enough as to make no difference. But he cannot leave Pendragon lands for more than a handful of hours a decade. The exact number is known only to him. He risked more than you know to come beg for my help."

Devlin said nothing, but his brow was drawn in that way that said he was lost in thought. Some of Neirin's tension was greatly abated by knowing that Devlin stood with him, would help him. He'd never had a friend like Devlin back when he was part of the clans. Too odd, too defiant, too arrogant, they had declared him. Losing Devlin or Midnight or Barra would be as bad as losing Troyes.

Barra came bustling back into the hall, and at some point he'd gone upstairs to dress properly. "I've breakfast ready in the kitchen."

"Thank you, Barra," Devlin said and swept off in his imperious fashion.

"Are you all right?" Barra asked.

"No," Neirin said, "but that seldom stops any of us. What's wrong?"

Barra hesitated, looking unhappy.

"What?" Neirin pressed.

Barra looked at him, silent for a moment, then slowly said, "Someone else kissed you."

"Oh, that." Neirin shook his head. "It was a ceremonial thing, that's all." He stepped in close, cupped Barra's face between his hands, and kissed him softly. "I love you, wolf-elf."

Barra covered Neirin's hands with his own. "I love you, too. Come and eat breakfast." He held fast to one of Neirin's hands as they walked, but though the frown had vanished from his mouth, it lingered in his eyes and remained there throughout breakfast and as they packed for the trip to Canterbury.

Dragons

They were just about to head out when the doorbell rang. Devlin scowled.

Barra sighed and went to answer it, returning a moment later with a calling card he handed to Devlin. "There's a woman who says she has a case of dire urgency."

"I don't help every fool off the streets—"

"Devlin," Midnight interjected.

Devlin cast him a look but ungraciously conceded with a bitten out, "Fine."

Barra slipped away again and returned escorting a tall, handsome woman dressed in the glass of fashion but with her hair pulled back in a simple bun that lent a severe look to her demeanor. It was dark red, and her face was smattered with freckles, her skin a delicate, pale brown. "Your Grace, thank you for seeing me."

Devlin set the calling card aside and settled into the chair he'd only just vacated. Midnight was still reclining lazily against the large window directly across from the sitting area while Neirin, Troyes, and Barra stood by the cold fireplace. "Miss Shelley, I am informed you require my assistance, but I am curious how you come to know my name. I am not at public disposal. My services are for Lord Tamor and those he requests I assist."

Shelley looked around the room, skin flushing as

she took them all in, gloved hands clenched tightly in her lap. "Forgive my impertinence, Your Grace. I found your name in my father's records and a few discreet inquiries affirmed you were still in the business of solving mysteries. I was not aware you consulted privately. Nevertheless, I hope you will help me, as you once helped my grandfather."

"I recall no Shelley."

"No, Shelley is my married name. My maiden name was Black."

"Black," Devlin repeated slowly. "That is an old name, and it was not I who once assisted them. That would be my grandfather. But I recall the case. A grimoire was stolen from your grandfather's possession, and I believe used to cast quite a few nasty curses."

She nodded, voice barely more than a whisper, "Yes, and that grimoire along with several other books are gone again."

Devlin sneered. "I see your family does not learn from their mistakes."

"You know nothing," the woman snapped, tears filling her eyes. "They were locked away. My father recently died." She looked at her hands, tears falling down her face. "I was contacted by a buyer in America interested in the tomes. He wishes to remain anonymous with all except me but has been in correspondence to reassure me the books will be in safe hands."

"I presume the buyer was not so trustworthy?" Midnight asked gently.

"No, my buyer is quite trustworthy." She sighed and dragged her eyes up. "But my husband... someone came by the house while I was out and painted a believable story about being there to retrieve the books. My husband handed them over, convinced he was doing the right thing."

Devlin's frown deepened. "Why would he fall for such a tiresome trick?"

"Because my buyer is the demon lord Sable Brennus, and the man who came by used the surname Brennus and had paperwork aplenty to prove himself."

"Brennus," Devlin replied, his eyes filling with storm clouds. "I see. Leave all the details with my assistant Barra. We will set to work immediately and be in touch when we have something. Who precisely did this man say he was?"

"Mstislav Brennus."

Devlin nodded, rose, and strode from the room.

Neirin rolled his eyes and went after him, leaving Barra and the other two to deal with the woman.

Predictably, Devlin was in his library, which, though impressive, paled in comparison to the one at Winterbourne Manor. He was scowling at a particular set of shelves filled with private journals and case accounts all the way back to the days of the first White, who had a long history of powerful magic and loyalty to the demon who eventually laid claim to London.

"What's wrong?" Neirin asked.

Devlin pulled out a book, rifled through the pages, then put it away and pulled out a different one. Some of his tension eased as he clearly found what he sought, though he didn't look particularly happy about it. "Have you ever heard the name Sable Brennus?"

"Not until today. Since when do you care about demon lords?"

"Brennus is an old name, a modernized version of an ancient Celtic name. They were once an incredibly powerful family of sorcerers—powerful enough to make my family look like pathetic dabblers. But in the late fifteen hundreds and early sixteen hundreds, they were brutally wiped out. Murdered one by one, every last man, woman, and child who possessed even a drop of their blood. No one was spared. The last man to be hunted down was Sable Brennus."

Neirin shook his head. "I don't understand."

Devlin set the book on his desk. "If you were to ask some of the few who still remember that day, they will tell you that Sable Brennus killed the person who annihilated his family. But my grandfather was there, involved in the matter because of the stolen grimoires, because the *real* Sable Brennus was desperately trying to stop the demon slaying his family—the demon who ultimately killed him, stole the name Sable Brennus, and wiped the Brennus family from existence. If you ask anyone alive today, they will tell you Sable Brennus is a demon lord in America. Few are the people who remember that Brennus used to be one of the most powerful sorcerer families in the world. Fewer still remember they were some of the cruelest, most ruthless bastards to ever live and the world is better off without them."

"So… the demon missed one?"

"I don't know, but that name, Mstislav, means vengeance, at least in part. Somebody is out for revenge."

Neirin snorted, recalling a case where that had been their exact belief, only to find they'd been played for fools the whole bloody time. "Or wants everyone to think that's the reason."

Devlin grimaced. "Yes, or that. Whatever the case, I intend to find out, as much as I hate to be dragged away from this matter with the dragons."

"I would prefer to have your help," Neirin conceded. "I will be the first to acknowledge my judgment may be clouded, though I will strive to overcome that. But I doubt this matter will take you long, and then you and Midnight can join us. I fear my matter *will* drag on, though it can't if there is any chance of saving the Holy Pendragon."

Devlin stared at him for a long time then nodded. "We will be swift. I do not think it will take long, not if the culprit is so bold. He wants attention and trouble, and such types are easily routed. Have a care with your dragons." He stepped around the desk, tucking the journal under one arm. "And I'm sure I do not have to tell you what I will do to you if you cast Barra aside in favor of that bloody prince."

Neirin's mouth dropped open. "Why would you even think such a thing possible? Have you finally gone mad, Winterbourne?"

"I saw the way you looked at him."

"You saw shock and the past," Neirin snapped. "I won't deny I was infatuated once, but *everyone* is infatuated with Avalon at one time or another. It's hard not to be, really. I love Barra, and if you dare to imply otherwise again, you will not enjoy what happens to you."

Delvin drew back, nodded tersely, and clapped him on the shoulder. "We'll cross paths again soon. Try not to get yourself killed."

"Do the same," Neirin called after him.

Devlin lifted a hand in parting and then was gone.

Neirin stared around the library and heaved a sigh.

How pathetic that old feelings were so apparent even to Devlin, who did his best to avoid ever admitting that feelings existed.

It *hadn't* ever been more than a boy's infatuation. He'd told the truth: everyone was besotted with the sad, lonely, mysterious Avalon at some point. There was too much pretty, childish romance spun up in 'the immortal prince' not to spin fantasies of being *the one* to Avalon. Eventually such nonsense was outgrown, turned to admiration and respect, and sometimes even true friendship.

He thought of how Barra, who'd noticed Avalon's kiss so easily, had looked so unhappy—but not remotely surprised. His breakfast churned unpleasantly in his gut. Did everyone believe him so fickle? So ready to cast aside the person he loved in favor of Avalon? He'd rather die than lose Barra. Even a chance to return to the clans was not enough to turn him from someone who had loved him despite having every reason not to, had loved him even when Neirin had not even a farthing to his name. When Neirin had been a right bastard to him when first they met.

But he was a banished knight, thrown out for disloyalty. A man proven disloyal once was a man who would be disloyal again.

"Neirin?" Barra called softly from the doorway. "What's wrong?"

"Nothing," Neirin replied and forced the unhappy thoughts aside for the moment. "Are we ready to depart?"

Barra nodded. "I had to pull the second carriage out of storage, but it's ready. Midnight and Devlin already left." He frowned as Neirin reached him and lightly touched his face. "You look so unhappy."

Capturing his fingers and kissing them, Neirin asked, "Do you think me disloyal in nature?"

"You?" Barra shook his head. "You're one of the most loyal persons I've ever known."

"I was banished for betrayal."

"You were banished because people are ignorant and afraid," Barra replied. "People see me and assume I'm a base, dirty mongrel with all the hostility of werewolves and fickleness of elves."

Neirin kissed him and shifted to press him up against the wide doorframe. He licked into Barra's mouth, tasted every nook and cranny of it, sucked on his tongue. He refused to draw away until they were both panting and Barra trembled against him. "I cannot say I'm sorry the rest of the world is comprised of fools, for if it wasn't, you might have chosen someone else for a mate, and I am selfishly pleased you chose me."

"Who has ever been capable of resisting a pretty, arrogant knight?" Barra asked with a laugh. "Especially one with a talent for coming to the rescue and an even greater talent for sucking—"

Neirin cut him off with a kiss, both of them laughing, curling his fingers around Barra's waist as Barra's fingers threaded through his hair. "I remember a time when you could barely stumble through a sentence intimating anything sexual."

"One loses modesty rather swiftly when sharing a bed with both a man and a dragon, neither of whom ever seemed to learn the words *modest* or *moderation*."

Neirin laughed and kissed his nose. "Don't remind me, or I'll torture myself with memories the whole of the carriage ride. But I do hope we have time soon to spend a night in excess again." He slid one hand down to palm Barra's cock, which was hard and jerked at his touch. He grazed kisses along Barra's cheek to nibble at his ear. "There's nothing like having a wolf-elf at my mercy, the way you stretch to take us both, and scream yourself hoarse."

"Stop that!" Barra hissed, face going bright red, because while he was much more relaxed and open than he'd once been, he'd likely never be quite as open and casual as the clans about such matters.

Still laughing, Neirin pulled away, took Barra's hand, and headed down the hall to where Troyes waited for them by the front door. His gold eyes gleamed and they'd barely reached him before Neirin found himself shoved against a wall and attacked with sharp, greedy kisses. His bottom lip split, but Troyes simply licked the blood away and kissed him again.

Turning away after a moment, Troyes dragged Barra in and kissed him too, and then Neirin needed to taste them on each other's lips. They stopped only when Neirin realized they were moments from stripping and fucking right there in the hall, which he would not stoop to because if Devlin found out, he would never let Neirin live down such uncivilized behavior.

"Come on," he said. "We're supposed to be working, however much I wanted to spend the day in bed." Pulling away was harder than he would ever admit, but he made himself do it all the same. Retrieving Avalon's sword, ignoring the tingle that shot through him whenever he touched it, he led the way outside and down the stairs to the waiting carriage.

Barra and Troyes swung up to the driver's seat.

Smiling faintly, Neirin climbed inside the carriage and settled in for the trip. He set the sword on the opposite bench and tried not to stare at it—but it was hard not to stare at a sword he'd only ever seen at Avalon's hip or, more often, as a necklace. Rarely, of course. He'd only ever seen the sword for his knighting, and when he'd been taken before Avalon for discipline.

But Avalon had always smiled or laughed and declared all forgiven. He'd always seemed more irritated with Neirin's parents than Neirin, though at the time and for many years after, Neirin had thought he was imagining that. Since being banished, he wasn't so certain. The memories of the whipping had faded, but he hadn't forgotten the look on Linden's face as he ordered it done, told the knight administering the lashings to keep going. They'd wanted to kill him, set an example.

It had been Avalon who'd called a halt and ordered them to throw Neirin out. And it hadn't been by accident that Neirin had been dumped where Troyes had been able to go for help.

Neirin stared out the window, thoughts and memories spinning. He could still feel Avalon's kisses like warm flutters against his cheeks. His lips.

More disconcerting was the faint stir of emotions at the back of his mind. Avalon's presence had eased since he'd vanished, so clearly it was something dulled by distance... But it was still there. Would he know if Avalon was in danger? Would Avalon know when he was in danger?

His face burned as he realized what else he'd been feeling strongly lately. Merciful heavens, he hoped Avalon hadn't felt *that*. How was he supposed to look Avalon in the face after the man had been privy to his sexual interludes?

The images that shot through Neirin's mind then made him choke and sputter. The *vividness* of them, the *clarity*. Far too detailed and bright to be wholly new, just how long had such inappropriate thoughts been lurking in the dark recesses of his own mind? He hoped Avalon couldn't see those. Neirin would die of mortification.

He should be ashamed of himself. He *was* ashamed of himself.

Thank whatever god felt sorry for him that he was alone in the carriage, because both Barra and Troyes would know the nature of his thoughts, if not the specifics, and he did not want to have to lie. There was no way Barra would be anything but hurt, no matter how central he had been in the illicit fancies.

Shoving those thoughts firmly aside, Neirin pulled out the books Avalon had given him—then realized he couldn't read in a carriage that had so little light. If only Devlin was near to hand to call up light... His thoughts trailed off as the sword shimmered, flashed, and suddenly a small globe of witch light hovered at the top of the carriage.

The faintest hint of amusement fluttered at the back of his mind. Embarrassment and terror washed through him. Just how much of his emotions and thoughts could Avalon read? Was he getting hints while Avalon was getting full, detailed images?

He stopped thinking about that as well, before he succumbed to panic and ordered the carriage turned around. He started with the green journal containing Avalon's notes. They were written in a beautiful script, though a few words were misspelled here and there, old languages clashing with his attempts to learn with the times. Neirin smiled, remembering all the books, papers, charts, and other paraphernalia in Avalon's enormous laboratory. Nothing lit up Avalon's face like a new book or treatise on some scientific discovery or shifts in laws, histories and accountings of other cultures, studies and theories, essays and the like. He'd once asked Avalon about a book he was reading and come away with a headache, having understood only that it was the greatest pleasure and the deepest pain to watch Avalon talk about things he would never get to see or do.

The first few pages were on Steward Linden, whom Neirin knew but only distantly. He was 119 years old and had replaced the previous Steward when she had asked to retire and returned to her family's clan in Germany. Linden had taken her place at the age of sixty-three. He was from the Durant family, a branch of du Lac—and he had always resented that he was not part of the du Lac family proper.

Linden had no magical aptitude, which was typical of du Lac. They traditionally abhorred magic, for though it had created the dragons, it was also their greatest weakness. Only Pendragon and le Fay dealt heavily in magic—and only Mordred, a branch clan of le Fay, was better than both, but they'd been rightfully banished for abusing their talents and putting themselves before the dragons.

The other two who had gone with Linden were names he only vaguely recognized: Beatrice Durant, likely a sister, perhaps a cousin... and the other was Rohesia le Fay. Well, that covered all the magic Linden could possibly need. No wonder they'd been able to smuggle the Holy Pendragon out.

That definitely confirmed they were headed for

the old le Fay territory, abandoned for many reasons, but mainly because the final striking down of Mordred, who had also lived in that area, had drawn too much attention to nightwalkers. The whole area was soaked in magic; nightwalkers of all kinds reported strange things happening to their spells and with their powers. Standing guard in Avalon's castle in his younger days, Neirin had overheard many a plea to Avalon to cleanse the area so the clans might reclaim it, but Avalon had always vehemently refused—and also refused to explain why.

So three knights, one of them a sorcerer, and they were hiding somewhere on unstable magic-rich ground. If anything was capable of breaking or twisting the intricate magic of dragons, the old le Fay territory was at least a good place to start.

Still, three knights was not much to stand against the whole of the clans... So either they were fools, or they had greater numbers on their side that had spurred them to action. Neirin bent back to the book, smiling faintly at every misspelled word, fondness curling through him. What must it be like to have seen your own language change so many times? Few were those who could speak languages lost to the rest of the world or slowly fading away. It was easy enough to change with the times when one lived in the world, but the clans were so hidden away...

So painfully hidden away. He had not realized the degree to which that was true until he'd spent more and more time in the rest of the world, traveled so much of it with Devlin. The clans needed to change, at least in part, there was no denying that. But stealing a Holy Pendragon was not the way to go about it. No good ever came from betraying the dragons. The surest path to success was remaining true to the dragons. Whatever his faults, whatever his mistakes, Neirin had never faltered from that path; he didn't care what others said about him.

Though by now they probably scarcely remembered his name, one more traitor to be quickly forgotten.

He sighed and continued paging through the book, but it contained only notes on the types of spells that might be employed, ways to recognize them, and methods for countering. .

No, there. That was a list of names. *Possible traitors*. Most of them were le Fay and du Lac, with further additions from Cross and Palimedes. Interesting. Cross was a branch of Corbenic, an old and almost blindingly loyal clan. Cross was usually the quiet sort. Palimedes was less quiet, but he hadn't thought any of them would turn traitor.

But then, he hadn't ever truly thought his own family would forsake him. He'd told himself he knew, but when that moment came, he'd believed they would stand by him. Instead, they hadn't begged for his life or even said goodbye.

Neirin sighed and closed the book, rested his head against the plush back of the carriage and gave his turbulent thoughts a rest. He could hear Barra and Troyes laughing, which elicited a smile. Soon he could go back to thinking only of them and whatever case they had taken up. After all of this, they certainly merited a break. Perhaps they could return to that beach in—

He nearly went tumbling as the carriage came to a sharp halt, but before he could open the door to ask what was happening, Troyes roared.

Snatching up Avalon's sword, Neirin threw open the carriage door and climbed out. Discarding the sheath, he hefted the sword and rounded the horses—and froze.

Four knights and their dragons stood arrayed across the road. The dragons' scales gleamed in the weak sunlight slipping through snow-heavy clouds.

Neirin's stomach clenched as he looked at a man who wore the face of his brother—a brother who must be long dead by now, already close to forty when Neirin had been banished.

The man stared back, eyes widening, mouth dropping open. Then he recovered himself, sneered, and drew the sword at his hip. "So it's true. You betrayed the clans to curry favor with a demon's pet witch to gain power and life."

Neirin laughed, letting his free hand drop to rest on Troyes's smooth head as he reached Neirin's side. He lifted the sword in his other hand and sliced the air with it. "If I am the traitor, explain why I am Acting High Steward of Clan Pendragon."

"Take that sword!" the man bellowed, and the dragons and their knights charged.

Barra, in wolf form now, crashed into one of the knights, knocking him to the ground, teeth sunk into his shoulder. The knight's dragon whipped around—

"Enough!" Neirin bellowed, trembling at the rush of power that surged through him, a strange certainty—no, a strange *knowing*—that he would be obeyed.

The knights swore and snarled and glared, but they fell to their knees and bowed their heads.

Barra let go of the one he'd injured and shifted into human form as he rejoined Neirin, standing close but far enough away he would not get in Neirin's way.

Neirin swallowed the lump in his throat and tightened his grip on Avalon's sword, hands slick with sweat and trembling. "Why do you betray Prince Avalon and the very dragons at your sides?"

"The clans stagnate and rot. We are meant to be glorious, to be held in awe by the world, and instead we hide like frightened children and wither away," Neirin's descendent said bitterly. He looked up, but looked immediately back down, face dripping sweat from even that small effort at defiance. "You left and look how old you are."

"I did not leave; I was thrown out," Neirin said quietly. "Long life is as much curse as honor."

The man's lips curled. "Forgive me if I don't feel sorry for all the people who hold their great power close and refuse to share it."

"Power shared too easily or too far no longer has the strength to do what it must," Neirin replied. "I respect your position, for you are not wrong: the clans do stagnate. But nobody loves the clans more than Prince Avalon, and you should have trusted that he always has their best interests at heart. Above all, the clans protect the dragons. They are the swords we wield; we are the shields that protect them. Look to your own dragons, their luster lost, their eyes drawn. They know what you do is wrong, but you ignore them. Why?"

"Because sometimes doing what's best involves pain!" snarled another man. "You're just another fawning bitch eager for any scrap Avalon throws you."

All of the dragons growled then, and tears stung Neirin's eyes as he realized he could feel their pain. Was this what Avalon felt? Was he always so painfully aware of all dragons, not simply Caliburn? Neirin could not wait to return the power granted him and have done. It would take a stronger person than him to stand as High Steward.

He wished with all his heart that someone else was there to do what he must now do. "Dragons, you are always allowed your choice. If you acted against instinct out of loyalty and fear of your lives, know you are loved and safe. If your hearts have changed, you are now free to confess that choice."

The dragons threw back their heads and roared, a long, mournful sound that set the tears in Neirin's eyes to falling. Beside him, Troyes roared with them, and he could feel Barra pressed up against him from behind, trembling hard.

One by one the dragons broke away from their owners and crept toward Neirin.

The knights lifted their heads and stared with wide eyes, tears streaming.

"Come back!" one of them howled, his cry echoed by the other.

But all in vain.

In Neirin's hand, the sword began to glow, the hilt almost too hot to hold. Words filled Neirin's mind, giving him a headache. Extending the sword, he spoke in a tear-roughened voice: "To the arms of Pendragon I return you, that you may find new hearts worthy of your love and devotion."

The dragons roared again as they were consumed by light. A breath later they were gone.

"No!" the knights screamed, surging to their feet, bolting forward, crying and begging.

Neirin sliced the sword out in a long, horizontal line, casting a crackling arc of light that dropped the four men to the ground. They sprawled on the ground, unable to move, loudly crying and begging for their dragons. Neirin strode up to the man who bore his long-dead brother's face and planted a boot on his chest. "How did you know I was coming?"

"We didn't," he said through his sobbing. "We were ordered to watch this road on the chance someone did. We noted the dragon."

"But not my power, which you should have, unless of course you were consumed by your own arrogance. You should have recalled that arrogance has always been the downfall of the clans. Even the great King Arthur himself was felled by thinking himself greater than he was and forgetting that the dragons are, above and beyond all else, a sacred gift to be treasured."

"I want—want—"

"It's too late," Neirin replied. "You betrayed your dragons and lost them as you should."

"You betrayed the dragons!" the man snarled.

Neirin shook his head. "No, I betrayed my family, but I always acted to protect the dragons. That Troyes stays by my side proves that. Where is Linden?"

The man remained silent.

"Tell me," Neirin commanded.

"Le Fay territory," the man spat out.

Neirin withdrew. "Rise."

The four men stood and he once more held the sword aloft. "I return you to Pendragon to face the judgment of Prince Avalon and the Round Table. May you face your punishment with grace and return to the clans' embrace."

They tried to reply but were consumed by magic before the words could form.

A heavy silence fell then. Neirin dropped the sword, no longer able to bear holding it, but before he could wipe away the tears on his cheeks, his arms were filled with Barra and Troyes. Neirin clung tightly, kissing first Barra and then Troyes, who whined and cried. "It will be all right," Neirin whispered. "I promise we will fix this, and those dragons will not remain alone and bereft." He hugged them tightly and kissed them again, and then he reluctantly pulled away.

Kneeling, he picked up the abandoned sword. It felt heavier than it had before, and the magic that thrummed through him burned.

Mordred

They reached Canterbury at a miserable hour of the night-morning, and Neirin was more than happy to leave Barra to handle the details of arranging a room in that deft, nigh-magical way of his. While Barra was busy with that, Neirin walked the streets, too keyed up to hold still. Troyes prowled close beside him, twitchy and unhappy to be confined to his human form because although Canterbury had a heavy Nightwalker population, the normal population was significantly larger.

He stopped as he came to a derelict yard, tucked well away from sight, nothing but decaying stone, ivy, and half-rotted doors. It smelled like alcohol, piss, and old magic. Taking a deep breath, he drew the sword and held it up before him, magic jolting through his body like the time Devlin had tricked him into touching an electric eel, the ass.

Light flashed, and then a ghostly image of Avalon appeared before him. He was dressed casually, nothing but trousers, a half-buttoned shirt, and a long, loose heavy dressing robe he'd left unbelted. His hair was barely bound by a ribbon, tumbling over one shoulder in thick, loose, messy waves begging for a comb—or fingers, his stupid brain whispered—to sort them out. "Your Highness."

"Steward," Avalon said softly. "I am tending the dragons now and am so very sorry you had to face that—and face it alone."

"I had Troyes and Barra. I am sorry those knights betrayed their dragons. Will the dragons be all right, do you think?"

Avalon shrugged and for the barest second looked every minute of his age. "Only time will tell. We shall do our best to find them new Owners. How are you?"

"Well enough. We're in Canterbury, and in the morning we'll push on to le Fay territory. If you're able to get further information out of those bastards, I'd appreciate it, though they seem the type of lackeys not to know anything important."

"I agree, but I have a few tricks." Avalon's smile was brief, but cold and sharp, sending a shiver down Neirin's spine. "I must return to them and the dragons, but if you've further need, I'll answer immediately. Have a care. I would not see harm come to you and yours. Troyes, see to your Owner."

Troyes growled, eyes glowing like shards of sunlight in the near-perfect dark, and Avalon's misty image faded away.

A throat cleared behind them, and Neirin turned with a smile as he sheathed his sword. "Barra, we were just on our way back to you."

Barra smiled, but it was stiff on his lips and didn't reach his eyes. "We're set for the night, and I even managed to have a light meal sent up."

Neirin closed the space between them and slid an arm around Barra's waist, drew him in flush, and dropped a kiss on his mouth. "You're magnificent."

That got him a real smile, crinkling eyes and everything. Neirin kissed him again, slower and sweeter, drawing back only when Barra's fingers threaded through his hair and soft whimpers filled his mouth. "Shall we take this indoors?"

"Since when are you the modest sort?" Barra asked with a laugh.

Neirin nipped at his lips. "I like to keep my wolf-elf happy, and he is generally happier when I'm not fucking him in public, or enjoying the view of my dragon—"

Barra covered Neirin's lips with his hand. "Stop that!"

Chuckling, Neirin sucked on his fingers, reveling in the shivers that drew out.

Troyes rumbled as he slunk up behind Barra and nipped at the nape of Barra's nape, which made Barra gasp and keen and writhe between them.

"As much as I enjoy flouting propriety, I do think this occasion calls for confining our activities to private quarters." He kissed Barra again, and as Barra stepped away, drew in Troyes, who clung to him tightly as he returned Neirin's kiss full measure.

Troyes kissed Barra just as eagerly, growling softly as he drew away and licked at Barra's wet, swollen lips. "Pretty wolf-elf happy now?"

"I'm always happy with you, Troyes." Barra said softly.

Neirin flinched inwardly but said nothing, only took Barra's hand and walked with him, Troyes falling into step at his usual place to Neirin's left.

Up in their room, a cold platter awaited them, and they all made quick work of the food and ale before stripping off their clothes and climbing into the slightly too small bed.

Firelight licked at Barra's skin, turning it gold and irresistible—but Barra had always been irresistible. Neirin had ventured out against orders again and again on the faint hope of seeing him just once more, though he hadn't been able to admit it to himself until the night he'd succumbed to the need to kiss Barra and banish at least some of the sadness that filled his eyes.

He hadn't thought his misbehavior would end with a near-fatal whipping and being cast out, but once he'd stopped feeling sorry for himself, he could only see himself as fortunate.

No matter how alluring it was to be working for Avalon and the clans again.

Neirin skimmed his fingers down Barra's beautiful body, tracing every dip and curve, marking the scars and moles he could find in the dark. He knew Barra as well as he knew himself, knew Troyes. Seventy-odd years as lovers left little room for mystery. Only the paths of Barra's mind still eluded him, but he sensed a thousand years would not be enough to unwind all those mysteries.

Barra gasped and shivered, head falling back to rest against Troyes's shoulders as he teased and tasted Barra from behind while Neirin continued his own ministrations from the front. Pulling his hands away, he set his mouth to retrace the path they'd taken, smiling at the fingers that tangled in his hair, winding in the long strands and tugging gently.

Ignoring the silent demand, Neirin put his mouth to Barra's cock instead, licking it thoroughly before finally taking it into his mouth and down his throat. Barra shuddered hard, his cries muffled, no doubt by Troyes's mouth or fingers.

When the tugging at his hair became more insistent, he slowly pulled off and worked his way back up, lingering at Barra's throat to lick the fading bruise Troyes had left there.

"Neirin..."

Chuckling, Neirin brushed a soft kiss across that lovely mouth. When that elicited a string of creative curses, he finally kissed Barra properly, tongue pushing into his mouth and tasting every crevice of it. He hummed approval at the mingled taste of Barra and Troyes. Breaking away, he leaned past Barra to kiss Troyes, which left his own lips pleasantly sore.

Drawing back, Neirin moved to sprawl out with his head on the pillow. Barra and Troyes stared at him hungrily, though he was relatively certain he wasn't half as interesting a sight as his lover and his dragon pressed together, bathed in firelight, cocks hard and eyes full of heat. Despite all his earlier thoughts and plans, right then there was only one thing Neirin wanted. "I have need of you, wolf-elf. Are you going to come attend me?"

Barra's breath hitched, a shiver visibly running through him. Troyes nipped his shoulder then withdrew with a growl and nudged Barra forward. Smiling faintly, Barra crawled up the bed, trailing kisses up Neirin's body, starting at the ankle and taking his time about it.

Neirin hissed when Troyes started on the other side, and his attempts to move were easily prevented by Troyes's greater strength. They didn't stop until he was begging and gasping, writhing uselessly as Troyes kept him pinned.

With a smug, pleased laugh Barra nibbled and sucked at Neirin's lips before finally kissing him properly, setting his lips to throbbing all over again, leaving them aching. Neirin had no complaints.

Pulling away, Barra fetched the lubricant they'd left on the bedside table. He settled between Neirin's spread legs and slipped his fingers down and back, teasing at his hole before gently pushing one finger inside. Neirin moaned, head digging into the pillow, hands flying up to grip the heavy headboard.

Troyes growled and bit again at Barra's shoulder before he shifted to put his own fingers to work, rumbling and nuzzling happily at every gasp and shudder his efforts extracted.

"Enough," Neirin said, pushing back on the two fingers now buried in his body. "I want you now, and I want to see Troyes fucking you."

Barra smiled and whispered, "Bossy," before withdrawing with a soft, fleeting kiss pressed to Neirin's chest. He slicked his cock and with agonizing slowness pushed inside Neirin's body, panting as he came to rest. A ragged cry filled the room as Troyes pushed inside Barra, and Neirin's moans joined Barra's as he drank in the beautiful sight. Seven hundred years could pass and seeing them together like that would still be able to take his breath away and shatter every thought.

After that it was all rhythm and heat, gasps and pleas, motions as old as time. Neirin clung tightly to the bed, meeting every thrust as Troyes's movements drove Barra's cock deep. Troyes came first, growls echoing through the room as he sank in one last time and bit down sharply on Barra's shoulder.

That tipped Neirin over the edge, and he reached up to drag Barra close and muffle his own screams in a wet, clumsy kiss. Barra's cries joined his as he found release.

Drawing back, panting as sweat began to cool on his skin, Neirin shifted just enough on the bed that Barra could lie beside him. Troyes crawled up to brace over him and bend to take a toothy kiss that split Neirin's bottom lip. Lapping it away, Troyes nuzzled his cheek and then shifted to kiss Barra before he crawled out of bed to shift and sleep in front of the fire like an oversized, scaly cat.

Neirin mustered the energy to draw the covers up then pulled Barra close and fell asleep breathing in the scent of the three of them that clung to his skin.

He would have gladly stayed there, safe and warm and happy in that little room, but morning and duty returned all too soon. Cleaning up in the washroom at the end of the hall, he returned and sighed as he saw the fine, dark blue and gray suit Barra had laid out. "Why that one? It's my favorite; I've only worn it twice. If I wear it today I have a feeling it will be the last time."

Barra's mouth quirked. "Suits are easily replaced."

"Devlin's tailors get a little too handsy for my taste."

"Deal with it," Barra replied with a laugh. He finished fussing with Troyes's green silk puff tie and wandered over to fuss over Neirin as well, smoothing down his gray and silver waistcoat and tweaking the matching paisley puff tie, securing it with a ruby pin.

As usual, Barra dressed much more plainly, though he wore the clothes handsomely. They'd all told him to stop dressing the part of servant. Times had changed enough nobody would care—assuming they noticed to begin with. But Barra could give even Devlin lessons in stubbornness when he set his mind on a matter.

Another seventy years and they'd probably crack him.

Neirin shrugged into his jacket followed by a heavy brocade frock coat, wrapped a silk scarf about his neck, and picked up the sword, content to carry it for the present.

Eschewing the hat Barra offered, he pulled on gloves and led the way outside. Horses waited for them outside, and Neirin swung easily into the saddle, sliding the sword into the holster intended for such a purpose. The fog was thick and limned with magic. Troyes growled softly as he climbed up behind Neirin. If Barra had been in wolf form, his growls would have joined Troyes's.

"Let's go," Neirin said quietly and led the way out of Canterbury proper into the fields and hollows, deep into shadows that normal eyes slid away from and forgot about. The sense of magic grew stronger, prickled and stung his skin. "Well at least there is no shadow of doubt that our traitors lurk here."

Barra grunted. "How do we get through? This isn't like your old lands. I can feel the wall."

"Pendragon lands have a similar wall. You simply never got close enough to it. Avalon tries to leave a stretch of largely untouched land that we guard more discreetly. But we are clan again for the present, and you very clearly one of us, so we should have no trouble passing through. The clans can restrict their lands to only their own, but Clan Pendragon can cross to all of them." He urged his horse forward through the swath of roiling darkness, heard a soft sigh from Barra and a growl from Troyes as they followed him through.

The stench of blood struck him like a blow across the face as they entered le Fay grounds. Troyes roared so loudly the sound thundered across the empty stretches of green around them. He shifted and ran off at full speed, his claws leaving tears in the earth.

"What—" Barra cut off as Neirin urged his horse to a gallop. A howl came a few minutes later, and then Barra was running by him and quickly catching up to Troyes.

The sound of Troyes's crying stopped Neirin cold, and he only barely noted the sound of someone else sobbing as he crested a hill—and stared in horror at the tragedy below.

Four dragons and one knight, wearing a frock coat in du Lac colors, lay on scorched, blood-soaked ground. Neirin's throat abruptly felt scraped raw, and he wiped futilely at the hot tears spilling down his cheeks. He dismounted, grabbed his sword, and sped down the hill.

Troyes twined around his legs, forcing him to stop. He rubbed against Neirin, seeking a comfort Neirin wasn't certain he could give. "Who would do this?" he whispered. "Who would slaughter four dragons?"

"Knights," said a bitter voice.

Neirin whipped around, hand going to the hilt of his sword and drawing it in the span of a heartbeat. He scarcely believed what he was seeing, but there was no mistaking those blackened eyes. "Mordred. Was this your doing?"

"Well, you *asked*. That's unique for a clan toady," the woman said, and wiped tears from her eyes as she stood. "No, I didn't do this. Whatever you narrow-minded arseholes think of us, Mordred has *always* stood by and for the dragons. Unlike the knights who did this, who bore le Fay colors and yours, du Lac."

"I'm no du Lac," Neirin replied, and sheathed his sword.

The woman sneered. "I know the look of a pure-blood du Lac, and by that sword, you're Avalon's new pet."

"I am merely Acting High Steward. What do you here, Mordred?"

She made a face, fierce demeanor dying as her shoulders hunched and tensed. "I am hunting two Mordred who have betrayed the dragons."

Neirin hissed. "So Mordred is involved."

"No!" She huffed, shoving back the long, loose strands of her wavy black hair. "I know we were approached by clan, but Chief Medraut threw them out."

"But couldn't bother to inform us," Neirin said bitterly.

Her sneer returned. "We owe you nothing, not after you cast us out for crimes we didn't commit."

"You betrayed the dragons!" Neirin bellowed. "You took what wasn't yours and you practiced forbidden magic—"

"We were trying to save the dragons, but you will never want to hear that," she snarled, tensing as though to attack.

Troyes growled a soft warning and moved to stand in front of Neirin. Barra remained off to the side, ready to cover from the rear or give immediate chase if she tried to run.

The woman rolled her eyes and lifted her hands. "I have no interest in picking a fight unless you are in league with the bastard knights who did this."

"I would sooner slit my own throat than ever take an action that brings harm to the dragons," Neirin replied.

Nodding, the woman replied, "I was hiding, watching them, hoping they'd lead me to the Mordred traitors I'm hunting. But they got into an argument and the dragons..." She sighed, shook her head, face etched with disbelief.

Neirin finished softly. "The dragons abandoned them, tried to leave."

"Yes. The knights tried to coax them back then tried to do it by force. One of the knights changed her mind, sided with the dragons, and tried to get them away. That's when everything went wrong... so horribly wrong..." She started crying again. "I tried to help, but I was too far away and acted too late. I never imagined..."

Neirin struggled against the bile rising up. It was against clan law to associate in any way with Mordred, but... "They stole a Holy Pendragon."

The woman's eyes popped open wide, mouth dropping—then she burst into frantic tears. "They can't do that! The dragon will *die*, why—why—"

Surging forward, Neirin caught her up and hugged her close. "We're here to get it back. I'm sorry you're tangled up in the mess." He drew back slightly. "What is your name? I am Neirin, this is Troyes, and my lover and associate Barra."

Barra shifted, came forward, and bowed to her.

The woman pulled out a handkerchief and cleaned her face, then she drew herself up. "I am Hasna Medraut."

Neirin bowed. "An honor to meet you, my lady."

"You'd be the first to say so," she replied, though the bitterness in her voice was milder than previously. "So how does a former du Lac, clearly an exile yourself, come to be Acting High Steward?"

"There is betrayal from every corner. What do you know of the Mordred who are here? Did they steal anything, grimoires or such?"

Her brows lifted. "Yes, actually."

"Let's tend the dead," Barra interjected, "and then we can compare notes and plan our next action."

Neirin bowed his head. "Yes, you're right. Come on Troyes, I'm afraid the duty of burning must fall to you."

He, Barra, and Hasna slowly heaved and pulled the heavy dragon corpses and that of the knight into a pile. His suit was definitely ruined by the time they were done, but Neirin was beyond caring. He knelt in the muddy ground and cupped Troyes head, hugging him close as Troyes cried. "You're a good dragon," he said softly. "There's none braver or stronger or more faithful than you. Let's honor our fallen brethren for the bravery and strength and faith they showed."

Troyes roared as Neirin pulled away and stood. Barra, back in wolf form, threw back his head and filled the air with a long, mournful howl. Approaching the pile of bodies, Troyes breathed fire. Very little in the world was resistant to dragon fire. Dragons of course were, but these ones were dead, the bodies already badly sliced, which meant they were as vulnerable as anything else.

Neirin pulled a kerchief from his pocket and covered his mouth and nose with it. The peppermint oil that scented it didn't block out all of the stench of burning flesh, but it cut the worst of it.

Barra drew close and took his hand, and Neirin clung to it as tightly as he could without hurting him. Sniffling drew his eyes, and he turned to see Hasna hugging herself and crying as she watched the bonfire. Abandoning his handkerchief, Neirin extended his free hand. She eyed him warily, but when he didn't withdraw the offer, stepped in close and clung to his hand.

Troyes finished breathing fire and came to curl up at Neirin's feet, crying loudly as the bodies burned.

By the time they finished, the sun was well in the sky and all the lingering fog had burned away.

"Let's go," Neirin said softly. "Will you travel with us, Mordred, or do you venture on your own path?"

"You would let me travel with you? As I recall, you could be killed solely for talking to me."

Neirin shrugged. "Mordred is guilty of much, but I'm bitterly aware of what it's like to be exiled for doing what I felt was right, and the important thing is the Holy Pendragon. We are united in that cause, which for now makes us allies. The more allies I have right now, the better."

She stared at him for several long minutes but at last gave a slow nod. "Allies for now, then, High Steward. I assume we are bound for Castle le Fay?"

"That seems our most logical course for the present."

Barra let go of Neirin's hand. "She can have my horse. I want to shift again, anyway, see what scents I can pick up."

Neirin cupped his chin and leaned in to kiss him. "Have a care, wolf-elf."

"Heed your own advice," Barra kissed his fingers then stepped back and shifted into wolf form. He woofed at Troyes, who prowled over to him and rubbed his sleek scales along Barra's russet fur. They ran off ahead, leaving Neirin and Hasna to catch up.

Smiling briefly, Neirin returned to his horse and swung smoothly into the saddle. When Hasna nodded she was ready, they rode off after the others. But werewolves and dragons were leagues faster than humans and horses, and it wasn't until they stopped several yards away from the lake of Castle le Fay that he and Hasna caught up.

"I'm not certain venturing so far ahead I cannot catch up to you is 'taking care'," Neirin groused.

Barra shrugged and cast him a fleeing smile as Troyes rumbled at his feet. "The mood we're in, it would take a score of demons to stop us. I assume whoever lurks in there is aware of our presence? At least, it seemed to me there was little point in stealth after all of our howling and roaring."

"Agreed," Neirin replied. He stared at Castle le Fay, which he'd seen in paintings and sketches, but never in person. It was even more eerie in reality than in oil and pencil, shrouded by mist and guarded by deep water, secluded on a small island that only boats could reach. The lake was not as large and impressive as the underground lake that fed Clan Pendragon, but it was close.

Though it had been abandoned for some time, the castle showed no significant age, but given the heavy, acrid taste of magic thick in the air, that came as no surprise.

"How are we to get across?" Hasna asked. "I see no boats and the water looks too deep to ford." She walked cautiously to the edge. "There's not even a gradual deepening, the water is too deep and dark to see the bottom even here at the edge."

"Le Fay and Mordred magic crafted the lake to be thus, if memory serves," Neirin replied.

"Yes," Hasna said. "Which I admire, but that does not make it any less frustrating."

Neirin dismounted, buckled his sword in place, and joined her at the edge. The water was dark as ink, shimmering at the corner of his vision. He looked at the castle, frowning thoughtfully. Stepping away from the edge, he pulled out the small green journal Avalon had given him, but it contained no notes on accessing the castle.

Marvelous. Some acting High Steward he was proving to be. His accomplishments so far were arresting lackeys and burning dead dragons. He was facing defeat by lake. He didn't know if it was better or worse that Devlin wasn't there to show him up and make everything look easy.

Snapping the book shut, Neirin tucked it away and returned to the edge of the lake. He drew his sword just to look like he was doing *something*—and nearly dropped it as the sword burned, flashed, and a beam of light shot out across the lake straight toward the castle. The slender beam spread out across the water, flashed and sparkled, then settled into a bridge that seemed made of moonlight and glass.

Neirin sighed and made to sheathe the sword— then thought better of it and kept it out. "Leave the horses." He stepped gingerly down onto the bridge, stamped on it, and took a couple more steps. "Seems stable enough, for now at any rate. He turned and offered a hand to Barra, who took it with a smile and hopped neatly down.

Hasna eschewed the offer and jumped down next to Barra.

Troyes stood at the edge and growled, clawing at the grass and casting Neirin a wounded look.

"Dragon, I have seen you face draugr, sorcerers, werewolves, and creatures far more dire than all of those combined. Get down here now."

Growling at him, Troyes nevertheless slunk down to the bridge and butted his head against Neirin's hip.

"Good dragon. Now let's hurry, for the longer we take, the more likely it is they will escape."

He remained tense the entire length of the journey, which was relatively short but seemed to take hours. By the time they stepped back onto land he was ready to scream.

But as they ventured up the long steps to the castle, they remained unmolested. The castle could have been deserted everything was so quiet. Had he made a mistake? Should he be looking elsewhere for them?

Magic sizzled along his skin as he passed through the raised portcullis but faded away as they crossed the ward into the keep. The enormous doors had been pulled completely open, baring the keep to mist and chilly air.

Inside, a small fire had been built in the enormous fireplace meant to warm an entire hall. A single long table and benches had been pulled from the wall and set close to the fire but not right in front of it.

No, the space directly in front of the fire had been reserved for a spell circle. Neirin scowled at the chalk. He couldn't read it in full, but he'd been around Devlin and magic long enough to pick out it was a transfer spell. "Damn it!"

He'd expected a fight, to be faced and challenged. He should have recalled he was working with cowardly traitors, men so desperate for a crown they would sacrifice the very creatures they wanted to control.

"They knew we were coming and fled," Barra said with a sigh. "I don't know why I thought they'd go with a more direct approach."

Hasna snorted and crouched by the circle. "That is clan thinking, little wolf. I would have expected you to be smarter than that, but perhaps you're affected overmuch by the company you keep."

Barra laughed.

Neirin could not decide which of them more merited a glare and settled on ignoring them. He went to the fire but saw nothing amiss with it, not even scraps from papers that might have been burned.

"Troyes and I will search the keep to see if anything was left behind elsewhere," Barra said, and slipped away with Troyes at his heels before Neirin could reply.

Sighing, Neirin turned back to the circle and Hasna. "I do not suppose you can read enough of that to tell us where they went?"

"At a glance, I can tell you it's somewhere here in England. More than that, I'll need a little while. I don't do transportation spells enough to have much of them memorized."

"I barely knew it was for transporting, so you are leagues ahead of me." Neirin left her to it to prowl the rest of the hall and the rooms beyond it.

The only thing of note he found were the leavings of a small dragon nest in the chief's solar, just large enough to hold a single egg. So the Holy Pendragon had definitely been here. At least he was on the right path, if woefully behind his quarry.

Dropping the nest leavings, he looked the solar over one last time—and spied a scrap of paper beneath the bed, like it had slipped from the bed and fallen between it and the heavy table kept beside it. He pulled it out, holding the old, fragile paper carefully.

The words were no language he could read, though he picked out a word or two of something that might have been Latin. A language he should know, but past the rites and rituals, his interests had always lain elsewhere. The runes were familiar, but like the circle, he knew only that they indicated a spell.

One edge was worn and ragged, like time and lack of care had caused it to come loose of the book to which it belonged.

He gave the room a third and final sweep then carried the paper back to the hall, where Barra and Troyes had returned.

Hasna looked up at the sound of his footsteps and rose. She tucked away a small black book in the folds of her skirt then brushed dust and chalk from her hands. "If I have read the circle correctly, our quarry has gone to Amesbury. Why, I could not say..." She frowned as they all groaned. "Clearly you know something I do not."

"That's werewolf territory," Neirin said sourly. "It is also close to Stonehenge. Why they require Stonehenge, I could not say for certain, but given it has been known to amplify magic, that would be my guess. But after our last altercation there, the Bruce pack told us to bugger off and never come back—or else."

"Well, hopefully we shall be able to contend with 'or else' because we've little choice in the matter."

Neirin nodded. "Let's get moving, then, because it will take us a good deal longer to get there, unless you want to attempt to transfer us."

"I wish I could, but I do not have the skills to transfer so many people."

"So they will probably be long gone from Stonehenge by the time we reach it as well." Neirin started to ball his hand into a fist and was stalled by the feel of paper. "Damn."

Hasna frowned. "What's that?"

Shaking his head, Neirin offered the paper. "I've no idea. It was in the solar along with the remains of a nest. I was hoping you'd be able to read it."

Her frown deepened as she took the paper. "This is from Mordred's copy of Morgana's Grimoire."

Neirin choked, and Troyes growled. Barra shook his head. "Morgana's Grimoire?"

"Morgana le Fay," Neirin replied. "The founding matriarch of Clan le Fay, and one of those responsible for creating the dragons. I thought her Grimoire had been destroyed."

Hasna looked sad as she examined the page held delicately in her hands. "It was, and most of the Mordred copy is gone as well. Only the Medraut family is allowed access to it. My family. They drugged my brother and his bodyguards and took it and a few other grimoires. All of the stolen books focused on either dragons or binding magic."

"It's a fool's quest," Neirin said. "Binding is the most complicated magic in the world, even I know that, and the way it works varies wildly from species to species. Dragons, demons, wolves... they all bond differently, and magically forged bonds are something else entirely, especially when you start mixing magics."

She gave him a pensive look. "For someone who cannot even read a spell circle, you seem familiar with the highest level, and most dangerous, type of magic."

"I'm well-acquainted with a damned good reason binding should not be done lightly. Shall we go?"

"Yes." Hasna tucked the paper away in her skirts, turned neatly on her heel, and led the way out of the keep.

Neirin offered a hand to Barra, who smiled as he took it, Troyes falling into step on Neirin's other side as they departed.

Family

It was pouring rain when they reached Stonehenge, though it had been clear enough when they'd set out. It was also cold enough Neirin's breath misted in the air.

Thankfully, it was also late, which meant dark, which meant no bloody tourists trampling all over something they didn't understand—something even nightwalkers didn't understand, not entirely anyway.

Neirin climbed out of the carriage and pulled up the hood of his cloak. It was an outdated bit of clothing, but a damned sight more useful for sloughing rain than anything current fashion dictated.

He turned to offer a hand to Hasna, but as usual she ignored him, stepping neatly down to stand beside him as Troyes and Barra jumped down from the driver's seat.

Troyes growled softly, but it was an easy, inquisitive, and happy growl. "Smell family."

Neirin quirked a brow. "You can't be—"

But even as he spoke, two figures came stepping out of the dark and mist, filling the air with the buzz and tang of wild magic. With every passing year, Devlin's power seemed to grow and grow, and Midnight's right alongside him. Even Devlin could not entirely understand why, though his strongest theory was that draugr grew more powerful with time and the bond between him and Midnight caused the same to happen to Devlin, which in turn fed more power back to Midnight, and back and forth it went.

"What are you doing here?" Devlin demanded.

Neirin's other brow went up. "What are *you* doing here?"

"Working, obviously."

"Can we work somewhere dry?" Barra muttered.

Devlin nodded. "Yes, I think that would be the thing to do right now. If our paths have crossed, especially here, then it would behoove us to figure out why before further steps are taken."

Neirin turned on his heel and climbed back into the carriage, followed by Hasna, Devlin, and Midnight. Devlin cast runes upon the carriage floor, and Neirin hunched, feeling the wretch that he had not been able to do anything about the rain beating down on Barra and Troyes, and Devlin had barely expended effort in helping them.

They rode back to Amesbury in silence, not speaking past the bare necessities until they reached the house Neirin had secured earlier, since of the group, he was the one least likely to draw attention. Though it was inevitable the werewolves would learn of their presence eventually. After Devlin had arranged for his carriage and belongings to be fetched from where he and Midnight had been staying, they settled around a large table in front of the fireplace.

"So tell me all that has transpired," Devlin said as he took a sip of tea that was mostly whiskey. He glanced at Hasna. "Who is our guest?"

"This is Lady Hasna Medraut, of Clan Mordred," Neirin said.

Devlin's brows vanished into his hair. "Mordred. The exiles that, if mentioned in your presence, turn you into a puffed cat?"

"*I* turn into a puffed cat?" Neirin replied, ignoring the way Barra and Midnight laughed, and even Hasna's lips twitched. "Shall we discuss the Dracula—"

"No, we shall not," Devlin snapped, sending the others into a fresh fit of laughter, because nothing was guaranteed to send Devlin into a snit like mentioning Seth Ashworth, the Dracula who enjoyed flirting with Midnight as often as possible. "Can we focus on our current problems please?"

"You started it," Neirin muttered, but when Barra cast him a quelling look, explained everything that had transpired since their departure from London.

Devlin's face was a thundercloud as he finished. "That is a lot of grimoires on binding that are going missing, especially if we include the ones stolen from my client. I do not yet see any other tie between Brennus and the clans, but I think it safe to say we will find one and Brennus is merely using revenge as a distraction."

"So what brings you to Stonehenge? Did you track Brennus this far?"

"No, I've not tracked Brennus at all. I am merely following reports of where he's been seen and where he is likely to go if he intends to use the more intriguing spells in the stolen books. If that trail has led here, then I think it safe to assume he is in league with the clans' traitors. If they are going to break the binding between dragons and knights, then Stonehenge is certainly a good place to try it. Also a stupid place to try it, but ambition and stupidity oft walk hand in hand."

Hasna frowned. "They must all be long gone by now. It took us most of a day to get here and they already had a day's start."

Devlin shook his head slightly. "I felt no recent activity at Stonehenge. A pity the rain kept Barra from smelling anything of interest. But hardly necessary, because they will not do anything before tomorrow at the full moon, because it lends strength and stability to places like Stonehenge, which needs all the stability it can get."

Seventy-odd years working alongside Devlin and Neirin had still failed to note something so stupidly obvious. His shoulders tensed. "I see."

Hasna scowled. "I should have noticed that."

Devlin lifted one shoulder. "I might have missed it save for Midnight, who keeps me acutely aware of such things."

Neirin didn't roll his eyes at that, but only just. Devlin attempting to be modest was laughable at best.

When he got a narrow-eyed look from Devlin, Neirin stared back blankly. Midnight chuckled softly and Barra sighed.

"So you think both our quarries will convene at Stonehenge tomorrow when the full moon is high," Neirin finally said. "I'm already getting a headache."

"Agreed," Devlin muttered, and Troyes and Barra looked equally unenthused. Given their last adventure to Stonehenge had entailed angering an entire wolf pack and Devlin's magic had been off for an entire month thereafter, the displeasure was warranted.

Troyes growled softly. Neirin reached out absently to stroke his hair, the back of his neck. His own neck prickled as he felt eyes intent on him, and he looked up just as Hasna looked away, a bitter expression fading from her face.

"It sounds as though there is very little for us to do

until tomorrow," Midnight said before anyone else could speak. "A bit of reconnaissance, but I can manage that well enough. The more the rest of you lay low, the better. I am astonished no one has come to make good on death threats."

Neirin frowned. "Astonished? I'm *alarmed*."

Devlin grunted in agreement. "They should have noticed us, though if we are actually fortunate enough in that they didn't, I will count my blessings. I think we should take advantage of the quiet and see about food."

Barra stood, not looking at any of them as he said, "I'll tend it."

"Would you like some assistance?" Hasna asked.

"I'll be fine, but thank you," Barra replied with a smile that Hasna tentatively returned.

It was the first real smile Neirin had seen from him in what felt like forever. He stood. "I'm going to update Avalon on our progress, see if he can lend any knowledge about Stonehenge. Then I'll help Barra with the food." He motioned for Troyes to stay, though reluctantly, and followed Barra out of the room.

In the hall, he nudged Barra against the wall and took a lingering kiss, skating his fingers lightly over Barra's body, hating how tense and too-still he was. "Is something wrong? You've been getting quieter and quieter."

"I just have a bad feeling about all of this," Barra replied. "Like something is going to go horribly wrong and we won't be able to walk away this time."

Neirin frowned. "We're dealing with people more dangerous than usual, I grant you that. We'll have a care, and I promise to keep my sniping at Devlin to a minimum."

Barra nodded, though he didn't look any less miserable. He kissed Neirin fleetingly then slipped away.

Sighing, Neirin followed in his wake, but outside, he turned in the opposite direction to find a quiet place to speak with Avalon. He could have done it in the room, but Devlin would have just started bickering, and Avalon seemed to make Barra unhappy too.

It also seemed somewhat cruel to do it in front of Hasna, though he shouldn't care about a traitorous Mordred.

He slipped into a narrow alleyway between two buildings and pulled out the sword. He stared it, still bemused that the most powerful magic sword in the world had been handed over to him so easily, in a matter of minutes, and with nary a thought.

But that wasn't true. Avalon had probably given the matter a great deal of thought. Was he satisfied with his choice? Was he regretting it? Would he be relieved to finally take it back and have done? How unpleasant it must be for him to rely on one traitor to catch another.

Maybe all of this would show Avalon, show them all, that Neirin was no traitor. He had always been a faithful knight of the clans. Maybe, just maybe, this would regain him a place. He doubted du Lac would want anything to do with him, though they'd obey Avalon if he ordered it so... But Neirin had been fostered to Pendragon for training and his turn at guarding Avalon and Pendragon lands, and he'd enjoyed Pendragon far more than du Lac. Perhaps Avalon would permit him to be a part of Clan Pendragon once and for all, at least honorarily.

Though that would likely entail an order to return fully and leave the rest of the world behind again. Which he most certainly wouldn't—couldn't—do. He had a family and a life here, and he'd rather die than leave Barra, Devlin, and Midnight behind.

No sense in worrying about problems that didn't, and in all likelihood would never, exist. But Neirin pressed his forehead to the flat of the blade before casting the summons.

Avalon was properly dressed this time, though only in trousers, shirt, and waistcoat, having at some point discarded his tie and jacket. His long hair was pulled back in an elegant twist of braids to a bun at the back of his head and reading glasses were perched on his nose. "Good day, Steward. How proceeds your search?"

"It's taken us to Stonehenge, and we've collided with another case that was brought to our attention," Neirin replied and explained everything to him.

"I expect no trouble from Lady Hasna, but show caution all the same," Avalon said when he was finished. "Mordred is not the traitor we seek, but they are not the sort to waste an opportunity when it is presented to them. Brennus is an old name, to be sure. I never met them, but tales were carried to me of their triumphs and abuses. They were once great contributors to magic; many a grimoire is filled with spells contrived by the Brennus line."

"They were also right bastards from what I've heard."

Avalon gave a short nod. "Yes, though my knowledge remains second and third hand."

"Do you think this thief we hunt is truly a Brennus?"

"I doubt it. That bloodline was well and truly wiped out. The only remaining is the demon lord who possessed the body of Ettore Brennus, stole the name of Sable Brennus, and destroyed the family. The name was a tool. I'm more curious to know the man's real identity. He must be a sorcerer of significant skill if he was hired to assist the clan traitors and thinks himself capable of breaking a bond as powerful as that of dragon and knight—and that dragon a Holy Pendragon, no less. Others have tried and failed in horrific, tragic ways. Mordred paid a dear price for their tampering."

Neirin nodded. "Any idea what spell or spells they may attempt?"

"I would wager they've created a new spell, which is foolish but likely the only thing to work, if anything could," Avalon replied, teeth worrying his bottom lip. Neirin dragged his eyes away, but everywhere he looked he fell back into staring. Gritting his teeth, he stared past Avalon's shoulder at the ivy-draped wall behind him. "It will be elaborate and require hours to prepare, check, and triple check, and I sincerely doubt they are foolish enough not to thoroughly check over their spell. One small error and there is no telling what might go wrong. A new spell, plus Stonehenge, plus the full moon..." Avalon's frown cut deeper into his face. He stepped closer, shimmering as the magic worked to keep up with his movements. "Be cautious. I would not see you or yours come to harm."

"We're always coming to harm," Neirin replied, lifting one shoulder. "I assure you, Highness, we've faced worse than this. I would not have you think me cavalier, but I feel we can handle whatever challenges come."

Avalon reached up to touch Neirin's cheek, the brush of magic burning against his skin and tinging through his body. Even translucent and made of magic, Avalon's eyes were dark, storm-filled clouds Neirin could never hope to breach or survive if he did. He regarded Neirin like he was someone who mattered, which was not a look he'd ever expected to see again on the face of someone from the clans—let alone the nigh-immortal figure who ruled them. "I gave you my sword and power because I have every faith in your abilities, but greater men than you have been felled by treachery and blades in the dark. I did not come to you for aid only to see you felled in the name of the family that betrayed you. Nor would I see your new family harmed. Please, for me, show utmost care."

Neirin's cheeks burned. He swallowed. "I-I will, Highness, I swear. That's why I came to you now, so we would be well-prepared. Devlin is a witch of no small skill, but even this is somewhat outside his realm of expertise."

"I will help as best I'm able," Avalon said softly, his hand falling away. He stepped away again, removed his spectacles, and tapped them against his lips as he thought, staring off in the distance at something beyond Neirin's sight.

After several minutes, he sighed and said, "As I said, it will be elaborate and time-consuming. The bonding of dragons is a powerful magic, as instinctive and beyond control as a demon recognizing his consort. It is the very fabric of the dragons, and to undo that will require blood at the very least. If they were merely breaking it, that might be the end of it, but they seek to *change* it, which is infinitely worse.

And that is merely conjecture, recall. They did not exactly leave their plans behind neatly written out for me." He looked at Neirin again, amber eyes glowing faintly. "An educated guess is still a guess."

Neirin nodded.

"So they will need blood, a true blood sacrifice, unless they've contrived something else. They will need the Holy Pendragon. They will need someone to bond with the dragon, though I presume that is Linden."

"Linden has a dragon, though. How could he bear to bond with another? Caliburn is magnificent, but I would never choose him over Troyes. Just the idea of it turns my stomach."

Avalon turned his head again, loose strands of hair brushing against his cheek. "Linden's dragon is dead. We found her body buried in a shallow grave just outside Pendragon territory. It looks like she was killed with magic, probably never knew what happened to her."

Neirin closed his eyes, feeling punched in the gut. Tears fell down his cheeks. "How could he murder his own dragon?"

"I don't know. In all of this, I hoped he still cared that much," Avalon said softly. "He was a good man once. I wish I had noticed sooner that his heart had changed. All the years that have passed, I am still very much a fool." His mouth was twisted in a sour smile as he turned back to Neirin, but it faded into a somber look when he said, "When you find Linden, grant him no quarter. I would have given him a fair trial and banished him, but no mercy is bestowed upon knights who murder dragons."

"As you command, Your Highness." Neirin bowed

his head, smoothly turning the sword in his hand so it pointed down and pressing hilt and hand to his heart.

Magic burned as fingers brushed the top of his head, and trailed down his cheek as Neirin looked up. "Thank you, Steward. Do not hesitate to call if you need me further. Remember: be careful." Then he was gone, leaving Neirin once more flustered and feeling cut open.

He sheathed the sword and headed off to find Barra, who was just coming out of the inn where he'd gone to purchase food. "Are you all right? No one gave you any trouble?"

"I got a few looks like usual, but nobody raised a fuss. None of them looked or smelled familiar, so perhaps for once we're lucky and enough time has passed no one knows to dislike us."

"That would be a nice change of pace," Neirin replied as he took some of the wrapped, steaming bundles and fell into step alongside Barra. "Smells wonderful." He turned to look at Barra when he didn't reply, slowed to a stop when he saw the unhappiness etched into Barra's face. "What's wrong? Did something happen you're not telling me?"

Barra shook his head, forced a smile that didn't reach his eyes. "No, I was left in peace. I'm fine, merely tired and worried. How did your talk with Prince Avalon go?"

"Well, I suppose," Neirin replied, stifling a sigh. "He thinks they are going to try to force the Holy Pendragon to bond with Steward Linden."

"Wouldn't he already have a dragon? Can a knight have more than one dragon?"

"There are knights, rare and powerful and dangerous, who can master two dragons. Linden is not one of them."

Barra's brows drew down. "So how is he going to bond with the Holy Pendragon, assuming they accomplish their goal and force it?"

"He killed his dragon," Neirin said, voice breaking on the last word. "Murdered her with magic—" He stopped in the street, pressing the fingers and thumb of his free hand to the corners of his eyes to stem the fresh tears.

"Oh, no." Barra whined and pressed against him as well as he could with both their hands full. "I'm so sorry."

Footsteps made them look up, and Troyes came barreling toward them, eyes bright with fear. "Neirin unhappy. What wrong?"

Barra took away the bundles Neirin held moments before Troyes crashed into him, trembling and crying.

"I'm all right, I'm all right," Neirin murmured over and over, though his hands trembled as he held fast to Troyes. "I'm fine, beloved."

"Not fine. Sad and sad and sad."

Neirin smiled faintly against Troyes's hair. "I'm not *that* sad."

"Sad about Prince. Sad about wolf-elf. Sad now."

"Sad about Barra?" Neirin drew back to stare at him in bewilderment. "What are you talking about?"

Troyes whined. "Wolf-elf sad. Neirin sad."

"I'm sad because knights are killing dragons and there's a Holy Pendragon at risk," Neirin said slowly. "The only ones keeping me from despair are you and Barra and the others. Barra doesn't make me sad."

"Neirin smell sad. Wolf-elf smell sad," Troyes said as he started to cry, turning his wide, wet eyes on Barra. "Wolf-elf no longer want?"

"What?" Barra's voice was rough, the word coming out cracked. "Troyes, I love you and Neirin more than life. I would have to be dead to no longer want either of you. That's not what's happening here. Now kiss me and help us carry this food in before an irate Devlin comes searching and does something unpleasant to us."

Troyes whined again but leaned in and kissed him hard, not releasing Barra until they were both heaving for breath. He licked away the blood on Barra's lips and nuzzled against him before turning to kiss Neirin as well. "Good Troyes? Good wolf-elf?"

"You're both magnificent and perfect," Neirin said softly. "I am sorry I gave you cause to doubt that. Now come, because our wolf-elf is right about Devlin." They split the bundles of food between the three of them and returned to Devlin, Midnight, and Hasna.

Neirin helped Barra lay all the food out and gave Troyes a platter of raw mutton before resuming his own place and making short work of the shepherd's pie and beer.

"So what did your royal irritant have to say?" Devlin asked.

Hasna laughed, sharp and short, before she cut it off with a swallow of ale.

Neirin started to snipe at Devlin about always maligning Avalon, then decided it wasn't worth the headache that would result. "He said they are most likely going to try to force the Holy Pendragon to bond with Linden, which they're unlikely to succeed at. But pretending they could manage it, they will need a blood sacrifice and a great deal of time, among other things."

"He didn't name a specific type of blood sacrifice?"

"No," Neirin replied.

Devlin's brow furrowed, eyes going distant as he lost himself in thought. "The closer to the purpose, the stronger the magic."

Neirin suddenly regretted all the food he'd just eaten. "Please don't mean what I think you mean."

"I'm afraid I mean exactly that," Devlin replied, looking up, meeting his gaze with haunted eyes. "At the very least, they are going to sacrifice a dragon. If they're as smart as I fear, they will sacrifice both knight and dragon."

"That's despicable!" Hasna snarled, looking ready to storm off right then and there to find heads to remove.

Troyes snarled, his eyes glowing so brightly they looked like torchlight. Neirin lunged out of his seat and slammed Troyes back down in his, grateful he was in human form because if he'd been in his true form, the room would already have been half-destroyed.

"We'll stop them," Neirin said firmly. "Troyes, don't worry, we'll stop the spell and keep the dragon safe. Prince Avalon will ensure the dragon finds a truly worthy knight, and we'll slay the betrayer. All right? Now eat, because you'll need your strength to save the dragon." He tipped Troyes's head up and leaned down to kiss him. "Come now, dragon, you are made of sterner stuff than this. Do not lose your composure."

Troyes rumbled softly, but subsided and resumed eating.

Taking his own seat yet again, Neirin drained his ale. "So what do we do now?"

Midnight chuckled, cutting off the reply Devlin had started to give. "We wait until tomorrow and then go on the attack. There's no time now for finesse, and finesse is not our style anyway, hmm? For now, it's long past time we rest after all the hard traveling we've done lately."

Neirin didn't roll his eyes, but it was a near thing. Devlin and Midnight were going to slip away to their room for the night to *rest*, his arse.

"I'll clean up," Barra said. "I'm feeling too restless to sleep quite yet, anyway." He didn't wait for a reply, merely stood and started piling all the empty dishes together. Neirin rose to help, but at the tense, unhappy look on Barra's face, subsided.

Midnight kissed Devlin slowly then slipped quietly from the room, Hasna following after him.

Neirin sighed and sat back in his chair. "Let's have it, then. I can see from the look on your face I'm about to get a dressing down."

"You're my dearest friend. I would no more see you hurt than Barra, but right now he is the one hurting, and you are the cause of it."

"Hell if I know why," Neirin said. "I haven't *done* anything. Whatever troubles him, he will not speak of it, and I know damned good and well that the harder I push, the deeper he buries it."

Devlin's mouth flattened. "You can't be that much of a bloody fool."

"Bugger off. Of course I'm not. He seems to think there is something between me and Avalon. But you were witness to the only kiss between Avalon and I, and even if there was a chance of something there, I would refuse it. I've not been clan for a long time and I have no desire to return, not even for Avalon. I explained this to you, or near enough, before we left. Must I rehash it?"

Devlin shook his head and rose. "No. I merely hate

seeing you both so unhappy, nor do I like being in the clutches of your bloody clans. What guarantees do we really have that they will not drag you back into their fold now you are second in command to their leader?"

"Avalon does not abide such behavior." Neirin turned his head to look out the window. "You do not seem to realize: Avalon has power enough to equal demons all on his own. Combine him with Caliburn, the power of the clans, and centuries of experience... If he wanted to force people to obey him, he could do it with all the effort it takes to blink. Surely you remember how it felt to be in his presence."

Lip curling, Devlin replied, "Distasteful is the word that comes to mind."

Neirin laughed. "Yes, I imagine it would be for a man who is used to being king himself, so to speak. But that is merely what he cannot help. Think about how much more devastating he could be if he made an effort. He takes such things very seriously—not unlike you, once upon a time, when you refused Midnight's affections over and over because you were in a position from which it was all too easy to take advantage."

"Fine, your point is made," Devlin said. "So you believe he will set you free again once this matter is concluded?"

"Yes."

Devlin rose. "Very well, then I suggest you drive home your earnestness to Barra as well as you have done with me. It's annoying and distracting to see the pair of you so distraught, though neither of you is as bad as your lizard when he's crying."

Neirin chuckled as Devlin left, the door banging shut behind him.

"Troyes bad?"

"No, of course not." Neirin pulled Troyes out of his seat and into his lap, nuzzling against him as Troyes shifted so he could rest his head on Neirin's shoulder. "You should recognize by now Devlin's peculiar ways of showing concern. He's worried about you."

"Bad knights. Broken dragons. Sad wolf-elf. Sad Neirin." Troyes whined. "Avalon miss, wants back. Can't go back." He sniffled and buried his face in the hollow of Neirin's throat.

Neirin nearly cried himself as he felt the warm tears on his skin. "You want to go back to the clan?"

"No. Yes. Both." Troyes sat up, eyes dark and wet and red. "Neirin sad, Avalon sad, Barra sad. Both miss Neirin."

"Avalon doesn't miss me. Avalon barely even knew me. I was one guard in hundreds. I stand out now only because I'm completely disconnected from the clans and somehow still alive after all these..." Neirin drew a sharp breath.

It had never occurred to him before because the idea was too ridiculous to believe. That he was still alive when normally clan did not live so long he had attributed to his life outside them, being surrounded by Devlin, Midnight, and other powerful elements of the Nightwalker world.

But Avalon had the power to grant extended life. Normally it was something he extended only to his Steward—and his Seneschal, once upon a time, before that position had faded from use.

That still made no sense, though. Why would Avalon grant him—and Troyes—extended life? How could he have done it without Neirin, or Devlin, noticing? Why, though, that was the question he desperately wanted answered.

Troyes growled softly. "Avalon *miss.*"

"All right, then, have it your way. It little matters, though. Whatever my regard for Avalon, my heart lies here, and I will not abandon this life to return to the one that rejected me. Now come on, let's go find our wolf-elf and tell him the same."

"Wolf-elf," Troyes repeated softly, affectionately, and slid from Neirin's lap to lead the way out of the room and in search of Barra.

Sacrifice

"I smell wolves," Barra said.

Midnight glanced ahead of them, seeming to see something despite the thick fog. Knowing Midnight, he probably did. Neirin had found him a bit alarming, even creepy, when first they'd met. It had taken very little time for that impression to fade, but as the years passed, Midnight gained a shade of that indescribable something that Avalon possessed. Like he was a secret no one would ever know. Devlin had something of that, but he was more like a wild witch of legend, a story people loved to whisper in delighted terror. Midnight was a myth so old even time had nearly forgotten the tale. They were both irritating prats in the day to day.

Devlin sneered. "So that is why they've been ignoring us. They've been waiting all this time, no doubt hired by our quarry."

"Or simply eager to join the fun when it means our blood might spill," Neirin added, and drew his sword, the ring of metal echoing through the dark, shrouded field. At his sides, Troyes and Barra growled.

Hasna drew her blade, a beautiful long sword that shimmered with magic and had a gleaming sapphire in the hilt. "Let them come."

Midnight gave a slow, soft, rippling laugh. "Yes, let them come." His eyes glowed, and the tips of his fingers looked more like claws in the faint light of

Devlin's lantern.

"Quell your blood lust." Devlin blew out the lantern. "I doubt any of these wolves recall firsthand why they hate us. They could merely be hired thugs like most wolf packs. Our goal is Stonehenge. Focus on that."

"It's quelled," Midnight said shortly. "Barra, Troyes, and I will clear a path for the three of you and guard your backs while you stop the spell. The moon is nearly in position."

Devlin nodded and abandoned the lantern on the ground. Reaching into his jacket, he drew a few runes and held them loosely in his closed fist.

Troyes prowled forward, Barra fanning out so they flanked Midnight as the three of them vanished into the fog.

Neirin's breath misted in the air, heart thudding as the sounds of fighting shattered the quiet. No matter how many times they did this, no matter the number of fights they survived... eventually there would come a fight they lost. He glanced at Devlin. "Shall we, then?"

"Carry on."

Brandishing his sword, Neirin plunged forward. The tangy, wild smell of wolf was growing thicker on the air, mingled with the damp, heavy feel of Midnight's magic, and the hot metal scent of Troyes. Two wolves snarled, but they turned into yelps and were replaced by Troyes's deep, echoing growl.

Then Neirin was close enough to see them: three against what must be at least thirty wolves, if not more.

One of them came at him and Neirin struck out— and nearly yelped as golden orange light arched out, slicing through the wolf before it ever actually reached him. The wolf whimpered and dropped.

Stowing his thoughts for later, Neirin pushed on, fighting through wolves and the occasional human. Witches, maybe, or alchemists more likely, but they fell faster than they could draw their spells. If they'd laid ambushes, they weren't working or he hadn't come to them yet.

Every now and then he saw a flicker of Devlin, casting and recalling and casting runes, throwing out fire and lightning and ice. Or Hasna, who moved with all the grace and power of a clan knight, as comfortable in trousers as she had been in a dress.

And then there was Midnight, who had always been the most dangerous of the five of them, neither alive nor dead, but a terrifying in-between. All the heart and vivacity of a living person, all the deadly power and remorselessness of a draugr.

A new wave of wolves came out of the dark, but they were no match for Midnight, Troyes, and Barra when they weren't holding back.

Neirin threw out another arc of crackling light, and then he, Devlin, and Hasna were through.

They were mere steps away from the outermost circle of stones.

A handsome man with pale skin and an artful tumble of glossy black curls came out of the fog and shadows. He bared his teeth. "Did you really think it would be that easy?"

Neirin surged forward, sword out. The man threw out runes, and Devlin bellowed as he tossed his own—

And the world burst with light, like being struck by lightning from every direction. Neirin screamed as he went flying back.

The man laughed, head thrown back, the sound echoing out across the night. It was an ugly, gleeful sound, threaded with smugness. "So it seems I was right."

Neirin wiped blood from where it was dripping from his nose. "Right about what?" He picked up the dropped sword in one trembling hand but didn't lunge a second time as Devlin gave a sharp, jerky shake of his head.

"Never you mind," the man said with another laugh. His gaze shifted to Devlin. "So you're the witch who walks with devils."

Devlin laughed in that *I'm more important than you and always will be* way of his. "Are they still saying that, after all this time? Here I thought people had finally grown tired of gossiping about the Mad Duke. Do you think your trifling ward will stop me? You haven't been listening to the right gossip."

"I think it will slow you down, which is all we need. Have fun with the draugr, I hear you like them—a little too much perhaps, but to each his own." He faded off back into the fog.

"Bloody fucking hell!" Neirin snarled.

Hasna huffed. "We need to get through that ward, but I've never seen one so—" She stopped, whipped around. "What is that awful sensation crawling over my skin like spiders?"

"Draugr," Devlin said, casting an absent look back the way they'd come. "Do not worry upon it. Our foes have a long way to go before they provide something that would actually constitute a challenge. Midnight and the others still consider this a lark."

"And they say Mordred are the ones not right in the head," Hasna muttered. "How do we get through this ward?"

Devlin reached into his jacket and cast his runes. They fell at the base of the ward, glowed, sent out lines of crackling light—then went dark. "Damn." He recalled the runes, kissing the last before returning it to the bag in his jacket.

From another pocket he withdrew a small silver case etched with the Winterbourne snowflake. Extracting a piece of chalk, he approached one of the enormous stones and began to draw. Neirin itched to do something, but he dare not lose himself in the fighting, and it was better to leave Devlin to his work.

"I thought we would beat, or at least meet, them here," Hasna said.

"So did I," Neirin said. "The night is still young, there was no reason for them to be here so early."

"We should have come last night, or earlier in the day, and waited for them," Hasna replied. "Stupid to wait until now when it is obviously far too late."

Devlin paused in his drawing to sneer. "What good would early have done? They'd have either prepared a nastier fight than wolves and draugr, or decided to cut their losses and vanish until they could try again. No, this was the best course for catching and stopping them, even if it means we enter in the middle of the mess rather than well before it. Now be silent."

Hasna huffed, but did not speak, only cast her eyes back toward the sounds of fighting that were slowly fading.

"There," Devlin said several minutes later. He dropped the remains of his chalk in the grass, pressed a hand to the intricate spell circle he'd finished drawing, and spoke the activating words.

The ward shimmered blue-green-yellow and with

a brilliant flash, vanished. Neirin surged forward, weaving through and around the enormous, ancient stones headed for the very center—

Just in time to watch Linden slit the throat of an unconscious imp and throw the body inside a spell circle. Linden looked up as movement caught his attention. His eyes widened, then narrowed, face filling with hate. *"You.* That's where Avalon turned for help? Why am I not surprised you're still alive? His precious little banished guard. Avalon's pathetic. What makes you worthy to be Steward, you—"

"Enough," said the man with the riotous black curls. He crouched at the edge of the circle and activated it.

Only Devlin's hand holding fast to his arm kept Neirin from charging forward to snatch up the egg at the very center. Soft, shimmering beads of reddish light filled the area, consumed the dying imp and the egg.

"Don't—you can't—you'll fucking *fail*—" Hasna howled. "You bloody fucking traitors! I'll kill all of you—"

"Stop!" Devlin bellowed at her. "If you interfere with the spell in the middle of it, you will definitely kill that dragon."

Hasna snarled again and turned around to focus her wrath on Devlin. "If we had shown up sooner, we could have prevented this."

"No, we would have merely delayed it," Delvin replied, and turned his attention back to the spell.

The light slowly faded, and Neirin's breath caught as he saw what now lay inside the circle.

As a baby, he looked to be only a few weeks old. The sacrificed imp was gone, along with the circle and anything else that might have been in it that Neirin had missed.

Devlin moved, casting out runes, and Neirin didn't bother waiting to see what they would do.

He ran as fast as he possibly could, sword out. He would die before he let those bastards have the baby. If they'd done what he thought, he would burn everything down before he let them have that child.

Power surged through him, and a rage that surpassed even his own. It felt like his body was not entirely his as he reached the baby, stood over it, and held the sword high. *"The Holy Pendragon is not for you!"*

The skies cracked and boomed with thunder enough that Neirin felt it in his chest. Lightning licked at the clouds, and with another earthshaking boom, arced down to the sword, then burst out in crackling streaks of blue and purple light, striking Linden, Brennus, and the figures skulking in shadow.

It *hurt* to have so much power surging through him. Neirin hated it.

With a scream he yanked the sword back down and sheathed it. He knelt, scooped up the baby, and bolted back toward Devlin.

"Keep going!" Devlin ordered. "We'll protect the rear."

Neirin obediently ran, not stopping until he tripped over something and went tumbling down. He barely contorted himself in time to avoid the baby taking harm in the fall, landing on his back staring up at a dark, starless sky where the fog occasionally swirled and parted. Tears streamed down his face from fear and rage and relief.

He barely noticed when the others surrounded

him, twitched and jerked as someone gently grabbed hold of his head—and shuddered in relief as he realized it was Troyes trying to cradle Neirin in his lap. With a shudder, Neirin finally let him.

In his arms the baby was still and quiet, but Neirin could just barely feel the rise and fall of his breathing.

"Up, up," Barra said. "I can still hear them coming."

Neirin snarled and rolled to his feet, ignoring all the aches and pains that flared up. He handed the baby over to Barra and drew his sword. "Go, I'm going to deal with Linden."

Barra opened his mouth then snapped it shut again and nodded. "Be careful. Troyes, don't let him do anything stupid."

Kissing him hard and quick, Neirin turned and strode off back the way they'd come, Troyes at his side.

He didn't slow as he passed Devlin, merely cast him a look that said *protect them*. Devlin spared him an offended look as he continued on.

A man came out of the fog a few paces later, bloodied and charred, screaming in rage as he saw Neirin. "You! I remember whipping you! You're a worthless, traitorous cunt. Avalon should have let me kill you."

"You have some nerve declaring *me* a traitor," Neirin retorted, bracing for attack. "I may have brought outsiders onto clan lands, but it was to protect the clans. I didn't *murder my fucking dragon.*"

"I did it for the good of us all!" Linden bellowed. "Do you think I wanted—"

"I think you chose to murder your dragon!" Neirin snarled. "Troyes, kill."

Troyes roared, the sound as ominous and

resounding as the earlier thunder.

As a knight, and former Steward no less, Linden should have been better prepared, but all he did was turn and try to run.

"Stop!" Neirin called out once Troyes had him down on the ground, bleeding heavily and whimpering. He stood over them, staring into Linden's angry, pain-hazed eyes. "Any final words, traitor?"

"That he went to you for help, that he's trusted you with his sword and all that power he never gave *me* even after all my years of service—" He coughed, spat blood. "All he's proven is that he deserves to lose his throne."

Neirin gave a bare nod. Troyes growled and crushed Linden's throat. Neirin winced slightly but did not look away. When Linden was dead, he softly said, "Burn the body."

Troyes growled again but drew back enough to cast his flames over Linden's body. Neirin moved out of the way, standing silent vigil as all that remained of Linden du Lac, former High Steward of Prince Avalon and Clan Pendragon, burned away to ash that would be lost to the wind and rain and soil in a matter of hours.

When it was finally done, Neirin sheathed his sword and beckoned. "Good dragon," he said softly, kneeling to run his fingers over Troyes's gleaming scales. He was still unused to their unusual color, more reminiscent of Caliburn than what he'd known his whole life. "You're the most magnificent dragon in the world. I'd never trade you for anything, especially not something as mercurial as power." He hugged Troyes tightly, enjoying the scent of hot metal, the heavy weight resting on his shoulder, the rumbling he could feel rolling through his body as Troyes tried to comfort him.

Eventually he drew back and rose, giving Troyes's slick scales one last stroke. "Come on, we have other matters that need addressing, assuming Devlin hasn't already hidden the child away, named him, and bequeathed him a small fortune." He grinned briefly. "Do you think Midnight fears competition?"

Troyes chittered in amusement, tail swishing across the damp grass.

They found the others in the clearing where they'd begun the night, the lantern once more lit, held by Midnight. Barra still held the baby, but Hasna was looking the poor thing over closely, brow furrowed, mouth pursed.

"Something wrong?" Neirin asked.

"I'm not sure," Hasna said, and nearby Devlin looked equally vexed. "It shouldn't be possible for a dragon to shift at so young an age. He was still in his egg."

Devlin jerked a hand impatiently through the air. "I take it dragons and humans are not suitably compatible for a human to give birth to a dragon? Or, I suppose, a dragon to give birth to a dragon already in human form?"

"No." Neirin shook his head. "They shift to humans as a form of disguise and a way to bond with their Owners; the deception doesn't stretch that far. Dragons can only breed with dragons, which they always do in their true forms. They can't shift until they're at least a year old, and some can take as long as three years. Most don't really bother until they choose a knight. There's just no reason until then, in a dragon's eyes."

Hasna continued to stare hard at the baby, reaching out to touch it, giving the barest smile when it curled one tiny hand around her finger.

"So this ceremony was never about forcing the bond. It was about turning the dragon into a human..." Devlin frowned and shook his head. "To what purpose?"

"Holy Pendragons usually die within weeks of being born if they do not find a worthy knight. Most dragons don't match for years, when they're older. But Holy Pendragons are powerful enough that they need an Owner right from the start. By making him human... I think they might have given him more time to bond."

"More importantly, it gave them more time to find a way to force the bond. Damn. Even this should not have been something they came up with so quickly and gotten right on the first try." Devlin's gaze shifted to Hasna. "Unless they had a foundation to build upon."

Neirin stiffened. His eyes shot to Hasna. "What the bloody hell has Mordred been doing?"

Hasna sneered. "You think I'm telling *you* anything about Mordred? We've cooperated this long, Pendragon, but do not think that makes us friends. You cast us out for a perceived crime—"

"You tried to create new dragons!" Neirin bellowed. "You tried to create dragons that would match beyond the protections of the knights born and raised to care for them. You gave them to a world not fit to have them!"

"You're not fit to have them!" Hasna snarled. "You keep them sheltered and hidden away and ignorant—"

"Enough," Devlin cut in, stepping between them

and shoving them apart.

Neirin's chest heaved, but he bit his tongue and turned away, forcing himself to focus on the Pendragon, not an ignorant fucking Mordred. He took the baby from Barra and cuddled him close. Now that he wasn't overwhelmed by magic and fighting for their lives, it was easy to feel the power of a Holy Pendragon. It was soft, sleeping, but there, and when the baby opened his eyes, there was no mistaking their brilliant amber color. "Hello, little Pendragon." He looked up. "We need to return the Holy Pendragon to Avalon."

"One thing at a time," Devlin replied. "Let's get home, where I can better assure our protection, and then we will contact Avalon and sort this mess out once and for all. The bloody sorcerers got away from me, and I'm not comfortable doing this exchange anywhere else. Into the carriage, everyone, we've dallied long enough."

Neirin obeyed without further word, holding the Holy Pendragon close as Devlin, Hasna, and Midnight climbed in with him. He would rather be with Barra and Troyes right then, but he'd endure until they were safely back in London. Or did Devlin mean *home*? "Are we going to the townhouse or the manor?"

"The manor, of course," Devlin said, and dropped runes on the floor of the carriage.

Neirin didn't bother to ask after the spell he'd cast; no doubt it was a protection of some sort. Instead, he closed his eyes, carefully held the baby close, and succumbed to the exhaustion washing over him, content that his friends would keep the Holy Pendragon safe while he regathered his strength.

When he woke again, it was to see the familiar

grounds of Winterbourne out the carriage window. He groaned and tried to clear the fog from his head. "How long did I sleep?"

"Hours and hours," Devlin replied quietly, gesturing to where Midnight and Hasna were fast asleep. "We've traveled nearly nonstop since leaving Amesbury. The only significant stop we made was to sort out food for the baby when he started crying."

"Blood and milk?"

Devlin looked pained. "Of course you knew that. We tried to get an answer from Troyes, but I don't understand dragon and he got cranky quickly."

Neirin laughed softly. "How would he know? Troyes mated a few times, but the kits were hardly given to his care, and he wouldn't remember what was given to him. It's only in the first few weeks they require the exclusively liquid diet, and a mixture of goat milk and blood has always worked best. The blood on its own is too much. Then ground meat so it's nice and soft, and once they get their damnable teeth in, they eat normally. You should have woken me to ask."

"We tried," Devlin grumbled. "You would not be woken. Frankly, you should be dead."

"What do you mean?"

"I mean whatever magic you used by way of that sword was powerful. Obscenely, alarmingly powerful. You could not pay me to muck with such magic—"

"No one pays you anyway."

Devlin sniffed, offended at the very idea of being paid for his work like a common laborer. "My point is that magic is beyond you, even merely serving as a conduit. It's beyond *any* human."

"To throw around lightning? You do that all the

time."

"No, I cast magic that resembles lightning, or occasionally manipulate lightning already present when I decide it's worth the risk. Which I haven't for at least thirty years as the last time I tried it I was unconscious for hours."

Neirin's mouth tightened. Even with it thirty-odd years in the past, he hated remembering that day. "So what did I do?"

"I don't think it was you, I think it was your damnable prince."

Sighing, Neirin replied, "So what did *he* do?"

"He *summoned* lightning—summoned a storm, in fact, which I have never heard of a human doing." Devlin's frown deepened as he tapped a knuckle against his lips.

Neirin shrugged. "He's the most powerful person in all the clans, with centuries of life to his name, and a legacy of magic users and their knowledge. The sword itself has powers untold. If anyone could manage such a feat, it would be him. We can ask about it when we contact him about the Holy Pendragon. If nothing else, he would consider the explanation a favor owed."

"I suppose that will have to suffice, but it makes me dislike him all the more. He let that bastard nearly beat you to death, he toys with your affections now, and who knows what he will do or demand next."

"He is not toying with anything," Neirin said with a sigh. "Why does everyone treat me like some besotted idiot on the verge of betraying my lover?"

"Because you *are* a besotted idiot, whether you realize or want to admit it or not," Devlin retorted. "But on the verge of betrayal? No, I do not think so.

You're honorable. You would simply cut ties, which is what we all fear will be the case."

Neirin smiled faintly. "Come off it, Winterbourne. You'd help me pack my bags."

"You're a bloody arse if you think so."

"Already have them packed, then," Neirin said, and laughed when Devlin kicked him.

They subsided after that, though Neirin would have preferred not to be left to his thoughts.

Thankfully they reached the manor proper a few minutes later.

Winterbourne Manor was enormous, though modest by the standards for such things. It should have a full staff to see to its maintenance and care, but that required Devlin trust people to be in his house unsupervised, and he most certainly did not. Where necessary, he had Barra bring in people to work for a few days, then sent them all running again. Much of the house was, in fact, closed up, and it was easy enough for them to tend the remaining rooms themselves.

Neirin accepted the hand Devlin offered and climbed out of the carriage, the baby still fast asleep in his other arm. He followed Barra up the steps and into the house, the wards tingling as he stepped through them.

Their gathering point was the library, and Neirin headed straight for it as much as he wanted to crawl right back into bed. He could not remember ever feeling so tired, not even after the month they spent contending with succubi. Spare him ever again being Avalon's conduit.

He settled in his favorite chair by the fire that Devlin lit with the flash of a rune and watched sleepily as the others filtered in. Troyes shifted to dragon form and lumbered across the room to him. He nudged gently at the baby, snuffled in satisfaction, then lay down at Neirin's feet and promptly started snoring. Neirin smiled faintly, an ache of affection in his chest. If he ever considered treating Troyes the way Linden and the other traitors had treated their dragons, he hoped someone had the sense to kill him before he tried. Devlin came in last, carrying a sleeping, heavily cloaked Midnight. He set Midnight in a far, dark corner of the library on a long, green velvet settee, brushed his fingers along Midnight's cheek before turning away and going to close all the curtains to keep out the sunlight that was very nearly Midnight's only weakness.

Only Barra was missing, but he arrived several minutes later bearing a tray of food, because no matter the circumstances, Barra always thought of everyone else first. He brought a plate over to Neirin before setting to work feeding everyone else. It was only when Neirin and Devlin both chastised him that he finally helped himself and took a seat on the footstool he moved to set beside Neirin's chair, resting his head against the plush edge.

When they'd all eaten, minus, of course, Midnight, Devlin pushed his plate away and said, "Let's get on with it then, and have done. What do we do to call forth the mighty prince?"

Neirin rolled his eyes, handed the baby off to Barra, and drew his sword. He held it before him, and moments later Avalon's translucent form appeared before them. He was dressed for sparring this time, in old-fashioned tunic, hose, and mail, hair braided and secured in a knot, face streaked with dirt and sweat, a bruise forming on one cheek. He was still panting as he said, "Hail, Steward. You had need of me earlier. I hope all is well now?"

"Yes, Highness," Neirin said. "Linden is dead. The sorcerers who assisted him are currently on the run, but we will be tracking them down. We have the Holy Pendragon, though the situation is unusual."

Avalon frowned. "What's wrong?" Barra stepped forward and Avalon's eyes widened. "That can't be..."

"It is," Neirin said. "We saw it happen right before we attacked. I wish we'd been able to get to them before they cast the spell, but our plans did not go as we had hoped."

Avalon did not tear his eyes away from the baby as he said, "Tell me everything."

Neirin explained everything as best he could, with the others filling in their own accounts. Whenever someone spoke, Avalon turned to look directly at them, causing all of them to stumble or stutter briefly—save Devlin, who glared throughout and was never less than snippy. Which only made Avalon smile, which just further soured Devlin's mood.

In less serious circumstances, Neirin would have enjoyed watching someone get the better of Devlin. Right then he rather wished they'd both behave.

But Devlin was the last to recount his version of events, and silence fell in his wake. Avalon walked over to Barra and reached out to the baby, who opened his eyes briefly and made a soft, rumbling-purr sort of sound before slipping back to sleep. "I cannot believe they managed it with a Holy Pendragon. I knew Mordred had done it with their lesser dragons—"

"What are you talking about?" Neirin demanded.

"You know nothing about it!" Hasna snapped at

the same time.

Avalon cast her a reproving look, and with a huff, she jerked back and looked away, folding her arms beneath her breasts. "I know more than you can possibly imagine. It little matters right now, save Mordred's work was used as a foundation to accomplish this deed." He sighed and withdrew to stand once more roughly in the center of their gathering. "I am glad you all came to no harm in the end, though I am most sorry, dear Steward, that serving as my conduit taxed you so. When you come to Clan Pendragon to return the Holy Pendragon, I will see you are given a restorative."

"Thank you, Highness. We'll leave soon to return him to you."

"Why can't you simply come here and take him and spare us a long, arduous, dangerous journey?" Devlin demanded. "Surely you have a few minutes or even seconds to spare to fetch your errant dragon."

"I wish I did, but I used all my spare time to contact Neirin. I cannot leave, not without a great cost that must be paid by another, which I will not ask, no matter how much you growl at me. I could bring you here via magic, but Neirin is too exhausted to be a conduit anytime soon. I must also release Neirin from his vows and you are all due worthy recompense for your deeds."

Devlin sneered but said only, "As you please, Highness. Let's go back to the magic you have artfully avoided discussing in detail. How were you able to summon a storm?"

"The sword has abilities even I scarcely understand. I prefer not to employ them, but we all do what we must, Your Grace."

"Still avoiding, but that's all right. I'll figure it out on my own and then we shall be having a conversation you will not be able to avoid, Your Highness."

Avalon gave a slight bow of his head and turned back to Neirin, stepping closer to him. He frowned slightly, reaching to brush his fingers along one cheek. "Are you certain you're well? I should have warned you ahead of time that I could do such, but I did not think it would become necessary."

"I'm perfectly fine, Highness. It's nothing a few good nights of rest won't fix. But thank you."

"Thank you," Avalon said, then swept his golden eyes over all of them again. "Thank all of you. I am greatly in your debt—even yours, Lady Medraut, and I pay my debts. I will see you at Clan Pendragon a few days hence. Take utmost care. Farewell."

Devlin cast a scathing look at where he'd stood. "I cannot wait for all of this to be over." He strode off back across the library to scoop up Midnight and carry him away. At the door, he paused and said, "Lady Hasna, I will show you to your room if you would like to follow me."

"I'm grateful, Your Grace, thank you." Standing, she followed him out of the library, leaving Neirin, Barra, Troyes, and the baby.

Neirin smiled at the baby, reaching to gently touch his hand, and looked up at Barra—who was staring off in the distance, a deep frown cutting into his handsome face. "What troubles you?"

Barra shook his head. "Noth—"

"If you say nothing again, or try to fob it off as exhaustion or the mission, I will lose my temper," Neirin snapped. "You cannot still think, after all I have said and done, that I would forsake you for the past that forsook me? Do you have so little trust in me after all these years? Is there nothing I can do to convince you that my heart resides with you?"

"A measure your heart resides with me, and I've never had cause to complain about that," Barra said slowly, voice ragged, eyes glistening as he stared at a bookshelf across the room. "But I know how you look when you are in love. Do not insult me by saying I am wrong about something with which I am intimately acquainted."

Neirin opened his mouth but closed it again.

Barra did not appear to notice. "Every time the subject of the clans comes up, you have that look. When Avalon himself comes up, it is definitely there, as vivid and beautiful as when you look at me and Troyes. I knew from the day we became lovers that eventually, be it days or months or years, you'd return to the clans, to your Avalon. That moment is finally here, but you cannot expect me to take it gracefully. I should be content that I had you, and Troyes, for more than seventy years, but I find I am not that selfless. I just—" His voice broke then, but before Neirin could catch him up, he'd fled across the room, the door slamming shut with an echoing bang behind him.

"Am I truly so despicable that my betrayal has been assured for seven decades?" Neirin asked no one in particular, his eyes stinging. First the clan threw him out for betrayal, and now the man he loved most had apparently been waiting several decades for the day he too was inevitably betrayed.

Troyes whined and padded over to him. Neirin dropped to kneel on the ground and clung tightly to him, let the tears fall. "At least I'll always have you, beloved. The rest of the world seems to have no faith in me, though I foolishly thought all this time some people did, but there is always you."

Growling, Troyes withdrew and shifted, then held him close again, licking and kissing away all the tears. "Neirin good. Best. Loves all. Loved by all. Have faith. Wolf-elf scared." He whined and hugged Neirin tighter.

Neirin clung tightly, but despite the assurances from Troyes, who couldn't lie even if he wanted, all he could hear was the heartache and resignation in Barra's voice. All he could see was the tears in Barra's eyes, the devastation etched into the lines of his face.

Even Devlin had constantly called him into question.

Was he truly so reprehensible a person? How could he be so oblivious to his own horrendous nature?

What the bloody hell was he going to do now? It felt far too much like Barra had just told him goodbye, but he would not return to the clans, either, certainly not like this. Even pretending Avalon would take him back, how could he do exactly what Barra had apparently expected of him all these years?

He had the sinking, wretched feeling there was nothing for him to do but leave and start again somewhere else. The very idea of it hurt more now than it had when he'd been banished. Barra and Devlin and Midnight were his family, his home, more so than even the clans had ever been.

What was he supposed to do, where was he to go, when all the people he'd loved and trusted always expected him to leave?

The Mongrel Wolf

Retreat

Barra made certain the baby was asleep before slipping into the hallway. He started to head for his room but stopped as it belatedly struck that he may not be welcome there anymore. His room before Neirin and Troyes had been at the opposite end of the house, where he was closer to the doors so he could go running easily whenever he wanted.

He sniffled, trying futilely to hold back tears. He hadn't meant to sever his relationship with Neirin, had secretly dreamed a thousand scenarios where he punched Avalon in the face, or outwitted him, or proved in some grand and glorious manner that a lowly wolf-elf bastard was infinitely better than a beautiful, mysterious prince Neirin had been devoted to long before he met Barra.

Ha. If he wasn't already crying he'd probably start laughing hysterically.

"Barra."

He jumped, only then registering Devlin's scent, and hastily wiped tears away with the heels of his hands. Looking up, he opened his mouth—and couldn't figure out what to say.

"What's wrong?" Devlin asked with unusual gentleness. "Are you and Neirin still at odds?"

"I think I may have just accidentally declared us finished," Barra said, fresh tears running down his cheeks.

Devlin sighed softly and pulled a kerchief from within his jacket, pushing it into Barra's trembling fingers. "Tell me."

In sniffling, hiccuping words Barra did so.

When he was done, Devlin pushed his fingers into Barra's hair and gently ruffled the mop of curls. "I remember a time when you would never have spoken up so, though I wish it had not been such a heartbreaking matter that drove you to it."

Barra just cried harder.

"Come now, I do not think it's as bad as all that. There is no doubt Neirin loves you and does not want to be parted from you, so simply tell him you did not mean your words to sound so." More quietly he muttered, "When the bloody hell is Midnight going to wake up?"

Barra laughed a little bit, shaky and weak. "Not for several hours yet, I'm afraid. And there seems little point. Neirin can protest all he likes; we all know how much he has always wanted to return to the clans. Some days it hurts to see how much pain his banishment still causes him. How could I ever ask him to reject this chance to rejoin them, especially as he still clearly has the favor of his prince?" It didn't matter what the stories said; in the real world handsome knights didn't choose mongrel wolves over beautiful princes. Especially a prince like Avalon, with his sad eyes and tender touches, the affection in which he so obviously held Neirin.

After seventy years together, Barra shouldn't be this upset. Neirin should have died years ago. They could have fallen apart for one reason or another over the span of seven decades. It was more time than most people could ever dream of.

But he wasn't far off from a hundred himself, and his elf blood and nightwalker life meant he could live at least thrice that. He had hoped, despite all the painful realities telling him otherwise, that Neirin and Troyes would be around for most of it, had dared to start to believe when Neirin inexplicably did not age as expected.

Now here they were, in exactly the place he'd always feared, losing Neirin to the one person Barra had never been stupid enough to think he could compete with.

He tensed in surprise when Devlin abruptly hugged him tight, tried to remember when, or even if, Devlin had ever done so. Then he shuddered and held tight to his oldest and dearest friend, the one person to believe in him when everyone else called him names, threw him out, refused to let him in, told him over and over that he was an embarrassment who should have been put down as an infant. Before Neirin and Troyes, before even Midnight, it had been just him and Devlin.

"I've never known you to give up without a fight," Devlin said gruffly. "Do not start acting differently now."

"Against a prince and the clans? What chance does a mongrel like me have?"

Softly but with steel, Devlin replied, "Better than you credit yourself or him, or have you forgotten in all of this that it was *you* who provoked him to the behavior that earned his banishment?"

"It was the dragons."

Devlin chucked his chin, smiled faintly when Barra looked up. "It was the pretty wolf-elf he stole kisses from at least as much as the dragons. Certainly I was not the one charming him. Now come along and let us fix this mess the two of you have made once and for all, because I for one am bloody damned tired of the dramatics."

"Oh, I think you and your draugr still have us bested. At least I did not spurn Neirin's affections for years and years—"

"Enough," Devlin cut in, casting him a warning look.

Barra laughed and felt moderately better as they headed down the hall to the stairs.

A blast of magic, a scream of pain, and Troyes's deafening roar drew them to a startled halt for a beat—and then they were both rushing down the stairs bound for the library.

The door had been burned away, and more flames were licking at the floor and furniture, the books thus far spared only because of the spells Devlin kept on them.

In the middle of the room, Troyes was fighting against several werewolves and three sorcerers, his beautiful scales smeared with blood, gore, and ash. Barra bellowed and shifted, throwing himself across the room.

"Get away from them!" Devlin snarled—then made an awful wet, sucking sound that stopped Barra cold.

He turned around, watched in frozen horror as Devlin dropped to his knees and toppled completely over, a knife sticking out of his stomach.

From upstairs, loud and clear though it should have been muffled by the distance and heavy walls of the house, came a long, piercing, gut-wrenching scream.

Barra dragged his eyes up and stared at the man

who'd just killed Devlin: the sorcerer from before with the pale skin, slick black curls, and eyes that glowed with magic. The man leered, face filled with triumph and cold, smug satisfaction. "Call for help, little wolf, call for help before the rest of your friends die like this pathetic witch." He kicked Devlin in the head, and Devlin rolled over onto his side, eyes full of pain and rapidly fading life as he stared at Barra, one hand clutched to the gaping hole in his gut.

Devlin passed out as Midnight burst into the room with another piercing scream. He did not pause, went straight for Devlin, eyes alighting on the sorcerer. With another bellow of rage Midnight attacked—and the rage turned into pain as he walked into a spell cage none of them had seen.

Hasna came bursting in then, wearing only a nightshirt and wielding a sword. As she stepped into the room, four more wolves appeared behind her and before Barra could call a warning, they were upon her.

No, no, no. They didn't lose like this. They were better, smarter. They always came through. They didn't lose like *this*. They didn't end in tragedy.

Barra turned back to the wolves, but even Troyes was lost beneath the mess. He ran toward them anyway, desperate to find someone he could save, desperate not to end this night alone—or to at least die with his friends, because even if they survived the fight, there was no way they'd escape the rapidly spreading fire.

Troyes lay curled protectively over Neirin, sprawled on the floor in a growing pool of blood. Another, smaller pool was forming from a gash on his head. His sword—Avalon's sword—lay nearby.

The baby. They were here to take back the Holy

Pendragon. All of this for one dragon? No wonder Avalon had been so desperate to get him back, if this was what happened when a dragon was stolen from the clans.

Someone slammed into him, and teeth sank into his throat. Barra snarled, jerked and twisted, fought off the wolf—two—three—that attacked him. Tearing away, dripping blood and limping badly, he dragged himself over to Neirin. He screamed as he shifted, far too battered to be doing such a thing, the shift contorting and worsening his injuries.

He wrapped one mauled and bloody hand around the hilt of the sword, tears streaming down his face. "Avalon, *help.* You have to come and help. They're going to win, if they haven't already. Avalon! Please, you have to come!"

A cold, smug laugh rolled through the room, and dread filled Barra's stomach as he realized he'd played right into their hands. God, he was so fucking *stupid.*

Magic shimmered, flashed, and that ghostly image of Avalon appeared. He looked around, dismay and then anger filling his face. He stared coldly at the sorcerer, or so it seemed, but Barra was no longer capable of even keeping his head up, could barely keep his eyes open.

Avalon dropped to his knees, one shimmery hand covering Barra's on the sword. "I need life. I cannot leave my lands. I'm out of time. But I can leave my cage for a day if you'll give a year of your life."

"Do it," Barra managed then coughed and spat out blood. "You can have it. One year of my life to grant you freedom for a day. It's yours."

Magic scalded through him, turned to ice, and left him dizzy and disoriented.

Then someone was helping him sit up, clutching gently at the sides of his throat. Barra dragged his eyes open and stared into eyes that were dragon amber, deep with age and brimming with a sadness that made him ache. "The bargain is struck and sealed," Avalon said. He kissed Barra's cheeks then brushed a softer kiss across his mouth. "Rest, now. I'll set all to rights."

"It's about time," said the dark-haired sorcerer— Barra could not remember his name, something hard for him to say correctly. "I've gone to a lot of trouble to get to you, Avalon."

"Well, you have me now," Avalon said coolly, and in the light of the flames, wearing old-fashioned breeches, shirt, and waistcoat, he looked every inch the mysterious prince most didn't believe existed. He threw out a hand, and the sword beneath Barra's fingers jerked, pulled free, and flew to Avalon's hand. He held it loosely at his right side and crooked the fingers of his left hand. "Caliburn."

Barra stopped breathing for a moment, too stunned to move even that much, as out of shadows and fire walked a dragon even more beautiful and stunning than Troyes. He was even bigger than Troyes, with golden scales that glinted and gleamed in the light of the flames.

Caliburn growled softly as he came to stand at Avalon's side.

The werewolves had gathered in a circle around them, growling, snarling, tensed to attack.

"I need him alive," the sorcerer said.

Avalon threw his head back and laughed—then stopped and said coldly, "Kneel."

All the wolves, even the sorcerers, dropped to their knees.

"Kill them," Avalon said.

Caliburn growled again and lunged.

He moved too fast for Barra to entirely follow, snapping bones, tearing out throats, throwing wolves into the walls. The other sorcerers managed to cast a handful of spells, but every last one slid off of Caliburn like oil spilled on water, and moments later they joined the growing pile of corpses.

Avalon lifted his sword and with a flash of blue light and chilling wind, the flames went out. He turned his attention to the last remaining sorcerer. "Caliburn."

But as Caliburn launched himself across the room, the man vanished.

"The baby!" Barra said, spitting out more blood. "He's upstairs, that bastard—"

"Enough now." Avalon dropped to his knees and caught Barra before he could topple to the ground. "This battle is lost, but I will ensure you all live to be needlessly angry about it. The Holy Pendragon will have to be reclaimed another day. Rest now, sweet wolf. You've done more than enough."

Barra tried to say something in reply, but all he could do was sigh as oblivion finally got the better of him.

~~*

He woke up to a barrage of unfamiliar scents: fragrant greenery, yellow roses, amber and sandalwood, silk and damask, old wood, and beneath all of it was the tang of hot metal.

It took a moment to realize that everything was dark because heavy bed curtains had been drawn, blocking out the rest of the world. Muted light slipped through the cracks. Shoving away the blankets, Barra crawled across the enormous bed and climbed out.

As cool air washed over his body, it struck him he was very, very naked. Barra looked frantically around, eyes finally landing on a dressing robe and a pile of clothes that weren't his. Wherever his clothes were... Well, as to that, they were probably beyond salvaging.

He pulled the clothes on. They were a trifle big, and at least a century out of date, but clean and warm— and quite beautiful, all various shades of blue with trimmings of gold that taken together reminded him of a twilight sky.

There were also shoes that fit remarkably well, only the barest bit too large, and clocked stockings. When he was dressed, he combed his fingers through his hair, fussed with the cuffs a moment... and then made himself stop dithering and head for the large door on the far side of the bedroom.

More unfamiliar scents washed over him as he pulled the door open. The door itself was made of heavy wood, with time-worn metal bands across it. It made him think of a castle, as did the stone walls and the elaborate tapestries lining the hall. The wall sconces had been converted to gas lanterns, an oddly modern touch that made the rest of the place seem all the stranger.

He pressed the heel of his hand to his forehead, fruitlessly attempting to ward off a headache and trying to remember what had happened that led to him waking up naked in a mysterious castle.

Barra closed his eyes. He remembered... arguing with Neirin, fleeing like a coward, talking to Devlin...

Devlin. Stabbed. Neirin and Troyes taken down by

werewolves and sorcerers. Hasna, too. Midnight bound in that awful spell cage. Tears streamed down Barra's face. Were they all dead and he the only survivor? What had he done to merit such an unspeakable cruelty?

This battle is lost, but I will ensure you all live to be needlessly angry about it. The Holy Pendragon will have to be reclaimed another day. Rest now, sweet wolf. You've done more than enough.

Avalon. He'd begged Avalon for help and he'd come. *One year of my life to grant you freedom for a day.*

Barra swallowed, clutching at his shirt with one hand, the other covering his face as tears of relief and hope replaced the anguished ones. Avalon had said he could save everyone, so maybe they were all still alive.

A soft growl rolled down the hallway, ran through him more intimate than a caress. Barra sniffled and wiped his eyes, slowly looked up—and froze as he saw Avalon's dragon, Caliburn, prowling down the hall. His heart jumped into his throat. The only other dragon he'd ever seen was Troyes, and his impression from Neirin was that all dragons looked much the same.

Then Neirin had been made Avalon's Steward and Troyes had changed in appearance, grown stronger in power. Still he was nothing like Caliburn, who shone with a golden sheen and seemed to fill the hallway and make everything in it smaller.

In the weak, wavering light of the hallway, there was something strange about his back. It didn't look right, seemed to have extraneous, loose pieces that shifted oddly...

Caliburn gave a low, deep chittering sound that Barra had learned long ago was a dragon laughing.

Then the wrong-looking parts of his back shifted—and spread. Barra stumbled back in surprise, mouth dropping, eyes going wide. Caliburn had *wings.* In the confines of the hallway he'd only barely opened them. Given enough space, their span must be enormous.

Folding the wings in close against his back, Caliburn resumed prowling toward him with that slow, lazy gait of a dragon who knew he had all the time in the world to catch his quarry.

The urge to run or bare his throat clawed at Barra, but he held himself perfectly still as Caliburn drew close, the tang of magic and hot metal filling his nostrils and pimpling his skin. Caliburn rubbed against him like a cat, circling slowly, nuzzling and rubbing and nudging.

When he was finally back in front of Barra, Caliburn gave a soft, rolling growl and heaved up on his back legs—and suddenly a person was standing in front of Barra. Rather, a person was towering over him by at least a full head. Caliburn in human form had dark brown, red-toned skin and hair shaved close to his scalp. He wore trousers and a shirt, nothing else, not even socks. He did wear a truly remarkable amount of jewelry—several bits in each ear, a gold hoop through one nostril, even a gold ball in his chin, though Barra could not begin to imagine how that was possible.

Just visible through the gap in his shirt were more of those little gold balls embedded in his chest like a strange necklace. Actual necklaces of gold, silver, pearls, and jewels hung just above them, with a snugger one of gold that practically looked painted on his throat. Caliburn rumbled softly in amusement, making Barra's face burn, and lifted a hand heavily laden with rings and bracelets.

His skin was hot, almost unbearably so. Barra shivered, still fighting the overwhelming urge to run or surrender.

Caliburn said something, his voice deep and soft, but Barra did not understand the words.

Barra shook his head slightly. "I don't—" He licked his lips, swallowed. "I don't understand you."

Caliburn frowned slightly, brow furrowing, then said haltingly, "Good you are awake, pretty wolf."

What was it with dragons never using his name? "It's Barra."

Grinning in an unmistakably mischievous way, Caliburn replied, "Wolf-elf."

Barra sighed, smiling faintly, though doing so hurt. He'd been so focused on Avalon, he'd forgotten about Caliburn. He bet they were magnificent together, in all ways. Why would Neirin and Troyes continue to settle for him when they could have everything they'd really wanted, and what they wanted was so magnificent? He couldn't even be resentful, couldn't muster hate. That would be so much easier.

But all he could feel was heartache.

"That is what they like to call me, yes," he said softly. "How do you know that?"

Caliburn scoffed in that uniquely dragon way that expressed so much about dragon opinions on the intelligence of everyone else in the world. "Come see friends."

Barra's breath hitched. "They are alive, then?"

Giving him an offended look, Caliburn turned away, shifting as he did so. He led Barra down the hall to the archway he'd come through before, down a curving staircase to another, slightly warmer hall that was lined with beautiful rugs and windows of stained-glass.

At the end of the hall were three doors, two of them painted dark blue and one maroon, all with the same old-fashioned look as the room he'd come out of. Caliburn nudged open the maroon door.

Several beds filled the large space. They were small but elegant, not the depressingly uniform and utilitarian ones usually found in medical places. The wretched smells of a hospital were absent, too, the sharp smell and feel of magic in its place. Wards and other spells Barra didn't know shimmered occasionally on the walls.

In two of the beds, pushed together so they could hold hands, were Devlin and Midnight. Both were naked, though currently draped in sheets. He could just see the bulk of bandages around Devlin's stomach. He looked far too pale, but he was breathing and Midnight was still there.

Caliburn rubbed against his hip, and Barra realized he'd started crying again. "They're alive, thank you, thank you, thank you." Was it acceptable to hug Caliburn, or would that violate some massive etiquette? Dragons seemed tactile in nature, if Troyes was anything to go by, but surely there were rules about touching *the* dragon.

The sound of the door opening drew Barra's attention, and he turned to see a stately woman with long, gray-blonde hair bound in a bun and wearing a slightly old-fashioned gown bustling in. She stared at him in surprise then shook herself. "Master Barra, you're up and about." She cast a look down. "Or did His Most Holy Impatience ensure that you accidentally woke?"

Caliburn growled softly, tossing his enormous

head and flicking the tip of his tail.

"He didn't wake me," Barra said. "I am flattered you know my name, my lady, and most apologetic I do not know yours."

She smiled. "Lady Wendy Pelles, of Clan Pelles, currently assigned as Master Healer of Castle Camelot."

"It's an honor to make your acquaintance. Thank you for tending my friends. I know it's against the rules to have non-clan on your lands. And I know Neirin..."

"The rules are what Avalon, and occasionally the Table, say they are. You are his honored guests, and Sir Neirin, you, and your compatriots did a great service in trying to rescue the Holy Pendragon. I won't lie. Not everyone is pleased Sir Neirin is here and was made Acting High Steward, but no one will cause you trouble. If some fool should try, you've only to tell His Highness or speak with the guards."

"I'm fairly certain we did no service at all," Barra said. "We tried to save the Holy Pendragon but only failed miserably."

"You nearly died doing so, from what little I have heard, and certainly you did more than anyone else has managed," Wendy replied. "But come, I'm sure you'd like to see Sir Neirin and Troyes. These two were the most dangerously wounded, between His Grace's stab wound—the blade both poisoned and cursed—and Lord Midnight suffered greatly from the curses woven into the spell cage His Highness broke him out of. They're kept sedated to help them heal faster, though we ran into some trouble when we tried to space them out."

Barra's lips twitched. "That does not surprise me. If Midnight cannot feel Devlin, he tends to get upset fast. It's a byproduct of his draugr nature."

Wendy nodded and turned toward the door. "This way to see Sir Neirin and Troyes." Out in the hall, she nodded to the blue door on her left. "Lady Hasna is there, but only Prince Avalon and I are allowed in the room until we are convinced she is not here on nefarious purpose. His Highness protested, loudly and crudely, but the council would not be moved. I am sorry, I am certain you would like to see her."

"I do not know her well, but she did fight alongside us, even though she and Neirin had every reason to be at great odds. Is she all right, at least?"

"She is well enough to be moved out of the healing hall, but the council won't permit her anywhere else," Wendy replied with a sigh.

Barra didn't roll his eyes, but he very badly wanted to. Instead, he followed quietly as she led him through one of the blue doors. This was another healing room, but with only a single large bed, bookshelves and a table. It made him think more of a room where someone could recover in comfort and peace, rather than the healing ward where Devlin and Midnight resided because they likely required frequent, if not near-constant, observation.

Rumbling softly, Caliburn prowled to the bed and leveraged up to plant his front paws on it, nostrils flaring as he examined the two figures curled up together in it. Fresh tears stung Barra's eyes as he looked at them, both Neirin and Troyes far too pale and still. Normally Troyes snored, but he was completely silent, the rise and fall of his chest barely discernible. "Are they all right?"

"Oh, fine, but they took quite the beating. We only moved them in here two days ago—same day we moved you out, in fact." Wendy smiled and patted his arm. "They're being kept sedated as well, though mostly because when we didn't do that, they kept trying to get up and do things because knights and dragons are nothing if not stubborn fools. They'll be asleep for quite some time yet, but they are healing very well."

Barra laughed. "I could not muster an argument against that even if I wanted."

Wendy smiled. "I will leave you alone, then, and tend to the others." She headed for the door and then abruptly turned around. "Oh, I almost forgot. His Highness was hoping to see you when you woke. It's not an urgent matter, however. If you are too tired to meet with him today, Caliburn will let him know."

Oh, god, no. Barra didn't want to see Avalon. Didn't want to talk to Avalon. Why couldn't he just *leave*? Slip away quietly while he still had some dignity to cling to. Before he had to see Neirin and Avalon surrender to everything that was in their eyes whenever they thought or spoke or looked at one another. "I'd be honored. I'll go see him after I've sat with Neirin and Troyes for a bit."

"It was nice to meet you." Wendy bowed her head and swept from the room, closing the door quietly behind her.

Barra stepped around the bed to stand by the side where Neirin lay, reaching out to touch his hand. Even too-pale and worn, he was still the most beautiful, enthralling person Barra had ever seen. Seventy years had only made him love Neirin more, and Troyes right beside him. How many mongrel wolves ever got to say they'd been loved by a noble knight and his dragon?

He picked up Neirin's hand and held it fast, pressed

a lingering kiss to the back of it, ignoring the stupid tears that wouldn't stop falling. Setting Neirin's hand back on the bed, he picked up Troyes's and kissed it in turn. "Take care of our knight, dragon."

Nothing else in a hundred years of life had been as difficult as it was to turn away from the bed instead of crawling into it.

Caliburn growled and butted against him, moved in front of him and pushed him back toward the bed.

"What are you doing?"

Huffing, Caliburn gave him another shove.

"Stop it," Barra said, and moved around him quickly, though he was well aware Caliburn was only letting him win for now. He'd been on the receiving end of a stubborn, determined dragon more than once. "Come on, it's rude to keep royalty waiting."

The sooner he spoke with Avalon, the sooner he could leave. He could deal with the manor, move everything of importance to the townhouse, and have everything ready by the time Devlin and Midnight returned home.

And maybe by that point he'd stop feeling like something had torn a hole in his chest.

Avalon

Four guards and their dragons stood in front of a set of double doors carved with dragons, knights, and other figures. They shimmered with magic, though Barra didn't doubt the real magic in them didn't give itself away so easily. Devlin's most dangerous wards were the ones no one could tell were there.

None of the guards spoke, but Barra was painfully attuned to derision and didn't miss the faint curling of lips that two of the guards displayed before catching themselves and returning to an impassive demeanor.

Caliburn growled, low and sharp, making all the guards jump and the two derisive ones cower slightly. The other two guards pulled the doors open, and Caliburn nudged Barra slightly forward before moving ahead of him to lead the way.

Barra hadn't known what to expect of Avalon's sanctuary. Something as beautiful, austere, and timeless as the man himself, perhaps. A slice of history that even the most expert historians wouldn't be able to immediately identify, maybe.

He definitely had not expected a gigantic room overrun by chaos. Bookshelves, cabinets, mirrors, and more lined the walls of an enormous round room, with stairs and ladders scattered about to access every nook and cranny. At the top of the enormous, echoing room was a dome of stained glass depicting vines and flowers, birds, and butterflies. Sunlight shone through them, casting colorful impressions across gleaming wood and intricately woven rugs.

In the center of the room was a circle of tables, each piled with different miscellany: books, scientific-looking equipment. Art supplies on another, and beside that a table on the verge of toppling from all the random clutter that filled it, discards and overflow from the other tables. Another was filled with all manner of fabric and sewing supplies, and another one that reminded him of Devlin's work room.

There were more tables and desks around the room, trunks and chests, couches, chairs, and settees. It was like someone had crammed together the libraries, studies, and laboratories of at least a dozen different homes. He wasn't sure where to rest his eyes, but looking around made him faintly dizzy.

"It's good to see you looking so well!" A familiar voice called out, but Barra still had to turn and turn until he finally spied Avalon on the second level, tucked into a corner in front of a shelf filled with loose papers, scrolls, and stacks bound in ribbon rather than proper books.

Barra's breath hitched, and he hated himself, but he was only human. Well, partly human. Whatever. He wasn't *blind* and Avalon was *beautiful*. Especially right then, in trousers and shirt and waistcoat, the long tumble of hair falling over one shoulder, barely contained by a sky blue ribbon that matched the flowers in his waistcoat.

Worst of all were the gold spectacles perched on his nose. Barra wanted to knock them off his face. Or just hit him. Or, gods save him from his own pathetic stupidity, gently remove them before pushing Avalon up against those shelves and kissing him senseless.

Avalon would probably have him hanged, or drawn and quartered, or weighted with rocks and thrown in the sea, or whatever it was Pendragon did to brazen mongrels.

Damn it, this was the man he'd lost Neirin to. Couldn't the world be kind enough to at least make Avalon easy to hate?

"Uh. Good afternoon, Your Highness." Barra shuffled, uncertain where to put his hands or what else to say or do. Nobody had ever thought to teach him the etiquette for meeting with a nigh-legendary prince who'd taken his lover.

Avalon laughed and headed for the nearby tightly-spiraled staircase, clattering down it fast enough that by the time he reached the bottom, his ribbon had been lost. He looked around briefly, huffed when he did not see it, and with a shrug crossed the madcap room to take Barra's hand in one of his own. Tucking the spectacles away in a pocket, he took Barra's other hand as well and leaned down and kissed each of Barra's cheeks. "You are my friend. You need not address me so formally."

"I could not take a liberty not granted..." Barra trailed off. "You probably *did* grant Neirin that liberty, and he simply refuses."

"Yes, precisely," Avalon said with a smile, and squeezed his hands gently before letting go to sweep his hair off his shoulders. "You are feeling better? I would not have you pushing yourself; your injuries were not as severe as the others, but they were not insignificant either. You are welcome here for as long as you care to stay."

"I'm feeling much better, thank you. I appreciate the offer, but I should probably be on my way.

Winterbourne Manor was badly dam..." He paused at the look of sorrow that overtook Avalon's face. "What's wrong?"

Avalon bowed his head. "It shames me to say that I was not able to save your home. I extinguished the first fire, but while I was taking all of you to safety, that sorcerer stole the Holy Pendragon and set fire to other parts of the manor. By the time I realized, I was too late to save it. The books in the library survived, which is truly remarkable spell work, His Grace's skills are not exaggerated, I—" Avalon shook his head. "We have put the books in storage until His Grace can let us know what to do with them, but there was nothing else left to save. I offer my most abject apologies, useless as they are, and will spare no expense to see that a new home is built."

"That's for Devlin to decide," Barra said, ducking his head to hide the fresh tears. He'd loved Winterbourne Manor. It was their *home*. The townhouse was where they spent much of their time, but that was because it was the easiest place from which to work. When they needed rest and respite, the manor was where they went. Gone. Damn it, he did not want to keep crying, but his home was *gone.*

And poor Devlin, he didn't even know yet, wouldn't know until he woke up, and what a terrible thing to be greeted with. It was all he'd had left of his family; it was going to break his heart.

Arms wrapped around him and pulled him close, enfolding Barra in the scent of expensive silk, sandalwood-rose cologne, and hot metal. God, how pathetic was he that he was so easily accepting comfort—and actually feeling comforted—by *Avalon.* What was wrong with him?

"I am so very sorry," Avalon murmured, and Barra swore he felt a kiss brush across the top of his head. "I will do what I can to make reparations, though the most beautiful house in the world cannot make up for the lost memories." He drew back, wiped Barra's tears away with his thumbs, and kissed his brow. "Come, come, I will have tea brought. Caliburn, you will *not* go back to napping. That's all you've done all day. Get up at once and do something useful or healthful."

Caliburn growled and didn't move.

Avalon sighed and shook his head as he cupped a hand beneath Barra's elbow and all but dragged him through the room to a table and benches set in a rounded nook. It overlooked a beautiful little garden with more flowers than he could count, scattered with birds and butterflies.

Barra looked back across the room, sweeping around it until he spied where Caliburn had sprawled out in front of the enormous fireplace, precisely as Troyes had done a thousand times. The only difference was the wings that drooped lazily on either side of him, carrying a rainbow sheen in the webbing where the firelight bathed them.

"I hope he has behaved himself."

Barra jerked, flushed as he realized he'd been caught staring, and turned back to Avalon. "He's beautiful, in dragon and human form. I didn't know dragons could have wings. I just assumed they were all like Troyes."

"Caliburn is the only one with wings now. My father's dragon had wings, so too my eldest sister's, but they died when my family died, and no dragon since has had them, not even Holy Pendragons. Did you say you saw his human form?"

"Yes," Barra replied, shoulders hunching. "Should I not have?"

Avalon laughed and smiled. "That would not be for me to say, even if I was inclined to try. Caliburn does as he pleases. It's only that he rarely bothers to shift. He hasn't done so for months. He must have been quite eager to impress you."

"Impress me?" Barra's face burned and god, could he just leave already? He was tired of floundering and stumbling and faltering. "Why would your dragon want to impress me? I'm nobody."

Caliburn growled, the sound rippling through the room, and cracked one eye open to glare their way before he drifted off back to sleep.

Avalon smiled fondly at him before shifting his gaze back to Barra. "Nobody? Not by half. Setting aside that every person is of value, and you're quite remarkable even if you had no attachment to the clans, you *are* Neirin's beloved and he is my dear friend."

"I..." Barra stared, too confounded to think of words, let alone voice them.

The smile faded. "Is something wrong?" Avalon asked.

"I don't know, anymore," Barra said. "You treat me like a friend and call me his lover, but I've seen—I know he's always wanted to return to the clans." *To you* he could not quite make himself say. "I really think it best if I go. Someone should get the townhouse ready and see about replacing some of the more important items lost in the fire before Devlin wakes." He wouldn't cry again. He *wouldn't.*

His hands curled tightly in his lap, shoulders hunching further, as he heard Avalon stand and move to his side of the table. Avalon knelt in front of him, took Barra's hands and unfolded them, gripping them gently but firmly as he met Barra's eyes. "It seems I am destined to cause you one distress after another when I mean nothing of the sort. I do not deny I hold Neirin in great esteem. It is rare for me to form friendships. People are intimidated or grow weary, and the older I get, the harder it is for me to connect to anyone, especially when clan do not live the extraordinarily long lives that most nightwalkers do.

"Neirin was a rare friend, for all there was always a certain amount of proper distance between us. I would gladly fight to have him brought back into the fold of the clans—if that was what he wanted. But he loves you dearly and has always longed for freedom besides. He would not enjoy returning to this strict, rigid life, and I would never ask it of him. He loves you, and I have no designs to upset that. I would see you both happy. So please, rest at ease on that point and know I would call you friend, too."

Barra sniffled and bobbed a nod, blinking futilely against threatening tears. Avalon brushed them away and rose to return to his seat. A moment later the door opened and servants came in bearing trays full of tea and food. When they had gone again, Avalon poured them both tea and said, "Now, then, our friends will be asleep and otherwise incapable of resuming the hunt for quite some time yet. They suffered magical damage as well as physical, and that is not repaired in a day. In the meantime, I have several hours left of the time that you were so immeasurably kind enough to gift me." When Barra started to protest, Avalon lifted a hand and added, "Desperate times, desperate measures, I know, but to sacrifice a year of your life is still an extraordinary kindness. I do not want to squander it and was hoping you would continue the hunt with me."

"I'm more than happy to help you catch the bastard that almost killed us and destroyed our home," Barra said, smiling, the first real smile he'd felt since tasting and smelling Avalon on Neirin several days ago. "Just tell me what you need of me."

Avalon's golden eyes flashed, seemed to burn, before he shook himself and the heat was gone faster than it had appeared, leaving Barra confounded as to whatever that had been about. "Mostly I am lacking information. I assume that was the Sorcerer Brennus who is tied up in this mess."

"Yes, that was him. But Linden is dead, so I don't know why he would still care about the Holy Pendragon. No..." Barra frowned, something nagging. *Call for help, little wolf.* "You!" he burst out, head jerking up. "He wanted us to call for you. He was so smug when you showed up; I remember thinking I just kept making mistakes. He doesn't care about the Holy Pendragon save as a means to you. But why?"

"I could not say," Avalon said, looking away to stare at the garden beyond the windows. "Power, I should think, or he is working for some figure we've yet to meet. It would not be the first time."

Barra frowned. "If he's after you, or working for someone after you, then it's even more important that you remain here."

"My friends nearly died doing me a favor I most definitely did not deserve," Avalon replied. "I'll be damned if I sit here safe and sound when I can, for once, spend several hours out in the world helping to fix the problem. It's less than a day. Caliburn and I shall be fine."

Barra tried to imagine Avalon and Caliburn on the streets of London, or anywhere else for that matter, and closed his eyes at the utter disaster it would be. Neither one struck him as the subtle type, and Caliburn didn't even seem terribly familiar with modern English. Their looks alone would draw attention. This was going to be infinitely more difficult than Neirin and Troyes when they were first adjusting. At least it would only be for a day.

And he was wearing modern clothes; that was a start.

"Well, you are the prince," he finally said with a weak smile. "If you desire to venture out, I can only acquiesce and enjoy your company, Your Highness."

They way Avalon's face lit up, he didn't even mind they were probably going to get arrested, or into a tavern brawl, or some other disaster at some point. He was starting to suspect that Avalon's true power was that it was impossible to tell him no and watch that lovely face fall.

He still wasn't convinced that Neirin wouldn't leave him for Avalon and the clans when it was all over, but at least it seemed like both Neirin and Avalon were obtuse idiots. That was infinitely bearable to Avalon being a schemer planning to steal Neirin away, or Neirin lying in a useless effort to spare Barra's feelings.

"When did you want to leave?"

"As soon as possible," Avalon said. "I merely need to inform my jailers I am leaving and get properly dressed." He tugged ruefully at his hair. "I am constantly told I should cut it, but—"

"You shouldn't," Barra blurted, then flushed and

stared at his tea, desperately considering trying to see if he could drown himself in it.

Avalon only said, "Yes, that is what Caliburn says, and I value his opinion above all others. He can show you back to your room, where hopefully more suitable clothes will be ready by now, and escort you to the ward, where I will meet you shortly."

"Y-Yes, Your Highness."

"You aren't going to use my name, are you?"

He looked so crestfallen, and yes, that was definitely his real power. Nobody wanted to endure a sad Avalon. Gods have mercy on them all. "Avalon," Barra said, and could only sigh at himself when Avalon's smile made him want to melt.

Damn it all, he was supposed to hate this man. That shouldn't be so difficult.

Barra finished his tea and rose. "I will see you shortly. Thank you, for everything."

"Thank you," Avalon said softly, standing with him. He rested a hand on Barra's shoulder and leaned down to kiss his cheek. Why was he so touchy? It was driving Barra mad. As much as he hated it, he could all too easily see why Neirin was in love with Avalon.

He fled the room, barely remembering to wait for Caliburn once he was in the hallway. Almost groaned when Caliburn shifted. "You don't turn human, he just said that. Why are you turning human?"

"Only knights understand dragons," Caliburn replied as he stepped in close, big and beautiful. "Easier to communicate."

"What was that you spoke earlier?" Barra asked, desperately trying to focus on anything except the enormous dragon crowding him against the wall. Even Avalon, far from short, would be slightly dwarfed by

Caliburn.

Caliburn smiled and spoke in that strange language again, then said, "Long lost language of nightwalkers before they fell apart. Language of clans before they too forgot."

"I'm sorry it was forgotten," Barra said softly, swallowing as Caliburn just leaned in closer, his hands braced on either side of Barra's head.

Warm lips pressed against his. Barra squeaked in surprise, and Caliburn took full advantage, kissing him deeply and oh, gods, there was a piercing in his tongue, too. How was that even possible? Why would somebody put jewelry in their tongue?

Barra tore away, chest heaving, and ducked beneath Caliburn's arms, stumbling back down the hallway, desperate to get away from him. "Why— why—why did you do that?"

Caliburn cast him a look of frustration he knew intimately from Troyes, whenever he'd had enough of human stupidity. "Knight's wolf-elf."

"Neirin's, yes, I am," Barra said with a frown, flushing with shame that he'd let Caliburn kiss him— had kissed him back. "I'm pretty sure Avalon will kill us both if he catches you kissing me."

Caliburn muttered something then, looking and sounding annoyed rather than alarmed or upset. "*Humans,*" he said and pushed away, shifting back to dragon as he turned.

"I'm only part human, you know."

Flicking his tail and giving Barra a look that said he was painfully aware of that fact, Caliburn turned and walked down the hall.

Too bemused to do anything else, Barra followed him.

Back in his room, he found a great deal more in the way of clothing and other miscellany than had been there when he'd left—including various weapons, all of which he eschewed. He fought as a wolf or with his fists. Even the firearms that had become so popular amongst normals and nightwalkers did not interest him.

He stamped into good boots, grateful they fit remarkably well, and shrugged into a sturdy coat, lingering a moment more only to try and put his dratted hair in order. Giving it up, he followed Caliburn back out of the room and through the breathtakingly beautiful castle. It was like walking through a painting or a storybook.

Outside, the walls around the castle kept everything beyond from view. He could smell running water, which could be a river or stream, but that didn't seem quite right. A moat, likely. Barra laughed. Devlin was going to be so mad, rescued by a prince, recuperating in a castle. Midnight would be enchanted, which would just make Devlin crankier.

It wouldn't keep either of them from being devastated by the loss of the manor, but it might distract them a little bit.

The air was chilly and damp, and he was grateful he'd brought the coat. He pulled the collar up and looked at the dark clouds gathering. As cold as it was, they might just see snow.

Caliburn rumbled happily and padded back the way they'd come. Barra didn't need to turn to know Avalon had arrived but did anyway, smiling as he watched Caliburn rub against Avalon like the world's biggest cat. Avalon crouched, petted and hugged him, reminding Barra so much of Neirin and Troyes it twisted hard and sharp in his chest.

How could Neirin have left this behind? Everything he saw had Neirin in it; every moment that passed reminded him more and more of Neirin. He'd always known what Neirin had given up to help them, to stay with him, but he was only now realizing just how little he'd really understood.

But there was nothing he could do about that for the moment, nothing that any of them could do until Neirin and Troyes were awake.

He tried not to stare as they walked back toward him but was absolutely certain he'd failed. Avalon appeared ordinary enough in a proper suit and tie, and his hair in a long braid and neatly tied off with a strip of black leather. But his heavy coat gleamed here and there with magic, as did the black gloves he wore, and there was no mistaking the sword he held.

"I was thinking," Barra said as Avalon reached him. "There are things I need to fetch from the manor and secure in the townhouse, things Devlin hid away should the worst come to pass, which it certainly has. If you do not mind the delay in our quest, I'd like to tend to that. I assumed we'd be visiting the manor anyway on the chance we find some clue to help us contend with Brennus."

Avalon nodded. "Yes, it cannot hurt to explore there, and of course we can tend to whatever you need. My advisors are not pleased with me, but they seldom are. I have nineteen hours of freedom; that should be plenty of time to accomplish many things." He nodded at something across the ward. "I drew the proper spell circle earlier. Shall we be on our way?"

Caliburn growled softly as he fell into step just behind them. Barra's heart drummed in his ears.

Should he say something about Caliburn kissing him? Did Avalon already know?

He'd learned a long time ago that sometimes silence was the best policy, and right then didn't seem the time to change that policy.

Behind them, Caliburn chittered softly. Avalon cast him a puzzled look, which only earned a soft, playful growl, garnering in turn a huff from Avalon.

Gods, they were just like Neirin and Troyes, except maybe worse.

Avalon led the way into a small area walled off from the rest of the ward but still open to the sky. The ground was covered with slate as smooth as marble and which smelled heavily of chalk. Laid out on it was an elaborate spell circle, the marks so myriad Barra felt dizzy trying to sort them out. "I don't think I've ever seen one like this. Devlin's are much simpler on the rare occasion he uses them."

"Spell circles are mostly a waste of time for him, I would imagine," Avalon said. "Such a powerful witch, confining him to spell circles would be like boxing up a hurricane." He stepped into the circle and offered a hand, pulling Barra to stand close beside him when he accepted it. Caliburn sat at their feet, and with a softly spoken word, the three vanished.

Barra gave a pained cry and swayed on his feet as he saw the blackened remains of Winterbourne manor. The sight blurred as tears overtook him. He'd thought himself prepared for the sight, but that had been foolish thinking. Seeing it, really seeing it—there was no bracing for such a thing.

Gone, nothing but charred stumps and bits of stone walls, but even most of that had been reduced to rubble and ash by the strength of the sorcerer's fire.

Arms wrapped around him from behind and pulled him back until he was flush with Avalon's chest. Barra clung to his arms and cried into them, barely hearing the words of comfort murmured to him.

He startled when hands cupped his head and looked up to stare through wet eyes at Caliburn, and then Caliburn was hugging him, too. Damn them both, how were they making him feel better? That wasn't fair. It was so far from fair.

They pulled away as his crying eased, someone kissing away the last tears on his cheek. Barra flushed, and could not quite bring himself to look at them. "Sorr—"

"Do not say sorry, or I shall grow irate," Avalon said with a gentle smile. "I promise we will do what we can to avenge this and build you a new place to call home. I will be mad at myself for a long time that I failed to protect what was precious to you when all of you nearly died protecting what is precious to me."

"You saved our lives. I could ask for no more than that," Barra said. "This wasn't your fault. It was that bastard Brennus."

Caliburn growled softly and walked off toward the remains of the house. Avalon headed after him, and Barra made to do the same but drew up short. "Where did your sword go?"

Avalon turned back, reached into a pocket of his waistcoat, and displayed a small gold and silver charm in the shape of a sword, attached to a chain that fastened to his waistcoat much like a pocket watch. "A spell I mastered some time ago when the carrying of swords went out of practice. I know I cannot help but draw attention, but I do try to minimize it. Usually I wear it as a necklace, but this seemed more prudent today."

"That's impressive spell work," Barra said, flushing guiltily at his earlier thoughts of how much Avalon and Caliburn would stand out.

"Thank you." Avalon chuckled and nodded toward the ruins. "Shall we, then? What are we looking for?"

Barra took a deep breath, let it out slowly, and followed him. "Devlin buried a special box beneath the library. It holds family records, special grimoires, family jewels, other such items. We have made a number of enemies over the years, and the White family was making them long before they bore the Winterbourne title. Devlin always worked hard to ensure we'd be safe, but he also made certain the most important things he owned would survive the worst should it come to pass."

He looked around at the empty stretch of fields, all the auxiliary buildings that had been burned down as well. What point had there been to burning down the stables? It was all so malicious, vindictive. Barra couldn't wait to tear the bastard's throat out. "I'm surprise there's no one here poking around."

"I had the place glamoured," Avalon said. "I thought you would all like some privacy, and no one should be mucking around before all of you have seen it, anyway. I also wasn't certain what His Grace would like done, so it's all under glamour until His Grace says otherwise."

Barra nodded. "Thank you."

Avalon smiled. "I am happy to help." He looked around. "I don't suppose you know where the library is?"

"I can't tell," Barra replied with a sigh, looking around feeling stupid. He tried to picture the manor, but the remains were so disorienting, and he couldn't smell anything but burned house.

Caliburn growled and shifted, put his nose to the ash-drenched ground, and prowled around. He headed for the west side of the house, which was about as far as Barra could have narrowed it. But after a few minutes, he looked up and spoke to Avalon in a rapid fire series of chitters, barks, clicks, and growls. Barra had tried over the years to discern a pattern to it all, and even asked Neirin a few times, but all his attempts at learning dragon had proved fruitless.

"Well done, my fire," Avalon said as they headed for Caliburn. He reached out to stroke Caliburn's head, smiling at the preening that elicited.

Barra crouched by the spot he'd marked, wiping away soot and tossing aside bits of burned rubble. There. Carved into spelled stone was the Winterbourne crest, along with a series of runes that always signified Devlin when he cast them. "This is it. There's a trunk inside that contains everything, but I don't know how to get to it. Devlin spelled it so only he and those of his blood could access it. But given all that's happened, and that Devlin is still incapacitated, I'd prefer to get it now if we can figure out a way."

"Blood spells are nearly impossible to overcome, but only nearly," Avalon said with a wink. He pulled out a handkerchief and as he unfolded it, Barra saw dried bloodstains. He crouched and spread the stained kerchief on the stone, right over the crest. Several inches above it, he splayed both his hands. The gloves he wore shimmered with gold light that seemed to trace the lines of runes not visible otherwise. Several of them flared, connected by that gold light, some strange combination of a rune casting and spell circle.

He hadn't known that kind of thing could be done with *gloves*.

Avalon spoke the activating words and the glowing marks on the gloves flashed brilliant, blinding white.

The kerchief vanished, and with a resounding crack the stone split, crumbled, and turned into dust that covered the trunk it had been protecting. More magic rippled and gleamed, but a few more words and flashing runes, and that too all vanished.

"You keep saying Devlin is powerful, but it seems to me you outpace him by leagues."

"I am a few centuries old and have done a lot of studying and practicing." Avalon held up his hands and fanned out his fingers. "These gloves weren't made in even a decade, I assure you. His Grace may never match me in terms of sheer power, but he is no one to be trifled with either. Sorcerers must create a wind and carefully control it. Witches, true witches, need only trust the wind. Give it another century or two and His Grace will be the sort of witch they once burned for fear they'd become as powerful as demons. Caliburn, the trunk, if you please."

Caliburn shifted to his human form and leapt neatly down into the manmade hollow beside the trunk. Lifting it like it weighed no more than a sack of feathers, he tossed it up onto the ground.

"Marvelous. Come along, let's find a place I can draw a proper spell circle. Once I've sent this off to be secured at the castle we can carry on to London." His face brightened, making him look almost boyish. "I've not been to London for at least a hundred years, minus going to see Sir Neirin recently, and that hardly counts. The last time I was there properly, it was only for an hour."

"Why were you in London?" Barra asked, falling into step beside him as they left the ruins behind and crossed the field that had once been Devlin's back lawn but currently was burnt grass and shrubs. Even the boathouse by the pond was a victim of Brennus's vindictiveness.

Avalon smiled a bit sheepishly. "I was out of books and wanted to choose some new ones for myself. The other clans frequently send me such things from around the world, but there's nothing quite like stepping into a shop and browsing. I always reserve one hour of my time each decade purely for such things. You can see why I am so eternally grateful for your sacrifice." Sadness bled into his eyes for only a fleeting moment, but it left Barra wanting to cry again. Avalon hastened his step. "I think the family vault will do for drawing, come along." He hurried off ahead of them, and Barra glanced at Caliburn, feeling like an intruder to see the same sadness and longing that Avalon had tried to hide.

All that magic, all that power, all that knowledge the clans possessed, and no one could figure out how to free two prisoners who surely had suffered long enough?

Barra had no hope whatsoever of helping with that. He was just a mongrel wolf, which gave him many things, but magic wasn't one of them. Even if he could use magic, he wouldn't be able to break such a powerful spell.

Ensuring a sad prince enjoyed his few hours of unexpected freedom, though... that didn't require special skills, and he was good at taking care of people.

He wasn't quite certain still why he cared so much about the man who would inevitably walk off with

Barra's lover, but he wasn't going to keep wasting energy worrying about it. He'd sort out that problem when the time finally came.

For now, he'd focus on making Avalon and Caliburn smile.

Dinner

There was someone waiting for them on the front steps when they arrived at the townhouse.

"Lady Hasna!" Barra rushed up the stairs to her, taking in the strain around her eyes and mouth, the tight line of her shoulders. She was dressed in a suit a trifle too big, her hair tightly bound back and hidden by a cap. "Are you all right? You shouldn't be up yet. What are you doing here?"

Her lip curled, but she let Barra help her to her feet. "As if I was going to stay on bloody Pendragon land a moment longer than necessary. And trust me, the feeling was mutual, for all they'll be mad they won't get to subject me to *questioning* like they hoped."

"They were under orders not to question you," Avalon said, the words almost drowned out by a roll of thunder, followed a few seconds later by flashes of light in the swiftly approaching black clouds. "I was going to speak with you myself because I didn't trust them not to do exactly what they were trying to do while I was absent. That will be addressed when I return." He shook himself. "Are you certain you are well?"

Hasna nodded. "I'll be better if I can sit somewhere comfortable for a time, if you do not mind the imposition, Master Barra, but I am well."

"I'll make some tea," Barra said. He finished going

up the steps and placed his hand on the door. The spell there shimmered as it recognized him, and the door gave a muted click. Pushing it open, he glanced over his shoulder and motioned for the others to follow him.

Inside, he stripped off his coat and cast it over a chair to take care of later and hastened through to the back of the house to put together a tea tray. There wasn't much in the house, since he tended to only buy food in small amounts as it all too often went to waste when they had to run off to solve one mystery or another. But there was enough to ease hunger a bit until he had a chance to run out to buy food for a proper meal.

Arranging it all on a large silver tray, Barra carried it to the front of the house, where it was easy enough to follow the scent to where Avalon, Caliburn, and Hasna had settled in the rose parlor. He set the tea on the table in the center of the loose ring of sofa and chairs then took the dark rose and gold chair that remained.

They'd just poured tea and started to eat when Hasna reached into her jacket and pulled out a red envelope, Devlin's name on the front. "This was stuck to your front door, by the way. I am sorry I did not give it to you straightaway. I may be more tired than I realized."

"It's no matter," Barra said, frowning as he took it, turning it over and over, sniffing carefully for anything suspicious.

"I see no spells on it," Avalon said. "I am going to assume that is from Brennus, inviting His Grace to bring me along to my own demise or else the Holy Pendragon will suffer in my place."

Caliburn gave a soft little growl that made Barra think of how Devlin sighed when some young sorcerer tried something they thought was clever but which Devlin had seen a thousand times.

Barra turned the envelope over and broke the plain wax seal, pulling out a slip of paper. The handwriting was neat and brisk, the message straightforward. "Correct on every count. He wants to meet at Castle Mordred tomorrow at sundown. If you do not come, he will kill the Holy Pendragon."

"A bluff, since if he kills the Holy Pendragon, I no longer have any interest in him, and well he knows it." Avalon finished his tea and set the cup down with a hard clack that made Barra inwardly wince for the delicate china. "Does he think he is the first to play such games with me? I am no trifling boy full of ego and bloodlust, but if he wants to meet, then I am entirely in support of ending this matter. It has dragged on quite long enough, and I won't see anyone else hurt."

Hasna took a sip of tea and nibbled at a bite of lemon tart. "Your Highness, I frankly do not care what becomes of you, but if you die, there is no telling what turmoil will arise within the clans and the harm the resultant strife will bring to the dragons. It would be foolish in the extreme for you to go see him. Let Master Barra and I handle Brennus."

"No," Avalon replied. "He already nearly succeeded in killing you once; I'll not allow it to happen a second time."

"It's not for you to allow or disallow me to do anything," Hasna snapped. "It is for you to show some bloody fucking sense and let other people handle this for you."

Avalon's mouth set. "I am going. That is the end of the matter. I will not risk your lives again."

"That isn't your decision to make," Barra replied. "We have the same argument with Devlin, even after all this time. I put up with his protectiveness to a point, but only to a point. If you insist on going, then I insist you take us with you. Fair is fair."

There was silence for a moment, then Avalon conceded by bowing his head. "As you say, Master Barra. We shall all four of us go and route this villain." He refilled his cup of tea and took a sip then picked up a sandwich of smoked ham and gave it to Caliburn, sprawled on the floor at his feet. "In the meantime, we should devise our plan of attack."

"I am fairly certain the plan need only be you attack, we guard you," Hasna said.

"Having seen him in a fight, I concur," Barra added, laughing at Avalon's frown. "It's true and you know it."

Avalon conceded defeat with a sigh. "I would not have you putting down your own remarkable skills."

"That's why we'll be serving as your bodyguards, and may I be long gone by the time the rest of Camelot comes looking for our throats." Hasna finished her second cup of tea and smiled politely at Barra. "Apologies in advance for leaving you to face the wolves alone."

"I can handle wolves," Barra said with a laugh. He set his tea aside and rose. "I suppose we are going to need a battle plan moderately better than 'leave the hard part to Avalon'. How about I see to food for a proper meal and we can discuss it over dinner."

Hasna rose with him. "I will take care of fetching food."

"Oh, no, Lady Has—"

She held up her hands. "Please, I would like to. I am not accustomed to anyone waiting on me, and you are providing the home and the cooking. The very least I can do is obtain the supplies. If you'll write a list of what you require, I will see it done."

Barra smiled and nodded, bustled off to the office to write the list out. When he finished, he found Lady Hasna waiting in the front hall, every inch the modern gentleman. "Uh, would you care for different clothes, Lady Hasna?"

"Oh, I do this all the time," she replied with a smile, patting his hand as he handed over the list. "Drives my brothers mad. Even nightwalkers are damnably old-fashioned and rigid in their thinking sometimes."

"What do you mean *even* nightwalkers?" Barra asked, a hint of bitterness slipping into the words.

She made a face. "Yes, you do rather have the right of it. We're much worse than the normals in many respects." She tucked the paper into her jacket and resettled her hat on her head. "I'll be back in an hour or two."

"Thank you."

The front door closed behind her and Barra went off to find Avalon, not remotely surprised that he succeeded on the first try: the library. Caliburn had claimed Troyes's normal spot in front of the fire, which had been lit at some point.

Avalon had his stupid spectacles on and was reading something in the science section.

"What are you reading?"

Avalon looked up, his face filled with eagerness. "A new book on photography. I hadn't realized they'd developed a new process for developing the images, as well as made improvements for focusing—this is truly fascinating. I will have to add the book to my list of those I would like obtained. Are there others like it? Photography is so interesting. Normals are so clever. Nightwalkers tend to give them too little credit, I think. We would have never thought of something like this."

"Midnight often says the same things. He loves to roam the city, poking and prodding." It drove Devlin absolutely mad, though mostly because he felt Midnight was putting himself at risk. "I'm sure he'd be happy to collect things for you on his outings, if it's permissible for him to send them."

The happiness that filled Avalon's face hurt. "It's permissible. No harm now that you are all well aware of me and have helped the clans. I'm sure my jailers will fuss, but that's their way."

"Why do you call them your jailers?" Barra asked. "I mean, if it's all right for me to ask."

Avalon snapped the book shut and slid it back on the shelf, tucking his spectacles away in his pocket. "You may ask me anything you like. I call them my jailers because everyone forgets that I am a prisoner bound for the arrogance of his family, not a delicate boy shut away for his own good. They have very rigid ideas about what I should do, where I should go on my rare ventures out, and with whom I should speak and forge friendships. Heaven forbid I take a lover or two." He turned back to the shelves, his long, beautiful fingers flitting over the books as he read their spines.

Devlin rarely spared expense for anything, but he was particularly free with his funds when it came to books—a fairly common tendency amongst nightwalkers. They weren't quite regarded with the fervor of religious objects, but they weren't far off. Money was nothing to scoff at, but books were the real power and currency of nightwalkers.

Avalon drew one out and opened it, pulling out his spectacles again, a soft smile curving his lips as he sank into whatever he was reading. Barra turned away and left him to it before he did something he'd regret. He was ashamed of himself for thinking about it, especially after everything he'd said to Neirin.

But those words rang in his head. *Heaven forbid I take a lover or two.* It wasn't surprising that Avalon might have multiple lovers at once, only aggravating because it teased Barra with things that would never be possible. He could see Avalon and Neirin together. They'd be magnificent and beautiful and perfect for each other.

So perfect they had no need of a stray. He hardly knew Avalon anyway.

That hadn't kept him from kissing Neirin barely after they'd met.

Barra muttered curses as he went to add more wood to the fire. No wonder Devlin got cranky when the world got too quiet. All this silence and lack of work was sending him straight into Devlin-levels of brooding.

"Wolf-elf good?" Caliburn asked.

Barra jumped and screamed, whipping around, head cracking against the fireplace mantel.

Caliburn darted forward and pulled him away from the fireplace, cradled the back of his aching head. He whined. "I'm sorry."

"That was a complete sentence. You must be really worried about me," Barra said with a faint smile. "I'm fine. It sounded worse than it is. I promise, Troyes is often rougher on me than a fireplace could ever be. Well, short of burning me—that'd be difficult to overcome."

Caliburn growled low, his eyes flashing, and the hands gripping Barra tightened.

"Caliburn," Avalon said sharply.

With another growl, Barra was released, and Caliburn fell back to stand behind Avalon.

"Are you certain you are well?" Avalon reached out, fingers falling gently on his arm.

Barra jerked away. "Stop it."

"What?"

"Stop being nice. Stop being nice to *me.*" Barra pressed the heels of his hands to his eyes, but tears fell anyway. "You're as stupid as Neirin. I've seen the way he looks at you and the way you look at him. I know precisely how much you both care about each other—" Avalon moved toward him again, but Barra reeled away and fled to the middle of the room, wiping his eyes with one sleeve. "I wish I could hate you, but I can't. But that doesn't make this any easier to deal with. You being nice. Gracious. I can see why he loves you. I just wish you would both admit it and move on and leave me in peace."

"Barra—"

He fled to the kitchen, where he sat at the table and let out everything he'd been holding back ever since Neirin had returned to the townhouse smelling like dragons and magic with the taste of Avalon on his lips. It wasn't fair, but life wasn't fair. He could learn to live without Neirin and Troyes; that was life, too. But he wished they'd just have done with it. He might want to see Avalon happy, but that shouldn't entail gutting himself. Why had he thought he could handle this?

At least someone pitied him enough that they'd be dealing with Brennus in a matter of hours and then he could return to the townhouse and wait for Devlin and Midnight to return. He should probably be there when they woke, but they'd understand why he wasn't.

When his tears and energy were spent, Barra heaved himself to his feet and ran water to clean his face. He filled a kettle and fixed a pot of tea, then set about laying out what he would need to fix dinner once Hasna returned. Oh, he should make up a room for her.

Finishing his tea, he bustled off upstairs to prepare one of the guest rooms, putting sheets and blankets on the bed, opening the window to air the room out a bit, laying a fire, and giving the whole place a quick dusting. By the time he finished, he was sweaty and dusty, but no point in cleaning up too much because he was going to get even messier cooking dinner.

He headed back to the kitchen, where he found foodstuffs on the table with a note from Hasna that she'd be in the parlor reading until dinner.

Rolling up his sleeves and tying back his over-long hair, Barra set to work.

Three hours later he had a respectable, if simple, meal of roasted lamb, roasted potatoes, and asparagus. Nothing like what he'd put together on days he had more time, but hopefully nobody would mind the lack.

He hastened upstairs to change for dinner, flushing as he made certain to pull on good clothes—not too fancy, but better than he normally wore for a quiet night at home. He wasn't even certain why he was doing it. Saving face? Impressing anyone was already long past possible.

A few minutes were wasted fighting with his stupid hair, but he could only hide from a mess of his own making for so long. Drawing a deep breath and squaring his shoulders, Barra headed back downstairs and carried the food into the dining room. Once it was all arranged to his satisfaction, he fetched Hasna from the parlor before finally facing the library.

He quietly pushed the door open—and stopped, face going hot, feet frozen to the floor.

He'd been right, though: even Avalon looked small next to Caliburn. Pressed up against Caliburn. Trapped between Caliburn and the bookshelves, twined around him as Caliburn kissed him senseless. *Damn it.* Damn them all, and damn whatever higher powers hated him so much they had to keep making Barra's life so much worse.

Finally able to move, Barra slipped back out of the room and down the hall, doing it all again but making much more noise the second time around. When it was just Devlin and Midnight in there, he'd learned to knock and leave it at that. Why Midnight was so damned fond of misusing the library, he did not want to know.

He knocked loudly on the door, counted to ten, then pushed it open. Not quite able to look at them, he said, "Um. Dinner is ready. I'm sorry it took so long."

"Thank you," Avalon said quietly. "Nothing to apologize for. Devlin's library is magnificent." He smiled ruefully. "And while I admit I would have enjoyed exploring the city, this was much safer and so many of these books... I did not know they existed."

Barra nodded and fled, all the words he wanted to say sticking in his throat. In the dining room, he poured them all wine then took his seat. Avalon and Caliburn appeared a couple of minutes later, Avalon's hair loose where it had been bound before, with only another slip of ribbon to hold it out of his face. Caliburn was back in dragon form and rumbled happily to see the platter of raw lamb that Barra had left for him on the sideboard. Avalon put it on the floor then took Devlin's usual seat at the head of the table.

A heavy silence fell as they ate. They were supposed to be making plans, but Barra couldn't bring himself to speak, too afraid of what stupid thing would come out of his mouth next. He was exhausted from the tug and pull of wanting Avalon to be happy and needing the torment of Avalon and Neirin to stop.

It was Hasna who finally spoke. "Brennus is obviously a man of skill and power. Strange that I've never heard the name before. Mordred works hard to stay aware of the major players amongst nightwalkers. Currently the Black family is the most powerful in this part of the world, though much like Lord White's family, they are beginning to scatter and fade."

"Yes, he clearly is powerful, but I think his key advantage is in surprise and preparation," Avalon said slowly. "He's always several steps ahead. If we are to best him, we need to break that advantage."

"I do not see how that is possible. He arranged the meeting place, the time, and still has the Holy Pendragon. Why does he want you, anyway? It's clear you were his goal the whole time if he ran off with the Pendragon and now demands you in exchange... but why, Your Highness?"

Avalon shrugged. "I could not say. I rarely know why they do it."

Barra frowned and set down the fork he'd just lifted, food forgotten. "Does this happen to you often?"

"Once or twice a century, though it's been as many

as four," Avalon replied, pushing away his plate and pulling his wine closer. "There are always rumors and whispers about me. That is one of the reasons my jailers prefer to keep me close, the spell binding me notwithstanding. People hear those rumors and get notions into their head, and suddenly I'm being threatened again. No one can reach me, generally, but they take other clan members, the dragons, harmless normals who never should have been involved, all to bait me into exposing myself." He spun the wineglass between his fingers and thumb. "This Brennus is particularly vehement, but he'll be no more successful than anyone else."

"Is that the notorious arrogance that got you into this situation in the first place?" Hasna asked.

Avalon smiled faintly. "Maybe a little."

She sniffed, but a hint of smile curved her lips as she took a sip of wine.

"Should we worry about getting the Holy Pendragon back while you deal with Brennus?" Barra asked. "Or focus on watching your back?"

"Split up," Hasna said. "I'll watch His Highness, since magic is our main problem. I doubt the Holy Pendragon will be particularly guarded; Brennus doesn't care that much about him. You do that."

Barra nodded. "Very well. He said to meet him at Castle Mordred... do you not live there?"

Hasna's mouth flattened and she set her wine down hard on the table. "No. We were banished, and that meant we were no longer allowed on clan lands. They're all too interconnected for a banished clan to keep their home. Much of the clan has gone to the Middle East, where many of our family originally hailed from. I believe Prince Avalon's mother was originally of Clan Mordred."

"Yes, she was a sorcerer from Egypt, married to a knight of Clan Mordred who died a few years after they moved here to England. She later met and had an affair with my father, and died perhaps a year or so before we were cursed."

Barra wanted to reach out at the sadness that flitted across his face. He also wanted to beat his own face against the table. He settled for draining his wine but resisted refilling it, and made himself clear his plate.

"It's peculiar Brennus wants to meet us there," Avalon continued. "He must know that location gives me a distinct advantage. All the clan lands respond to me. I have more power on them than I do when I leave them."

"Maybe it's to lull you," Hasna said. "Or he has assistants who will also gain advantage. Recall I am here because I am hunting down traitor Mordreds." Her eyes fell to the table, unhappiness pulling down the corners of her mouth. "Counting all the Mordred killed so far, there are two left. The three of them together, at Mordred Castle, could cause many a problem for us. He's also probably doing it just to offend you. His ego seems at least as bad as anything Pendragon can muster."

Avalon twirled his wine glass again. "Let us hope so, because arrogance leads to mistakes." He took a sip of wine and set the glass down again. "I should..." Avalon swayed slightly in his seat, blinked slowly, then dragged his head up to stare at Hasna. "What did you..." He plummeted forward.

Hasna sprang from her seat and caught him by the chest right before he could land in his plate. On the floor, Caliburn gave a roar, but even as he heaved to his feet, he was toppling again.

Barra stared wide-eyed. "What in the hell did you do?"

"Saved my clan," Hasna replied as she rearranged Avalon in his seat so he wouldn't fall over again. She knelt to check over Caliburn, muttering to herself. When she was satisfied, she stood and brushed off her hands on her dark violet skirts. Where she'd gotten the clothes, Barra couldn't guess.

He shook his head. "Avalon will *kill* you when he wakes up."

"No, he won't, because he won't be waking up for several hours. By the time he does, it will be too late."

"That's not going to do Mordred any favors." Barra looked at Avalon, remembering his smiles and cautious eagerness, how damned happy he'd been just to have a few hours to see the world. How excited he'd been over something as simple as a book relating developments in photography. "Why would you do this?"

"Because he's being a selfish ass," Hasna snapped. "An arrogant, selfish ass. What do you think will happen if we go to Castle Mordred and he's injured or killed or kidnapped? They'll blame me, they'll blame Mordred, and what little is left of us will be wiped out. I'm not letting that happen. I'd rather His Highness be mad at me than all the clans furious with me."

She strode out of the room. Barra looked over Avalon and Caliburn himself before going after her. He wasn't remotely surprised to find her in the workroom off the library, a room of slate that perpetually smelled of chalk, magic, and Devlin's cologne. He stayed well out of the way as she worked. "What are you doing now?"

"Drawing a spell circle to send them back to Castle Pendragon, and I'll be affixing a note letting them know what Avalon tried to do so they'll be extra certain not to let him go anywhere." She rose, checked critically over her work for several minutes, then brushed off her hands. "Help me carry them in here."

Avalon was easy enough to move, but Caliburn was another matter. By the time they were finally done, Barra wanted to take a nap. Instead he stood by and watched as she activated the spell, an ache in his chest that what had likely been his last chance to speak with Avalon had been wasted in yelling at him and making battle plans.

He should have been relieved the matter would soon be over, that he could finally start dealing with the aftermath and moving on.

But as Avalon vanished, all Barra felt was regret.

Hasna turned to face him. "Shall we on to Castle Mordred?"

Barra nodded. Tucking away everything else he was feeling, he put all his focus and energy on the battle ahead. When the Holy Pendragon was safe, he could resume thinking about everything else. "I'll ready the horses."

Brennus

It was the kind of night where rain and gloom would have been apropos, but when they reached the old Clan Mordred lands, the sky was clear and there were glittering stars as far as the eye could see. If they'd been at Winterbourne Manor, he and Troyes would have gone for a run through the woods, possibly with Midnight tagging along in his raven form. After hours of running, they'd return to the manor exhilarated, often with Neirin on the back lawn waiting for them. Midnight would vanish into the house where Devlin waited. Neirin would grumble about grass and dirt, but he always surrendered to them wanting to stay outside.

One of many things he'd vowed not to think about, but the damnable thoughts slipped in whenever he let his guard down.

"The last time we approached a castle, we got a whole lot of nothing for our troubles," Barra said. "I would not have called that luck at the time, but we should be so lucky this time."

Hasna snorted but did not argue. "I will do my best to keep him occupied while you search for the Holy Pendragon."

"Are you certain you'll be able to escape? I cannot see him letting you go."

"We do not have much choice but to let me try, so the question is moot."

That was a no if ever Barra had heard one, and he'd heard quite a few such no's from Devlin and Neirin. Oh, how he wished for Midnight right then. He could be reckless when his blood was up, but most of the time he was cool and practical to Devlin's stormier nature.

On second thought, given Devlin's condition and that they were going to face the man who'd put him in that condition, it was better that Midnight wasn't there.

Barra smiled crookedly at Hasna. "I suppose we'd best be getting on with it, then." They dismounted and he quickly shifted, woofing softly in thanks as she secured the pouch he would need later to carry the baby while still a wolf. Once the horses were secured behind an old, crumbling cottage, they headed off further into the territory bound for the castle not too far off in the distance, just visible by the light of the full moon.

This was going to end in disaster, but Hasna was right: what choice did they have? They couldn't return to Pendragon even if he wanted to—it was too far away, they'd never get past the protections, and it was likely Hasna, at least, would be killed on sight.

And there was no time to call in favors from those who owed Devlin, nobody he trusted enough to bring them into the matter anyway. Or, as in the case of the demon lord, it was a mess they were better off not getting involved in.

So it was just the two of them against a sorcerer who'd already come far too close to killing them—who had failed only because Barra had been able to call Avalon for help.

Barra thought of Neirin, too pale and too still in a

strange bed, Troyes curled up beside him equally unwell. Of Devlin and Midnight, refusing to be parted even in sleep.

Of Avalon, damn him, beautiful and kind and heartbreaking.

If he and Hasna were the only two that could end this, then end it they would. The Holy Pendragon was not going to continue being used as a pawn in yet another round of a tiresome game.

He woofed softly, nuzzled at Hasna's hand, and ran off. He ducked into the woods as he reached them, following his nose as he wended around trees, over scrub, navigating roots and leaves, sending smaller animals running for cover, and leaving even larger ones nervous.

It took a couple of hours to make his way to the castle, but they didn't want to arrive too early and make Brennus suspicious.

Once he was clear of the woods, he moved more slowly, more carefully, wary of whatever might be watching. As he reached the castle, he crept up to the edge of the moat. Unlike Castle Pendragon and Castle Le Fay, there was no water here. It was the kind of moat filled with spikes and other unpleasant ends. Rather, it had been.

Currently, it was just dirt and a few scattered puddles from a recent rain shower. Getting down was difficult, and he mostly wound up falling and tumbling, but it got him to the bottom. Shaking off dirt and water, he found a patch of shadow and hunched there to wait.

An hour or so later he heard the pounding of a horse running along hard-packed earth, smelled Hasna on the air as she rode across the lowered bridge into the depths of Castle Mordred. Barra rose and loped around to the back of the castle, slipping behind a large boulder that, as promised, was not as flush with the wall as it would look from above. He stepped into the tunnel there and headed slowly down the length of it until he came to cold, damp stone and a stairwell covered in moss and crawling with various insects. He made his way quickly up the stairs, moving as quietly as he could manage.

He lingered at the top of the stairs, reciting Hasna's directions again. There were several doors and archways, but the one he needed was the middlemost on the right side. Heading through it, he climbed another set of stairs, these ones winding in a loose spiral. They smelled like old smoke and faded magic, with the barest hint of hot metal. Dragons had dwelled here once, in a quantity great enough their mark lingered even though the castle itself smelled of decades of disuse.

Once out of the stairwell he continued down a short hallway that contained only four doors. They didn't know where in the castle Brennus had stashed the baby, but Hasna had given him some educated guesses—starting with the rooms where once Mordred had practiced and studied and improved the magic that made them such a remarkable and dangerous clan.

He paused as a noise pricked at his ears and went perfectly still to listen for footsteps, voices, anything that might indicate he was about to be found. But though he strained ears and nose, he smelled nothing awry.

Not even, come to think of it, the Holy Pendragon. Well, he'd just have to venture on, anyway. He wasn't turning back because the danger was worse than anticipated. They'd tried to hide the baby even from his senses, so what. They'd had werewolves back at Winterbourne Manor. Obviously Brennus knew what he was about.

Barra doubted the bastard had bothered to account for a werewolf that was part elf.

Barra hesitated a moment longer, but there really wasn't any help for it. He padded up to the hallway intersection, which also had a large window, all the stained glass in it long ago destroyed.

He was only part elf, which meant those abilities were not as strong for him; most of the time, being a werewolf was just as useful, if not better. His nose went a lot further than every other sense he had. But there were some things that only the wind could feel, and right now he needed to know what the wind felt, and that was much easier to do without a wolf's heavy coat. Shivering in the damp, chilly air, he closed his eyes and opened senses he hadn't bothered to use for years.

The wind felt sour, stale, but he could feel the damp and freshness of the woods and fields. Not of use. He breathed in, breathed out, reached for the wind and coaxed it to him. Sweat beaded on his brow and his shivering turned into trembling. But he could feel dragons, fire and smoke and metal. He could feel magic, the burn of good brandy and the crackle in the air after a pounding storm.

He traced the feel of dragon, followed the thread of it, as it felt softer and sweeter, to a room further down in the castle. It was tangled with the feel of magic new and old, the bitter taste of anger and the acrid burn of fear.

Barra swayed and sank to his knees as he let the sensations fade. The clawing hunger to chase the wind, to feel and touch all it felt and touched, vanished with it. Barra sighed in relief, though a small part of him always felt a pang, too. The hearth nature of a wolf and the nomad nature of an elf were never easily reconciled, though in him, the hearth had eventually won out when he met a man willing to give him a home and call him family.

Swallowing against the lump in his throat, the ache in his chest, Barra shifted back to wolf and followed the images in his mind, threading through the castle to the little room where Brennus had stashed the Holy Pendragon.

Magic stung his nose as he drew close to it. Brennus was powerful, alarmingly so. In all their years of tracking down and stopping such people, Barra could not remember one as strong as Brennus. Well, maybe that priest who'd summoned an angel, but Devlin had always said Winsted's power was mostly wasted by his ego and the doctrine shoved down his throat.

He drew up close to the door and sniffed carefully, looking for any sort of weakness. Try as he might, though, there was no getting past that door without triggering the magic traps laid upon it. Huffing in frustration, Barra walked on further down the hall, his claws clicking softly on the cold stone floor.

A window. He heaved himself up, braced his paws on the sill and leaned out. Yes, the room had a window. Pulling back in, he shifted to human again, resettled the pouch meant for the baby, and climbed onto the deep, narrow windowsill. It barely had space for him, but barely was still enough.

Leaning out, he examined the rocky wall between the windows. Climbable, maybe. Hopefully. That was a long way down. Jerking his eyes back, he gave the wall another look over. It seemed doable. And did he have much choice? Devlin wasn't there to blaze through the magic with runes and willpower. Midnight wasn't there to trespass where no one thought to guard against a draugr with a heartbeat. Neirin and Troyes were not there to conquer with fire and might.

It was just him, a little wolf-elf of no special note.

He could distantly hear the sounds of fighting from elsewhere in the castle, could smell magic on the air. He needed to hurry up.

Climbing out, he started his slow, careful way across to the other window. His foot slipped, and Barra barely bit back a scream. He laughed shakily as he clung to the wall, willing away the trembling. How depressing that after all he'd managed to survive, his downfall might be a literal fall.

When he was mostly steady again, he resumed moving, step by careful step across the rough stone. Minutes felt like hours, and by the time his foot finally landed upon the window sill, Barra wanted to cry. He tumbled inside the room, went still, and after a few minutes passed without incident or even a change in the air, slowly stood.

The baby lay in a nest of blankets and old cloaks in the middle of the room, fast asleep and happily oblivious to all the trouble surrounding him. Runes shimmered on the floor around him, but as Barra tentatively reached past them he felt only warmth. So they were probably there to keep the baby warm— and likely from wandering off, though he seemed far too young to be moving on his own yet.

Barra slipped the baby into the pouch, sighing when he stayed fast asleep.

He eyed the window, then the door, then looked at both again. Standing, settling the baby comfortably across his chest, he approached the door. The wards tingled along his skin, rushed through him hot and cold, but they didn't *hurt*. But why would they? They were meant for keeping almost everyone out, not for keeping anyone in.

Opening the door slowly to minimize the noise, Barra stepped cautiously over the wards and back out into the hallway. He waited a couple more minutes, but all remained quiet save for the distant sound of Hasna and Brennus fighting.

Ignoring the urge to help her that clawed constantly at him, he put the baby down, shifted back to his wolf form, and got the pouch on properly.

Then he ran, sacrificing stealth for speed, dashing back through the castle all the way down to the secret exit into the moat.

Getting out of the moat was thankfully not as difficult as he'd feared it would be, thanks to boulders he was able to climb and jump from. He only just barely made it to land, and nearly toppled right back down, but he *did* make it.

Throughout it all, the baby slept on unperturbed. They must have laid a spell. Barra chuffed softly, shook himself to get rid of the worst of the dirt and grime clinging to his fur, and loped off toward the forest.

He was halfway there when the other wolves came after him, at least twenty of them coming from both sides. *Damn it.* Barra ran faster, trying to get into the trees where they'd at least have a harder time taking him all at once.

But he was no match for twenty werewolves by himself. Damn it, he'd been so close to succeess.

A wolf caught up to him, lunged, and Barra yelped in pain as teeth sank into his left haunch.

He went down.

The werewolf who'd caught him growled, its eyes shining a brilliant, vibrant blue. The other wolves drew close, surrounding Barra, growling and snarling. They could smell him, that he was half-elf, and it pissed them off. All these years later, no matter how the rest of the world changed, so many still hated him for being a mongrel.

One of them shifted and tried to take the baby.

Barra lunged with a snarl and sank his teeth into the man's wrist, cracking bone, tearing muscle, blood spouting and pouring all over them both.

The wolf jerked back with a scream of pain and three of the others attacked Barra.

The baby was taken away, and he was left battered, torn, and bleeding. He heaved to his feet, unable to rest his weight on one front paw.

A wolf knocked him back over, and then they were all running back to the castle.

Barra heaved himself up again and howled.

As the sound faded off into the night, it was answered by the cry of a raven.

Barra howled again, and the raven swooped so he could see it in the light of the moon. He limped off toward the castle, dizzy and nauseous, but like bloody hell was he going to stand by while Hasna was probably dead and Midnight was going to be fighting alone. He didn't know what he could do, given he'd already failed, but damn it, he was going to do *something*.

He hobbled across the drawbridge and into the keep, but toppled over halfway across the ward.

But the fight, as it turned out, came to him.

Midnight came blazing out of the keep, Hasna in his arms—too still, blood on her head and in her hair, but as Midnight set her down next to Barra, he could just barely see she was breathing.

Barra woofed at Midnight, but all he got in reply was a gentle touch to his head.

Not that he was surprised, given the look in Midnight's eyes and the way they glowed. He was in full draugr mode, bent only on protecting Devlin, the man who'd once unintentionally won the love and devotion of a child, a love that ran so deep that murdered child had become a draugr and sought Devlin out.

A child who'd grown into a man who would destroy the world without a qualm if that was what it took to keep Devlin safe.

Who had been stupid enough to let Midnight get loose?

Brennus appeared with a roar and a blast of fire, but Midnight threw himself out of its path and in the next breath was a raven.

Mist trickled through the ward, thickened into fog, and continued to thicken until Barra could not see his hand in front of his face. He nudged closer to Hasna, draped himself over her, and buried his nose in her long, tangled and blood-matted hair as he listened to Midnight and Brennus fight.

The last time they'd faced Brennus, he'd had surprise in his favor and had been smart enough—or lucky enough—to attack while Midnight was asleep.

Brennus screamed in agony, the sound resounding

through the fog. The scream turned into sobbing, high and terrified.

Thunder crack-boomed, and the fog was gone in the blink of an eye. In its place came rain—torrents upon torrents of sheeting, stinging rain, pounding down like its goal was to reduce the castle to dust.

A figure strode across the bridge, lit by bursts of lightning: Avalon. His sword was in one hand, and his magic gloves shimmered. The rain had pulled his hair loose to drape around him in a tangled mess.

Across the ward, Midnight had Brennus pinned to the ground, claws sunk into his shoulder. Brennus was bleeding from his stomach, the blood rapidly lost to the rain. Midnight glared. "What are you doing here?"

"I came to end this matter," Avalon said, voice audible only because the rain eased somewhat. "You should be with Lord Devlin."

Midnight snarled. "I'm going to kill this sniveling bastard."

"Then—" He broke off as brilliant blue light burst and blinded them all. Barra whimpered and closed his eyes.

When he opened them again, Midnight was lying in an awkward heap by the stables.

Brennus rose slowly, clutching his bleeding stomach with one hand, the other gripping his wounded shoulder. More blood dripped from his mouth and a cut on his cheek. "You arrive on a storm. How dramatic and appropriate, Your Highness." He laughed when Avalon merely regarded him in cool silence. "Do you wonder how I know? I—"

"No," Avalon cut in. "Secrets only stay secrets if those who know them are killed before they can share them. Somewhere some fool wrote down something he should not have, or fell into his cups and ran his mouth. I'm more interested to know why you give a damn."

"I need access to something, and you're the easiest way to get that access." His eyes gleamed, and Barra was equal parts relieved and frustrated that he had no idea what they were talking about.

Brennus threw out a hand, but so did Avalon, and it was Brennus who screamed and dropped to his knees, coughing blood and spittle.

"Hold still," Avalon commanded coldly. Brennus snarled, but even Barra couldn't move as Avalon's full commanding power filled the ward.

Avalon raised his sword and pointed it to the sky. Thunder boomed so loud it left Barra's ears ringing, and he barely closed his eyes in time to avoid the lightning he could see even through his eyelids.

When he opened them again, all that remained of Brennus was a blackened body amidst a heap of scorched, shattered stone. Barra was grateful for the rain that kept him from smelling it.

The rain eased to a soft shower as Avalon walked over to them and knelt. His fingers carded gently through Barra's fur, frowning as they came away blood-stained. "Little wolf, you seem to be trying to get yourself killed and that distresses me. Caliburn, get Midnight."

Caliburn growled softly from where he lingered by the gate and crossed the ward to Midnight. Shifting, he heaved Midnight over one shoulder and returned to the gate.

"Can you walk? I cannot carry both you and Lady Hasna," Avalon said.

Barra whined but slowly pushed to his feet. Avalon

draped Hasna over his shoulder and stood. He used his free hand to steady Barra as he limped alongside, and slowly they crossed the ward to join Caliburn. "I put the return spell circle on the drawbridge," Avalon said. "I would have been here sooner, but I wanted to make certain we had a way home."

It seemed to take hours to walk that short distance. When they finally stepped into the spell circle, Barra fell again—and this time he did not think he would be getting back up. If they wanted him somewhere else, they were going to have to carry him.

On that thought, he passed out.

Love

Barra woke up hot, sweaty, and sore, but sadly he didn't think it was for the reasons he usually woke up that way. He stared up at the ceiling and tried to sort out what wasn't right about it. His ceiling in the townhouse was blue, and dark green in the manor—

The manor that didn't exist anymore.

He was back in Avalon's castle. Bracing himself on one arm, Barra pushed himself to a sitting position—and swallowed with happiness and relief to see Neirin and Troyes fast asleep on the small sofa against the wall on the right side of the bed. Why were they sleeping there?

Climbing out of bed, Barra walked over to them, wincing with every step. Someone had clearly healed him, because he was in human form despite the fact he'd been too injured to shift. How long had he been unconscious?

He sat down next to Neirin on the sofa and gently rested a hand against his cheek, chest aching at the way Neirin smiled in his sleep. His eyes fluttered, blinked, slowly opened—and he nearly toppled them both off the couch as he jerked upright. "Barra!"

Barra smiled. "Were you expecting someone else?" A shadow fell across Neirin's face, and all right, given what Barra had said the last time they'd spoken, maybe that hadn't been the funniest joke. "Sorry."

"It's fine," Neirin said, and grabbed hold of him to

drag Barra into his lap. "You're all right. That's the only thing that matters to me." He kissed Barra hard, one hand sliding up to grip his hair, the other arm still warm and heavy around Barra's waist.

Barra whined and shuddered, twining his own arms around Neirin's neck and kissing him back like a starving man. Bloody hell, he'd missed Neirin. Drawing back, panting softly, he asked, "What about you? Are you both well?"

"Troyes is still a little tired, but yes, we're doing very well. You are the one who got into a second fight."

"Fight is too generous," Barra replied bitterly, looking away. "I never stood a chance either time. It was one sound trouncing after another." It had become painfully clear that when he was alone, he was completely fucking useless.

Neirin nuzzled his cheek, pressing a whisper-soft kiss behind his ear, fingers slipping beneath the soft, loose shirt he wore to caress his skin. "Nobody wins one against a pack of wolves, which is what Avalon thinks happened."

Barra's breath hitched at the mention of Avalon, his stomach turning and twisting into a thousand knots. "Yes, there were at least twenty of them. They took the Holy Pendragon. Did Avalon get him back safely?"

"No," Neirin said quietly. "He went back to retrieve him, but the wolves and baby were long gone."

"But Brennus..." Barra's mouth flattened. "There's someone else mixed up in this, like we feared. Brennus was working for someone—or maybe with someone, it's hard to tell. Either way, this isn't over."

Neirin nodded. "Though we still don't know why

they're after Avalon."

Memories flickered in Barra's mind, but he'd been in so much pain and the rain and thunder had been near-deafening... "Brennus said something about access, and he needs Avalon to get it. Avalon seemed to know what he was talking about, but neither of them elaborated."

"I see." Neirin sighed. "I haven't seen Avalon since I woke up and he showed me to your room. He went into his private chambers and has not left them since. His guards say he is refusing all visitors. He also broke the bond between us, meaning I am no longer his Acting High Steward. Whatever he intends to do next about the Holy Pendragon and the people hunting him, I fear he intends to do it alone." Sadness flickered across his face, echoing the ache in Barra's chest.

"We—we won't let him," Barra said.

Neirin looked up, surprise replacing the sadness. "Barra..." He reached up to rest a hand against Barra's cheek. "Did you really mean to leave me? To quit us so easily?"

Barra swallowed against the jagged bits of glass that seemed to fill his throat, eyes burning as he leaned in to rest his forehead against Neirin's temple. "I love you. I want you happy. I always knew that meant eventually you'd go back to Avalon. You're happy here, you light up in a way the rest of the world cannot hope to recreate. You're meant to be here with your prince and your dragons."

"Not according to them. I haven't had the warmest reception, you now. Minus Avalon and a small handful of others, every person I've encountered has been chilly at best. No familiar faces linger in Camelot, but they all remember my name and that I was thrown out. You may have noticed the clans have a hard time letting go of things." He drew back and brushed away some of Barra's errant curls. "I love you, and I long ago decided I'd rather have you than any of this. I won't deny my feelings for Avalon are not as faded as I always tried to convince myself. But you wanted me when I was nothing but a banished, beaten knight with nothing to my name save the clothes I wore. You've stood with me through all these years—"

"Years that Avalon gave you," Barra cut in, though admitting it just twisted in his chest like more shards of glass. "He loves you, too, you know. It's in his face as plainly as yours."

Neirin looked away, eyes closing. He drew a deep breath and let it out on a shuddering sigh. "Maybe. The fact remains he is not the one I've built my life with, and even he cannot simply do as he pleases in everything. Pendragon and du Lac would never allow me to rejoin the clans." He looked back at Barra, hurt and anger in the lines of his face. "At what point will you trust what I say instead of ignoring me? I love you, I'm choosing you, why can that not be good enough for you?"

Because there was too much hurt and longing in his voice, not quite buried. Because damn Avalon, Barra wanted to see him happy just as much as he wanted to see Neirin happy.

Possibilities teased at him, whispered seductively through his mind, but he knew a fool's wish when it tormented him.

"You're right," he finally said. "In your position, I'd be mad as hell you weren't listening to me."

Neirin smiled and drew him into a soft, lingering kiss, leaving Barra aching in ways sweet and hot.

A soft growl drew them apart, and in the next minute Barra was on his back on the floor, breath knocked out of him by the hot, heavy dragon pinning him down. "Tro—" He was cut off by a bruising kiss, lip splitting from Troyes's ferocity. Whenever he tried to move to get hold of him, all he got was a warning growl to hold still. Eventually, Troyes lost all patience and grabbed his wrists, spread Barra's legs and settled between them so there was no hope of getting the leverage he needed to break or twist free.

Not that he wanted to get free, he just wanted to touch, but Troyes was clearly not in the mood to hear that.

When he finally drew back, nuzzling and lapping away the blood on Barra's lips and chin, he rumbled, "Wolf-elf hurt, wolf-elf sad."

"Missed you," Barra said. "Are you feeling better, Troyes?"

Troyes just growled and resumed kissing him, letting go of his wrists so he could make short work of the clothes impeding his intentions.

Barra laughed and let Troyes have his way, though when they were done he'd probably drop right off back to sleep for several hours.

He yelped when Troyes abruptly pulled away and yanked him up to his knees, nearly sending them both toppling. But firm arms wrapped around Barra from behind, held him steady, and the last of his thoughts fled as a hot mouth sucked up a mark on his neck.

When his ruined clothes had been discarded, Troyes went back to eating at his mouth, sharp nails scoring Barra's skin, drawing out shivers and shaky moans. A rough, calloused hand wrapped around his cock, the other working harder at teasing the rest of his body: pinching his nipples and then rubbing away the sting, scraping along his neck and down his sides, right where Barra was weakest.

Neirin's hands spanned his thighs, then one slid further along to join Troyes's around Barra's cock.

The floor was cold, even through the rug they'd landed on, and his knees weren't enjoying being abused, but Barra was more focused on the hands and mouth rapidly driving him mad.

By the time slick fingers pushed inside him, he was trembling with the need to come apart, his lips so sore he whimpered whenever Troyes kissed him, but the loss of his hungry kisses was infinitely worse.

He cried out when Neirin's fingers were replaced by his cock, hard and hot, pushing into him carefully. Slowly, much, much too slowly. Barra clung to Troyes, who rumbled happily and leaned past Barra to kiss Neirin. Then Neirin was fully inside him, arms once more heavy and solid around him.

"Pretty wolf-elf," Neirin said, husky voice filling Barra's ear and making him whine. His hips moved in frustratingly tiny thrusts, enough to tease without being anywhere close to satisfying. "I'm not pleased we almost lost you, that we were so useless the first fight and sleeping warm and safe the second time."

"You—you're being—" Barra groaned, head falling back to rest against Neirin's shoulder as a quick, hard thrust shattered his thoughts. He panted, tried to regather the pieces. "You're being Devlin. Quit it."

Neirin laughed and thrust hard again. "Insults won't get you anywhere, wolf-elf, you should know that by now."

"Prat."

"Mmm," Neirin agreed, then said, "Dragon."

Oh, he knew that tone, but surely they wouldn't—

Barra shuddered as he realized they *would*. Neirin shifted to lean back, propped against the sofa, and settled Barra across his lap, stretched wide with Neirin's cock still buried deep. "Neirin, we haven't done this for weeks—"

"And yet I doubt you'll struggle," Neirin murmured in his ear before biting it playfully.

Troyes growled and kissed his way down Barra's chest, occasionally putting teeth to his skin, leaving a trail of bites gleaming with saliva. He teased Barra's cock, licked and sucked just enough to leave him writhing on Neirin's cock, making both of them moan.

Coating his fingers from the jar nearby, and Barra did and did not want to know where they'd gotten it, Troyes slicked his cock then gently pushed a finger into Barra's already stretched, filled hole.

"You're both evil—" Barra's words were cut off by Troyes's mouth again, a kiss ravenous enough it was like Troyes hadn't left his mouth bruised with a hundred previous kisses. Barra clung to him, shaking and moaning.

The finger withdrew, was replaced by the careful nudging and pushing of Troyes's cock, and for a moment Barra stopped breathing.

Then it whooshed out of him as he let Neirin take his weight, let them take *him*, content to close his eyes and focus only on feeling: the heat of the bodies pressing against him, the stretch and burn as he was filled by them both, the heady rush as they began to carefully move, fucking him slowly and surely, because even in this, knight and dragon had to do everything together.

Not that he was complaining. They moved in time,

back and forth, cocks rubbing together inside him, driving him to the brink of madness—and tipping him over the edge with a last hard thrust from Troyes and sharp dragon teeth in his throat, Neirin's softer mouth on the other side. Too much, too much. Barra screamed as he came apart, spilling over Troyes's skin.

When they came, he wasn't certain, as by the time the world came back into focus he was in bed, tucked between them. He felt exactly as sore as he'd known he would, but it was a well-sated kind of sore, even if he'd feel it less pleasantly with every step later. "Was that absolutely necessary?" he asked sleepily, smiling faintly.

Troyes rumbled in that *well, obviously* way of his. Neirin chuckled and kiss the spot behind his ear again. "Absolutely necessary. You're our wolf-elf and we won't have you doubting it again."

"You could have convinced me without rendering me incapable of walking."

Another chuckled, a soft kiss brushed across his mouth, and Neirin whispered, "But you're so very beautiful when you take both of us, caught between us with nowhere to go, helpless to do aught but fulfill our every desire."

"Spoiled rotten," Barra whispered, and sank happily into sleep, though he was still just aware enough to be ashamed of the fleeting wish to know how it would feel to be so helplessly, happily pinned between Neirin and Avalon.

Then that thought too was gone and lost to quieter, if equally wistful dreams.

When he woke again, the room was dark save for the flickering light of a fire. Troyes and Neirin were still fast sleep on either side of him, loosely holding each other's arms where they were stretched across Barra. Shaking his head, smiling fondly, Barra carefully extracted himself and hunted out some clothes. He wound up in the old-fashioned clothes he'd first worn about the castle, but they were comfortable and warm.

That accomplished, it was time to find some food. He cast a last look toward the bed, grinning at the way Neirin and Troyes had already curled around each other, and left them to their slumber.

It took him some time to find the kitchens, but when he did, it was easy from there to find the larder and fill a plate with bread, cheese, sausages, and even a fresh, tart apple. No one else was about, but given the darkness and the quiet, it was probably late at night or early in the morning. Hopefully nobody would mind he'd helped himself to the food.

After he'd cleaned everything up, he went in search of Hasna, Devlin, and Midnight.

He stumbled across Hasna in the great hall, speaking with a couple of knights and clutching a satchel, a large travel case at her feet. Barra frowned and hurried over. The knights bowed and faded off, leaving them alone.

"You're all right!" he said. "I was so worried when I saw you in the courtyard."

She smiled. "It's good to see you well, too. I am sorry we lost the Holy Pendragon again."

Barra's mouth flattened. "I had him. I was so close—"

"They were prepared, and we again underestimated just how ruthless they would be." She hesitated, then said, "Be careful, if you continue to help His Highness. I was barely conscious when he arrived at Castle Mordred, but I remember bits..." She shook her head. "If I am right in my suspicions, he is even more powerful and dangerous than people already believe." When Barra started to protest, she lifted a hand and said, "I do not mean that he, himself, is a danger. I mean that if he falls into the wrong hands, they will use him in terrible, awful ways. A sword is only as dangerous as the person who wields it, and I suspect there is more to Avalon's confinement than anyone knows."

"What do you mean?" Barra's brow drew down, heartbeat kicking up with worry.

"I cannot say, because right now it is only speculation, but if I am right, then it is not my secret to share. I am sorry."

Barra shook his head. "I understand. I remember some of it, what Brennus and Avalon said. Clearly it made more sense to you than me, but that's probably for the best. We'll be careful." He would also protect Avalon, because the man suffered enough and nobody deserved to be used and hurt.

"You'd be wiser to leave this mess behind entirely, but I think you have too good and kind a heart. I would stay for you, but I think it's best if I go."

"So you are leaving?" Barra asked.

Hasna nodded. "I do not think I can be of further use, and it hurts to constantly be around the dragons. Nor is Pendragon particularly happy to have me around." She smiled sourly, but it turned more sincere as she extended her arms and, as Barra stepped in closer, hugged him tightly. "It was a pleasure to meet you, Master Barra. You understand me better than most, I think."

"I do," Barra said, and squeezed her hands. "I am

sorry to see you go. I would—and will—gladly call you friend."

"I will write once I have a firm address, and if you are inclined to reply to my letters, I would enjoy that. I am moving to Canada, to join those of my clan that have recently moved there." She clutched the band of the satchel on her shoulder. "His Highness ordered I was granted funds—truly astonishing funds—to ensure Clan Mordred can settle well." She shrugged, looked down briefly, then back up with a shaky smile. "I did not expect that."

"I think Avalon would like to repair relations with Mordred," Barra said.

She shrugged again. "Maybe someday that will be possible, though I do not think it will happen in my lifetime. There is still too much bad blood. Are you going home soon?"

"I don't know."

"Whatever you do, be careful and do not let these clan fools treat you poorly." She hugged him again and kissed his cheek. "If you're ever in Canada, you would be welcome by Clan Mordred. Farewell, my friend."

"Farewell," Barra said, and walked her to the doors, watching as she stepped into a spell circle and vanished.

Turning around, he threaded back through the castle to the healing hall where Devlin and Midnight had been before. That room proved to be empty, however, so he tried the room in which Neirin and Troyes had been put.

He opened the door slowly, very much *not* wanting to catch Devlin and Midnight in the throes of the same activities he'd enjoyed a few hours ago.

But Devlin was fast asleep, and Midnight was

stretched out beside him reading a book, wearing the same sort of old-fashioned clothes as Barra—clothes that had been in fashion when they'd first met Neirin and been dragged, however briefly, into the world of dragons.

Midnight looked up at the noise and smiled brightly as he saw Barra. Dropping the book, he climbed out of bed and crossed the room to throw himself at Barra and hug him tightly.

Barra ushered him out into the hallway so they wouldn't wake Devlin. "Are you feeling better?"

"Nothing wounded but my ego," Midnight said with a crooked smile. "I thought I had that bastard, but he got the final blow in. If he wasn't already dead, I'd make damned certain I won round three." He laughed. "Probably for the best Avalon put an end to the matter. A pity I missed the show. He wouldn't say much about it."

"Lightning," Barra said softly, eyes going distant as he fell into the memory. "He arrived on a storm and called down lightning. There was nothing left of Brennus but a burned husk."

Midnight frowned. "That... Devlin's right, that's not normal. No human can just call down lightning and summon storms."

"What can?"

"Demons," Midnight said. "There are a handful of demons capable of manipulating the weather that way."

"Avalon isn't a demon. That's impossible, and anyway, by this point, certainly we'd know if he was a demon. That sort of thing is impossible to hide."

Midnight shrugged. "I agree he's not a demon, but there's a demon mixed up in this, and an incredibly powerful one. I wasn't kidding when I said only a handful can control storms. Princes of Hell, all of them." He grinned. "Whatever he is, once Devlin wakes up the mystery will be solved, whether Avalon wants it solved or not. He was already mad, and between the mess this case has become and the manor being a casualty of it, Devlin is going to be out for blood." His smile collapsed, and he blinked rapidly against tears. "I can't believe they destroyed our home."

Barra hugged him, and Midnight clung tightly in return, sniffling into Barra's shoulder.

"Devlin is going to be crushed," Midnight said. "It was all he really had left of his family."

"He still has you, and as long as he has that, he will always be content," Barra said, hugging him even tighter. "He gave up on the remaining Whites a long time ago, and this will just give him an excuse to build or buy an even more obnoxious house."

Still sniffling a bit, Midnight drew back and dug out a handkerchief to wipe his eyes and nose. "You're probably right, but I worry how long it will take him to get to that point."

"If anyone can keep him from wallowing, it's you," Barra said. "Devlin possessed not a single weakness or soft spot until he met a little draugr boy. He's been even more unbearable ever since."

Midnight laugh-cried. "Even after I got him to admit he loved me as something other than a ward?"

"Especially after that," Barra replied dryly.

Midnight's laugh then was happier and free of tears. "I think we would have killed each other one way or another without you as our intermediary, Barra." He leaned in and kissed Barra's cheek. "How are you?"

"Fine. Tired."

Midnight grinned his mischievous little grin. "Sore?"

"Shut up," Barra hissed, face burning.

That elicited bright, happy laughter, though, so he could not complain too much.

Midnight shook his hair from his face, though it didn't really do more than further tangle the long cascade of wavy, midnight-blue strands. "How are Neirin and Troyes? And Lady Hasna?"

"Lady Hasna has returned to her family, though she promised to write me. Troyes and Neirin are fast asleep. I was going to check on all of you, then see if I could speak with Avalon. Neirin said he was refusing all visitors, but..." He shrugged, not really certain what else he'd wanted to say.

"Are you and Neirin all right?" Midnight asked slowly.

Barra drew a deep breath and let it out slowly, staring hard at the stone floor as his thoughts tumbled and twisted. "Yes, and no. But I cannot sort out anything until I speak with Avalon again, and I had best do that while a certain bossy knight is still asleep."

"I'll keep everyone distracted as they wake. Hell, I'll probably need Neirin's help to keep Devlin from doing something drastic once he learns about the manor." He sighed. "I had best get back so he does not wake up alone. It was hard enough tearing away to go deal with Brennus." He hugged Barra again, wished him good luck, and slipped back into the bedroom.

With no further way to avoid the most confounding person he'd ever met, Barra headed off to confront Avalon.

As Neirin had said, however, Avalon was refusing all admittance. The guards, a different set than the four he remembered from the first time, looked miserable as they apologized for having to turn him away.

"Thank you, anyway," Barra replied with a smile and headed back the way he'd come, mind working as he tried to figure out how he might be able to get through to Avalon anyway. He wasn't remotely surprised to learn that when upset about something, Avalon got as broody as Devlin and Neirin. What was it with the commanding sort of men that they had to go sulk alone in dark corners and act like the world was ending?

He found a tower after a bit of wandering and climbed it all the way to the top, including the ladder that took him to the roof. The wind was bracingly cold, leaving him hugging himself and shivering, but even in the dull gray dark of earliest morning, the view gave him what he wanted: a rough layout of Castle Pendragon, especially the location of Avalon's domed room and everything that immediately surrounded it.

Of greatest note was a walled garden right off the dome, filled to overflowing with scores and scores of plants, from tiny flowers that were little more than blurs of color at a distance, to great oaks and other towering trees he couldn't immediately identify. He remembered it from when Avalon had invited him to tea.

Mentally mapping the location and the best route to it, Barra headed back downstairs.

It took quite a bit of backtracking and swearing, but eventually he came upon the place he wanted, grateful for the trees that just barely peeked over the edge to give themselves away. The stones were rough, uneven in enough places that scaling the wall was as easy as he'd hoped.

Wards were a problem, but he didn't feel any as he climbed, or even as he swung over the edge and headed down.

The soft, inquisitive growl that met him on the ground, however, was conceivably far worse than any ward.

Barra turned, fighting against the urge to flee or drop to his knees as Caliburn prowled toward him out of the shadows, gold scales gleaming in the fading moonlight, eyes glowing like shards of sunlight. "Um... good morning?"

Caliburn growled again, though this one was of amusement. He shifted as he drew close, and then Barra was up against the wall, trapped by the arms on either side of him. He stopped breathing as Caliburn leaned in close, nose trailing as he sniffed and scented, the rumble in his chest thrumming through Barra.

"Wolf-elf smells good," Caliburn said softly, the movement causing his lips to just barely brush along Barra's cheek.

Barra shivered, lust curling lazily through him. He felt like the worst sort of traitor, but there was no ignoring the unexpected *want* that Caliburn had just provoked. "I-I-I c-came to talk to Avalon. Get off me, dragon." Oh, god, he was treating Caliburn like Troyes and really needed to *not* do that. "I mean—"

But Caliburn only laughed and kissed his nose before pushing away and giving Barra breathing room. "Good wolf-elf." He waved his hand back toward the open doors Barra could just barely see through all the foliage. "Avalon inside. Scared. Sad. Lonely."

"Aren't you lonely, too?" Barra asked.

Caliburn shrugged. "I have Avalon. That is enough for me. Would like to see more than clan lands, but I have Avalon. Come."

Barra fell into step alongside him as they wove through the mazelike garden, finally coming to a beautiful stone patio framed by roses with large French doors filled with stained glass rather than the usual, ordinary glass.

Inside the contained-chaos of Avalon's private chamber, Avalon was stretched out on a settee in front of the fire, a glass of brandy on the floor within easy reach. He was wearing only a dressing robe, and that barely closed. His long hair fell over the back of the settee like a waterfall, catching the light of the fire. It wasn't hard to tell what he and Caliburn had recently been up to, even without Barra's nose to give it away. He flushed hot, that damnable *want* spiking again, making Caliburn rumble beside him.

What sort of backstabbing bastard was he, to constantly doubt and question Neirin when he was himself distracted by the man Neirin loved? Maybe that was why he doubted Neirin—he knew he couldn't even trust himself.

"Where did you run off to, dragon?" Avalon asked, dragging his eyes open. He froze as he saw Barra. "What are you doing in here? I told them nobody was permitted entrance."

"I used the garden," Barra replied.

Avalon narrowed his eyes, irritation and amusement on his face before both were wiped away. "I see. You should go."

"I wanted to make certain you were well and apologize for losing the Holy Pendragon again. I also wanted to apologize for Hasna's drugging you."

"She already did," Avalon replied. "Her actions were not your responsibility. I always tell myself I will not fall for that trick again, but that was easily the tenth time I have done so." His mouth twisted as he looked away, stared at the fireplace, and reached blindly for his brandy. He drained the contents in one long gulp, dropped the glass on the rug, and stood. He pulled his robe closed, but not before Barra caught a glimpse of things he would be remembering for a very long time. "You should go. Sir Neirin and Troyes were most happy to see you again, Midnight is doing exceedingly well, and I imagine His Grace will be awake by no later than midday. You have all done more than enough in assisting me this far."

"You ask for our help and then discard us the moment things prove to be more difficult than any of us predicted? We're not *that* bad at our job. You killed Brennus, but now that we have a better of idea of what we're up against, if not who, we'll do better."

Avalon smiled weakly. "I have every faith you would, but be that as it may, I am declaring the matter closed. Go home."

"No," Barra said, and crossed the room to grab his arm as Avalon tried to turn away. "Whatever's really wrong, let us help."

Something flickered in Avalon's eyes—bleakness, yearning, maybe, but then it was gone, replaced by a hard, cold look that made Barra want to sigh and roll his eyes. "Of what help would you possibly be? Twice now you've almost gotten yourself killed. The Mad Duke himself is still lying about unconscious, and clearly Neirin and Troyes have lost their fighting edge in the years since they were thrown out for disloyalty.

Desperate times called for desperate measures, but I am no longer so desperate. I have asked and said nicely, and now I am ordering less nicely: go home, you are no longer needed or wanted here." He pulled his arm free and stormed off across the room, vanishing through a door Barra hadn't seen before.

The words stung, there was no denying Avalon had known exactly how to land his blows, but they were also exactly what Barra had expected the very moment he'd seen that look come over Avalon's face. Clearly Avalon had either forgotten, or was not aware, that Barra was long used to men who liked to do things *for your own good.*

"Not a bad performance," he said as he cast a look at Caliburn. "Devlin still does it best. Neirin hasn't tried it since the day I finally lost my temper and punched him for it. I'm sure he'll revert to bad habits eventually, but for now he's behaving."

Caliburn smirked a bit.

"Should I wait for him out here, or go in there?"

"Here. Won't like you in bedroom. Hurt too much."

"Hurt too much? Why would it hurt—" He broke off as the door opened and Avalon reappeared, the dressing robe belted now, but his hair still a long, loose, beautiful mess. He scowled when he saw Barra. "What are you still doing here?"

Barra shrugged. "You're going to have to try harder at being mean if you want to make me leave that way. Nobody can be meaner or colder than His Grace the Duke of Sulking and Brooding when he wants to do what he thinks is best for everyone else."

For a moment it looked like Avalon might laugh, but in the end it crumbled into a look of anguish that was itself quickly banished under a shaky blankness. "I see."

"What's really wrong, Avalon?" Barra asked. "Why won't you let us keep helping you?"

Caliburn growled softly, and Avalon's dark, sad eyes shifted to him. They stared at each other for a few minutes while they had some silent conversation. But in the end, Avalon's mouth twisted and he jerked away, a stubborn set to his shoulders as he once more addressed Barra. "I went to Sir Neirin to help me rescue the Holy Pendragon."

"Which we haven't done yet, so let us continue helping you."

"No. The situation is not remotely what I thought, and in all of this, the Clan clearly has been used and manipulated. Though I'm glad it rousted the traitors in my midst, it's only part of a larger, more dangerous game, and it is a game I intend to play alone—for your sakes, and my own."

"We would never do anything to hurt you, Avalon, you must know that." Barra swallowed, those golden eyes searing through him. It hurt to meet them, but it would hurt more to look away. "You confuse the hell out of me. I wish I could hate you, but I can't. I want to help, even if that means I go home alone at the end of it all."

Avalon's sadness deepened, and beside Barra, Caliburn growled softly again and shifted the slightest bit closer to him.

Barra's breath caught as Avalon reached him, the ache in his chest hurting so deeply his eyes stung. The sadness, the bleakness, etching lines into Avalon's face and putting shadows in his eyes, twisted through him sharper than any knife. He shuddered as Avalon's hands cupped his face. Licking his lips, Barra said,

"Avalon..."

"If you think Neirin is the only one I've come to love after all these years, you're an oblivious fool, sweet wolf." Avalon kissed him, lips soft and warm, tasting of brandy, hot metal, and magic. "If I could have you both here with me, I would, but centuries of life have taught me much. It is time for you and your little family to go, and I am sorry that I dragged you into my mess. I was selfish and weak. I will not continue to be so. Return to your knight and dragon. Take care of them for me." He kissed Barra again then pressed a last kiss to his brow and stepped away. The hot touch of his fingers lingered, and the press of his lips felt like it would never fade.

Tears fell down Barra's cheeks as Avalon withdrew. "You can't mean—Avalon—" He broke off, frustrated the words wouldn't come.

Avalon reached into the pocket of his robe and withdrew something.

Runes, Barra realized too late. "Avalon, no—"

The runes struck him, and the hum and sting of magic washed over him. Light flashed, and when Barra could see again, he was back in his room. Neirin sat on the bed, playfully kissing Troyes, who stood between his splayed legs.

They both went still as they realized they were no longer alone and rushed toward him in alarm.

Neirin swept him up. "What's wrong? Are you all right?"

"I don't think I am," Barra said, and pressed the heels of his hands to his eyes. "Avalon—"

"You saw Avalon?"

Barra nodded, and once he was finally able to speak properly, related all that had happened—all of it, even the strange encounter with Caliburn, and the kiss from Avalon.

Neirin's face was drawn when he finished.

"I'm sorry," Barra said. "I got so upset with you, and said all those things—" The words were halted by Neirin's mouth, a warm, firm kiss that just made him cry more. "Neirin..."

Smiling, looking entirely too pleased under the circumstances, Neirin replied, "You cannot expect me to find complaint with the fact that you and Avalon are not entirely averse to each other."

"You *cad*." Barra thumped him on the chest. "You arrogant bastard! Here I am distraught and your mind is filled with smug, dirty thoughts!" Barra thumped him again. "I should toss you out the window. *Stop looking so pleased with yourself.*"

Catching his wrists and pinning them to his own chest, Neirin kissed him again and said, "I'm sorry, I was trying to tease so you would not be so upset. I won't lie, it was hard not to think about how nice it would be to have you both. But I knew that was arrogant and selfish and cowardly of me, and I meant it when I said I chose you."

"But it would have hurt to walk away from Avalon again."

Neirin hesitated, then seemed to let go of whatever he was still holding back and nodded. "Yes. I loved him then, I love him now."

"It's not hard to see why," Barra said softly. "However, as you arrogant types are so inclined to do, Avalon seems to have made the decision for us."

Laughing, Neirin kissed him hard, then Troyes, and then Troyes kissed Barra. "My heart of hearts, if there is one thing I have learned in all these years, it is that every arrogant prat on the planet has a wolf-elf or a Midnight to put them soundly in their place. If anyone could storm the keep and conquer the lonely prince trying to lock us out, it is you." He kissed Barra again, lingering, smiling into it all the while. "Though if you will take a bit of advice, I think it is time for us to retreat and come at the problem from our own angles. Devlin was here a short time ago; he and Midnight went to see what remains of the manor. Then we were going to convene to work out what to do next."

Barra slumped against him and buried his face in Neirin's throat, happier still when Troyes pressed against him from behind. "I will gladly heed that advice."

Neirin kissed the spot behind his ear. "So you went on and on about giving me up, *letting* Avalon have me, when all this time you were thinking the same naughty thoughts as I."

"Keep being smug and see what happens to you." Barra smiled as he rose to his full height. "I think we're all mad."

"We already knew that," Neirin said, and kissed him one last time before drawing back and taking his hand. "Let's go home, wolf-elf. There is revenge to plan and mischief to plot."

On the heels of Troyes's happy growls, they departed.

The Captive Prince

Storms

Rain fell drearily, as though it was damned tired of falling but had no choice.

Avalon might have been projecting slightly, but he didn't much give a damn. He drained his latest glass of brandy and refilled it, annoyed when the decanter ran out before the job was half done. Whatever, he'd call for more soon.

He should not have kissed Barra. He really, really, *really* should not have kissed Barra, or admitted so much, but if there was one thing centuries of life had hammered home, it was that he was a bloody fucking fool. All the same, he shouldn't have done it. There was a world of difference between pining for something, spinning fanciful thoughts about it, and having it for a single, too-brief moment and knowing viscerally what he would never have.

Not that he should have ever been pining after Neirin or Barra, and definitely not Neirin *and* Barra.

But it had been just as sweet as it was painful to have them both in Castle Camelot, no matter how brief their stay had been. The few hours he'd spent out in the world with Barra would be a memory to warm him on the coldest, longest nights.

He gulped down the last of his brandy and rose unsteadily to cross the room to the bell pull. When a servant appeared a few minutes later, he lifted his empty decanter. "Bring more. Be liberal about it."

"Yes, Your Highness." The servant—Michelle, if he wasn't mistaken, though he hadn't bothered to look—faded off, leaving him once more alone.

Completely alone, as Caliburn was mad at him and was somewhere else in the castle.

Avalon couldn't blame him, not entirely, not when Caliburn had wanted them to stay just as much as Avalon. If he thought he could bear it, Avalon would do everything in his power to see that Caliburn went to someone more worthy, not some chained monstrosity doomed to solitude until his long life finally came to an end.

But even if he could quash his selfishness long enough to bear it, that wasn't his choice. It was Caliburn's, and the foolish dragon had chosen him, and chose him still, though Avalon felt increasingly unworthy with every year that passed.

The brandy arrived just as he was about to lower himself to the port. He thanked Michelle, mustering a smile to do it, and then was alone again.

They would have stayed. They would have helped. Neirin loves you. Barra wanted to love you.

I told you to leave it alone, Avalon replied. *We both know how well my relationships always end.*

You always choose people too weak. These two aren't. Neirin was a better steward the brief time he did it than the last dozen. Look how long he's loved you already.

From a distance. Everything is easier to do at a distance. Look at how much harm they've already come to just by being close. I would not see them killed, or see them fall apart because I wedged myself into the middle.

Caliburn sighed—audibly, and in the next beat the

just-refilled glass of brandy was pulled from his fingers. "Ava."

"Don't call me Ava," Avalon grumped. "You know I like it and am weak and I already give in to you far too often, you spoiled dragon."

"Ava."

Heaving a sigh, Avalon flopped back on the settee and stared up at the ceiling. "You know I couldn't ask them to stay. Why do you seem determined to make me hate myself over it for the rest of my life?"

I want you happy. I want us both happy. They could have done that.

"They could have been killed, they could have been used against me, they could have grown to hate us like so many others. I'm tired of loving people who only wind up hating me. I'm not saying I don't deserve it, but I am damned tired of it."

I think you need to face the matter you have avoided for too many centuries, and deal with the rest when that problem finally no longer weighs you down.

"Stop being smart," Avalon muttered, turned onto his side to scowl at the fire. "I hate it when you're smart."

Caliburn chuckled and sat down behind him, pushing Avalon's dressing robe down to press a warm kiss to his shoulder. "Ava."

"I hate you." Avalon twisted back around, reaching up as Caliburn moved to settle over him on hands and knees. Curling his hands around Caliburn's head, Avalon dragged him down into a kiss. Whatever happened, no matter the years that passed, he had Caliburn.

Nothing was as familiar and right as Caliburn's kisses. He would know Caliburn's touch if he was deaf and blind. Loosing his hands, Avalon trailed them down to Caliburn's shoulders, lingering there to enjoy their broad mass and fine muscle, then trailed further down to admire the even more impressive chest, tugging at the hoops in Caliburn's nipples, gold and ruby where Avalon's were silver and emerald. "Cali..."

"Ava..." Caliburn murmured, sucking on his bottom lip before kissing him properly again. Pulling away slowly, he reared back so he was sitting across Avalon's thighs. The firelight bathed his skin, gleamed in his gold jewelry.

"You're still the most beautiful thing in my world," Avalon said. "Fuck me, dragon."

Caliburn rumbled soft and low, shifting them until he was settled between Avalon's thighs. They'd fucked only a few hours ago, shortly before Barra had appeared and ruined what little peace Avalon had managed to find, so it was easy for Caliburn to slide right back in and settle into the hard, brutal fucking Avalon wanted—needed.

Neither of them lasted long, and right then that wasn't the goal, anyway. It took only moments for Caliburn to come, buried deep inside him, Avalon's thighs burning from the stretch and the hands gripping him bruise-tight.

The excessive quantities of brandy he'd imbibed made him dizzy and too-hot, especially with the fire piled on top of everything else. The room spun, and his vision blacked out briefly. When he could see everything properly again, Caliburn had flipped them on the settee and consigned the dressing robe to the floor.

"I'm going to regret that brandy in the morning," Avalon mumbled against Caliburn's chest.

He got a growl of agreement in reply, but also fingers tracing up and down his spine. They came to rest lightly on his ass, which made him smile. "What are we going to do, Cali? I thought Brennus was the end of it, but there is someone else in the mix. I have no idea who or what or why."

They need access, and you were easier to reach. You know who that means. Go see him.

Avalon's stomach clenched at the thought. "I suppose you're right: I've put it off long enough. But how about not when I'm drunk?"

Caliburn grumbled at him, but did not argue, and Avalon finally let alcohol and exhaustion and warmth pull him into sleep.

He woke with a scream in his throat, but he was long used to being thrown out of sleep by nightmares. Throwing back the heavy blankets, he padded out of the bedroom and into the bathing chamber and quickly scrubbed himself clean.

Returning to the bedroom, he went through another door to the room where all his clothes were kept—piles and piles of clothes, from times long gone all the way up to the latest fashion—and dithered over what to wear. What did one wear in such a situation?

Perhaps it would be best if he picked out what he wanted to die in.

You're being melodramatic.

Am I?

He felt Caliburn's sigh and then heard soft footsteps shortly before Caliburn came up behind him and wrapped him in a loose embrace. He pressed a kiss to Avalon's shoulder, his throat, and his cheek. "You worry too much, even after all this time."

"I'm seldom wrong about my worries," Avalon

murmured in reply. He went over to the section holding his suits and finally selected a black one with green and amber touches, standing still as Caliburn fussed over putting the matching jewelry on him.

When that was done, Avalon sat at his dressing table to contend with his hair. He picked up his brush, but it was plucked from his fingers with a soft rumble and a fond smile, Avalon happily left Caliburn to tend it. He closed his eyes and sank into the pleasure of someone else expertly combing and brushing his hair, the deft way Caliburn pulled the heavy strands into a trio of intricate braids and then wound those together at the back of his head.

Opening his eyes, he beamed at the results. His only addition was an emerald and amber comb in the shape of fully bloomed roses. Rising and turning, he drew Caliburn down and kissed him deeply, wishing he could drag them both back to bed and pretend the rest of the world didn't exist for a little while.

But there were questions needing answers, and a meeting he could no longer avoid, not if he hoped to keep loved ones and the clans safe.

He shrugged into a long frockcoat of dark hunter green and wound an amber and black paisley scarf around his neck. Finally he pulled on his sorcery gloves, tucked his charmed sword into an inner pocket, and a chalk case into an outer pocket. "I suppose I'm as ready as I'll ever be. Are you certain this is a good idea?"

I'm certain it doesn't matter whether it's good or bad. It's necessary.

Avalon sighed. Going up to the second level of his library, he paused halfway down the long row of shelves and pulled out a single volume. He cast on it the same charm spell he used on his sword and slid it into yet another pocket. Then he led the way into his magic room, made entirely of smooth slate, and nothing in it save a small table to hold the books and notes he was working with. At present, there was nothing on it but a small lamp.

He lit the lamp and crouched on the floor to draw the spell circle. It was one he'd drawn at least a hundred times, and probably thrice that, but always in the end he turned the coward and erased it, retreating once more to his haven.

This time there would be no retreating. Not when Neirin, Barra, and the others had all nearly died because of him—Midnight, Barra, and Hasna twice. No matter how scared he was, no matter how likely it was he was about to be killed.

Who knew, maybe the clans would be better off without him.

Caliburn growled and leaned in to bite him.

Hissing in surprise and pain, Avalon shoved him out of the way and finished the spell circle. When it was ready, he triple checked it from habit then rose and brushed chalk from his hands. He stepped into the circle and held out a hand. When Caliburn took it, Avalon pulled him into the circle with him.

He took a deep breath and released it slowly, repeating the exercise four more times before he finally was able to speak the activating words.

They appeared in a dark, stormy town of clapboard buildings and mud. One building seemed central, a two story affair in better condition than all the rest, spilling brilliant light despite the gloom everywhere else. Thunder rolled and rippled through the sky above, and Avalon swallowed nerves a man his age really should have been beyond feeling. Crossing the street, steps splashing in the muddy mess half flooding it, he climbed the stairs and pushed the door open.

It creaked quietly, but still a woman appeared from a door at the far end of the entryway. An imp, by the feel of her, and a powerful one. Her eyes were mismatched, one blue, one green. She eyed him warily. "Can I help you, my lord?"

"I need to speak with Lord Brennus. Tell him Avalon has come to see him."

She nodded and departed, but returned after only a moment, wide-eyed and far less composed. "He'll see you now, Your Highness."

"Thank you," Avalon murmured, and let her take his coat when she offered, removing the objects within before handing it and his scarf over. She offered a drink, but he demurred. He was rattled enough without compounding the matter by adding alcohol.

She directed him up a short flight of stairs. He could hear people in other rooms, the sounds of gambling, drinking, and sex. Powerful magic prickled along his skin—wards and other protections, along with spells for light and warmth.

The door pushed open easily when he reached it, and only the presence of Caliburn close behind gave Avalon the strength to step into the room.

It was a quiet but handsome place, all the wood smooth and dark, the street-facing wall lined with windows that ran from the center all the way to the top. There was a large desk, an even larger table, several bookcases, and a large, heavy safe in one corner. Next to it was a door that probably led into a bedroom, and a smaller door that likely led to a water closet.

Leaning against the desk was Sable Brennus, the demon Cadfael, Prince of Storms. His skin was similar in tone to Avalon's, perhaps a shade or so darker, his hair a wild tumult of black curls, his eyes like storm clouds. He wore a suit at least as fine as Avalon's, in black and silver and gray, with touches of red peeking out at the cuffs and waistcoat and the ruby in his tie.

"Prince Avalon Pendragon," Sable said in a deceptively mellow tone, a hint of lost accents in his voice—fourteenth century Italian, fourteenth century Egyptian, the barest dusting of sixteenth century French, and notes of relatively modern German and British. "I always wondered if I would meet you."

"I was never certain you wanted to." Avalon took a wary step further into the room.

Sable's mouth twisted, and he looked off into the distance. "I was never certain, either. Violate is not a term normals, or even many nightwalkers, would think to apply to what Arthur did to me, but amongst demons and a few others, it would certainly be counted the worst sort of violation." His stormy eyes turned back to Avalon. "If we had crossed paths a few centuries ago, I might have killed you. I might have killed all of you, right down to crushing every last fucking egg. But you are not to blame for Arthur's sins, and even he did not fully appreciate what it was he truly did. Humans are rather stupidly oblivious that way, but any demon will tell you humans are the truly dangerous ones."

"All the same, I am sorry."

"You're just as much a victim as me," Sable said. "It's not your apology to make." He pushed off the desk and rose to his full height. Thunder boomed all around them, and in the window behind Sable, lightning flashed with blinding brilliance. "So what finally brings you to see me?"

Avalon licked his lips. "Someone kidnapped a Holy Pendragon to get to me. Twice now friends of mine have nearly died trying to get the dragon back. The man said he needed access to something, and that he needed me to get it. I can only assume he means that he needs access to something of yours, and it is blood sealed, and my blood is easier to get than yours, for all I am the one in a hidden castle." Though he could feel even more acutely now all the heavy wards and traps that Sable had laid on the place. Even the street was not somewhere to tread lightly if the intent was to trifle with Sable and those under his protection.

Sable chuckled, and the thunder seemed to rumble with him. "How cute. They can't get to my books, and they can't get to me to circumvent my seals, so they somehow learned of..." He pursed his lips, regarding Avalon thoughtfully. "My son? I suppose that is the most accurate term, though it's not quite right. And they thought to use your blood. Do they think me an amateur? That won't work. It would take a great deal more than my blood to get past those seals. But by all means, let them hammer away and die trying."

"They're after books?"

"Grimoires, many of them worth killing for, certainly, a few that would do the killing should they be opened. I collect them, you see. If I do nothing else while I am on this plane, I will collect every last damned grimoire written by foolish, reckless, ambitious humans and see they're never again used to violate and abuse the rest of us." Lightning flashed in his eyes and out the window behind him.

"A goal I fully support," Avalon replied. "I have the

one they used to create me." The one they used to summon Sable centuries ago and tear away a piece of him.

The hole was there, if one knew to look for it. The barest sliver of empty space in his aura, a thread of essence gone forever, and poured instead into a womb where a babe had only barely begun to form. His parents had been so proud of what they'd achieved.

At least until it finally dawned on them that a child who was part demon, a child who had the power and strength and might of a demon, also had the weaknesses of a demon.

Avalon could not see auras the way a demon could, which had always disappointed him. Thunder and lightning came when he was suitably upset, or when he purposely called it. Magic was a parlor trick.

And though he was not as tightly constrained to his territory as a true demon, neither could he entirely leave it. He did not need a consort, though he ached for one all the same to complement and strengthen him. Caliburn was his most faithful companion, but he was a dragon, and so it wasn't the same.

Sable looked at him, eyes filled with hate and hunger. "I want it."

"It's yours. Freely given." Avalon reached into his jacket, withdrew the book and broke the spell on it, and held it out.

Thunder rolled. "Thank you." Sable crossed the room and took it, carried it over to one of his bookshelves and slid it into an empty space. Returning to them, he stopped a couple of paces away from Avalon. He glanced down at Caliburn, who growled softly in greeting. "Handsome dragon. I've not seen a gold one since Arthur summoned me."

"Caliburn is the last remaining gold," Avalon replied, chest hurting as always when the subject came up. He had hoped his siblings would weather the years, become a stronger family for suffering together... Instead it had torn them apart, and they'd all hated him in the end, like it was his fault his father had done something he never should have, like it was his fault he needed a territory.

Sable sighed softly and looked up, meeting his eyes. "The men who came seeking my books gave no real names, and I never cared enough to learn them."

"One used the name Brennus to steal grimoires from the Black family. He did look something like you. I killed him, but I don't know if he had relatives."

"I see," Sable said. "I will look further into the matter if you desire."

"If you can do so without drawing attention. I want the Holy Pendragon back, and the bastards responsible dead. Brennus already is, but I have no inkling at all of the other one, or ones, involved. They knew the clans well, knew exactly how to manipulate and use them to draw me out." He pressed a hand to his chest, feeling the tug of his territory as his freedom ticked away. "I only have a couple of hours left before I am forced to return."

"I envy you the freedom," Sable said levelly. "I will see what I can learn and contact you." He reached up and cupped Avalon's head, pressing his thumbs to Avalon's temples. Something hummed and resonated, then seemed to click, or unlock.

And suddenly he was aware of Sable in a whole new way. "What did you do?"

"Mentally linked us. It's not the natural telepathy

your dragon possesses, but it does the job. Now I think it's time for you to go. I am not sorry we've finally met, but your presence makes me uncomfortable."

The words stung, more than Avalon had expected for all he'd been braced to hear those very words or something much like them. "Of course. Thank you for your assistance, and for not killing me on sight." He turned to go, reaching out to rest one hand on Caliburn's head.

"A word of advice," Sable said just as he reached the door. Avalon turned back. "Your energies are frayed and ragged. You are not me, to need a consort in order to stabilize on this plane. You've already gone twice as long as I will before hell drags me back if I do not find my consort. However, you do need shoring up, or I think eventually you will go mad and die—and not quickly or peacefully. There are patches where you've recently interacted with your consorts. Two of them, which is unusual, but not without precedent. I suggest you draw them close and keep them there, for your sake and theirs."

Avalon opened his mouth, and then closed it again. "I see," he said at last, heart speeding up, the constant ache of longing in his chest spiking and twisting.

Sable stared at him another long moment before adding, "You do not make me uncomfortable in a bad way, necessarily, but I have enough to do without succumbing to paternal instincts that normally are completely foreign to a demon."

Avalon let out a cracked laugh. "I will endeavor to see our paths do not cross again."

Thunder shook the building and lightning rippled in Sable's eyes. "Oh, we'll meet again, my little princeling of storms. That is inevitable. Go now, and have a care."

"Farewell, my lord."

Avalon retrieved his belongings and then fled to the streets, where he huddled in an alleyway, bent nearly in half as he tried to remember how to breathe and fought valiantly to keep the contents of his stomach right where they were. Caliburn pushed into his hands, rubbing against him, and Avalon gave a shaky, sobbing laugh as he crouched in the muck and clung tightly.

My son. Paternal instincts.

Of all the ways Avalon had imagined his encounter with Sable Brennus, he'd never seriously thought Sable would acknowledge him as some sort of son. There really *wasn't* a better term for it, but Sable would have been well within his rights to deny all claim, or to treat him as some sort of monster or abomination.

That was certainly what his family had considered him after the constraints of the curse had truly settled in, after decades and decades of being prisoners on their own lands. All because the dragons, and the strange, powerful undercurrent of magic that governed and was governed by the dragons, had decided that Arthur and the rest of them deserved to be punished for their arrogance and cruelty in violating a demon and turning a human into something they were never meant to be. For intending to use him like a tool, with none of the respect they bestowed on the dragons. If he could not leave his territory, neither could they.

"Let's go home," Avalon said, and hugged Caliburn one last time before standing and taking them home.

Back in his sanctuary, he discarded his suit in favor

of a favorite pair of breeches and a worn, soft and comfortable shirt, over which he pulled on a maroon and gold dressing robe lined in brown velvet.

You should talk to them. Ask them to come back. Cadfael said it himself: you need them and they need you.

"They'll be fine without me, without all the chains that come with me," Avalon said. He wandered through the main chamber of his private space, pausing at a table filled with a seemingly random assortment of odds and ends—including an ornate, gold-framed mirror. He waved a hand over it, and a muted, just ever so slightly blurred-at-the-edges image appeared: Barra and Neirin kissing, both of them already half undressed.

Avalon dismissed the image and set the mirror down. He was not so mad from isolation that he felt it appropriate to invade privacy. He liked to check on them from time to time, but if it wasn't something he would glimpse walking down the street or passing through a shop, or similar, he always stopped watching.

Though even that rule had given him plenty to see in drips and drabs. A few seconds here, a few minutes there. Enough, over seventy years, to love Neirin all the more and fall at least a little in love with Barra. They called to him, and he had always wondered if his demon side had something to do with that.

Now that he knew it did, he wasn't nearly as happy or relieved as he'd thought he would be.

Could he go and talk to them, ask them...

But just the idea of it cramped his stomach. He tried to imagine it, telling them he was some strange, impossible child of a demon. That they were his consorts. Avalon laughed, shaky and sad.

Definitely not.

Why are you so certain they would react poorly?

Who wants to be told 'love me and stay with me forever or I might go insane and die'?

Caliburn snorted and went over to stretch out on the warm stones in front of the fireplace. *The little wolf was right in that you have a bad habit of doing what you think is best for everyone else. How about you ask them and trust them to make their own decisions? After all these years, I would think you'd be past making the absolute worst decisions for yourself.*

Avalon snapped his fingers and spread his palm to catch the reading glasses that appeared. Tucking them into the pocket of his robe, he headed up the spiral staircase to the second level. He walked down the row of shelves until he reached the books he sought: three whole shelves of demon lord compendiums. These were only for the last three centuries. The rest were in storage. Settling his spectacles in place, he perused the shelves for the volumes he sought: *Consorts, Index.*

It was not a book he'd ever had much occasion to use—only twice, in fact, when trying to remember a bit of information while reading other books. He carried it over to a bookstand and flipped gently through the old pages.

Sure enough, there was an entire section labeled *Dual Consorts.* The list was short, only four instances in the recorded history of demon lords. The last case had been in the seventeenth century, a man and a woman who'd been consorts to the demon Rabdos, who'd later been killed and his territory eventually overtaken by werewolves.

Avalon closed the book and returned it to the shelf, then removed his spectacles and tucked them away.

Oh, look, another excuse not to talk to them has trickled away.

Be quiet.

You should know better than that. You are my beloved prince, but you are also a fool. If you spent less time fretting and hiding and more time doing, *you would be a great deal happier.*

"I don't want to put anyone else in chains," Avalon whispered. Even without the demon bit, so many of his lovers eventually went from loving him to feeling obligated to love him because guilt made them reluctant to leave him alone. They always, always eventually resented that he could not leave, would never be able to leave... and that one resentment always spawned a hundred smaller ones.

How much worse would it be when it came with the chains of demon and consort?

Talk to a demon with a consort and ask them if it feels like chains. Honestly, Ava.

"I know," Avalon said miserably, leaning against the bookshelves and staring up at the stained glass dome. But knowing and believing were two different things, and he didn't remotely believe that Neirin and Barra would be different from all his previous attempts. He'd rather die than see them come to hate him the way so many others had.

He wanted you, that first meeting.

What?

The little wolf. I could smell it, feel it. He saw you up there and wanted you. He likes your hair almost as much as me. Not that Neirin is any less weak.

So were several others.

You are the son of a demon, literally something that is meant to be impossible. I would think you of all people would know that anything can happen, and that one chance in a thousand is still one chance. All those relationships that did not hold, there must be one that will, and I think if you stopped being afraid and tried, you would find these two are the relationship you have been seeking.

"Don't," Avalon said, voice cracking. "We've been alone for so long, don't you bloody dare get my hopes up just so this attempt can fail miserably like all the rest. I will never forgive you if you get my hopes up only for them to be dashed upon the rocks."

Caliburn growled and heaved himself up, lifted his head, ears fanning out wide in aggravation. Even his wings fluttered, a true sign Avalon was about to find himself carried to the roof and pitched off it.

I only did that once, and you were perfectly fine, as we both knew you would be. Get down here.

Avalon pushed away from the shelves, wiped his cheeks, and slowly headed back down to the main floor. He skirted the tables and piles of stuff that he always meant to put away but never got around to, and sank to the floor as he reached Caliburn. Nothing soothed and warmed him like being enfolded in Caliburn's arms.

Are you done?

I suppose.

Will you contact them and see if they will come visit and talk?

Maybe.

Avalon.

Yes, all right. Not tonight. Tomorrow, when I feel a

---

bit more grounded.

Fine, Caliburn said with an admonishing rumble. *Promise me.*

Avalon drew a deep breath and let it out slowly. He felt sick to his stomach and his heart felt like it was going to pop, but he hadn't survived all these centuries by ignoring his infinitely wiser dragon. *I promise.*

Hellspawn

He should have worn a different suit; the one he'd chosen was all wrong.

Caliburn laughed in the back of his mind. Though it had killed Avalon to leave him behind, it had seemed safest.

And if everything turned out as horribly as he feared, Caliburn would be angry and hurt on his behalf, and Avalon wasn't certain he could manage both of them at once.

"Shut up," he grumbled as Caliburn kept laughing and teasing. Climbing the stairs, he fussed with his suit and hair one last time. Leaving it even partly loose, as he had this time, was always a pain, but he would press any advantage he had.

Quit stalling.

Quit talking. Reassured by Caliburn's warm, fond laughter, Avalon rapped on the door. He'd come at twilight so that the entire household would be awake; it struck him as cowardly to arrive when one of their members would be asleep, even if he'd come to speak with only two of them.

The door swung open just as he was starting to think no one was home—or he was being ignored.

Midnight's pale, pretty face filled with surprise. "Your Highness! I admit you're the very last person we expected to see."

"I did not expect to come, but... matters have

changed. I would like to speak with Sir Neirin and Master Barra, if I may."

"They're not awake yet, but you're welcome to come in and wait." He grinned mischievously and waggled his eyebrows. "Be warned there is a foul-tempered beast prowling the grounds, however, who may not give you terribly warm a welcome."

Avalon didn't laugh, but only barely. "I appreciate the warning. Thank you." He stepped inside as Midnight motioned for him to do so.

"I think they'll be most happy to see you," Midnight said as he closed the door. His long, wavy hair tumbled about his shoulders like it had been loosed from a ribbon by impatient fingers. "I'll show you to the green room and then go—"

"What. In the *bloody hell.* Is *that* doing in my home?" Devlin demanded from the door he'd just stepped out of, a large book clutched in one hand. He glared at Avalon. "We've had more than enough of you, and I'll thank you to bugger off back where you came from."

Midnight lifted his eyes to the ceiling then turned to face Devlin. "I think you're being overly harsh."

"I think you're too soft like always." Devlin shifted his glare back to Avalon. "What the buggering fuck do you want? First you beat him to death, then you play with them both and nearly get them killed before tossing them out. What do you intend to do this time? String them along before killing them yourself?"

"Heartbeat—"

Devlin barreled on. "Of what possible interest could they be to you really? You are more than six centuries old, they are barely past one century, never mind that Neirin was barely more than a child by comparison the first time you tossed him out."

Midnight drew himself up, a glint in his eye that made even Avalon wary, though he'd never seen it before. "You're a fine one to pick apart who should be loving whom. Or did you forget you are the one fucking the man you raised from childhood after bringing his draugr corpse back to some semblance of magic-induced life?"

Devlin stiffened, eyes frigid as winter as he looked at Midnight. "You want to side with that despicable hellspawn, go right ahead. But I will not be party to this, and if any of you had sense left in your thick heads, you would toss him out for good." He turned around, stepped back into the room he'd come from, and slammed the door shut.

"Well, that went well," Midnight said with surprising cheer.

I shouldn't have come. Avalon drew his shoulders up and tamped down on his hurt, not remotely soothed by Caliburn's silent reassurances. "I should probably go." Especially in light of that *despicable hellspawn* crack. Devlin had clearly figured it out, damn him, and if his opinion was so scathing, how much better would the others be?

"Why, because Devlin is in a protective snit?" Midnight scoffed. "I will corner the beast in his lair and pet him until he calms down." He winked. "The green parlor is straight down the hall, turn right, second door on the left. I'll go fetch Neirin and Barra. It's too bad you didn't bring Caliburn." He pouted slightly. "Barra said he had wings."

Avalon managed a smile at that. "He does. If we get the chance, he will be more than happy to preen for you."

Midnight echoed the smile. "It won't take me but a moment to fetch them, Highness, and I'll make certain tea is arranged, as well. And please, don't worry a moment about Devlin. He's been worried about them, and he knows seeing you will make them happy, but he always has to growl and snarl first." He motioned down the hall and headed for the stairs.

Still far from convinced he should be there, Avalon nevertheless followed directions to the green room. There were several chairs and a lovely pale green sofa, but he moved to the little window and looked out eagerly over the street. It was still early enough in the evening that people walked about, carrying packages, dinner, walking dogs... a beautiful carriage, a cheaper hackney...

What must it be like to be able to see the world change firsthand? He could remember when the Tower of London was only a couple hundred years old. Could remember London when it was smaller. Remembered so many things, some clearly, some vaguely. But he'd only seen it in stolen moments, most of his knowledge of the world confined to books and whatever else his people thought to send to him.

He turned from the window at the sound of shouting, and frowned as he strode toward the door and pulled it open. He stepped into the hall—and was grabbed by the throat and slammed into the wall. "This is your fault," Devlin snarled, his hand squeezing painfully tight, cutting off Avalon's ability to breathe. "I don't know how yet, but I know you're the one to blame. Where the fuck are they?"

Avalon held perfectly still, hands resting against the wall, fighting the urge to struggle even as his vision began to falter and his chest to burn.

"Devlin!" Midnight shoved him hard, sending both Devlin and Avalon crashing to the floor.

Avalon gulped in air, trembling as he huddled on the floor, gently holding one hand to his bruised, aching throat. He looked up at Devlin and rasped out, "What—" He broke off coughing.

"They're gone," Midnight said quietly. "Neirin, Barra, Troyes. They're not in their room. It's like they just walked out. But a window is open, and the wards there were broken."

"Nobody should be able to break my wards so easily, and definitely not without my noticing it," Devlin said, fingers flexing like he was contemplating choking Avalon a second time. "Where the fuck are they? I will not ask again."

Avalon shook his head and whispered, "I don't know. I came to talk to them about—about me, and why I tried to push them away. This must be related to the Holy—" He broke off coughing again.

Midnight gently helped him up. "Come on, we'll go to the kitchen and I'll fix you some tea." He cast a look at Devlin that put Devlin's earlier chilliness to shame. "You are free to return to your library, Your Grace."

Devlin looked like he'd been slapped. "Midnight—"

Ignoring him, Midnight bustled Avalon away through the house to the warm kitchen in the back. There was no staff, but that didn't surprise Avalon. Devlin was clearly the suspicious sort and probably didn't care to have people around whom he did not fully trust or could not watch closely.

Once he was sitting at the table, Midnight bustled around the kitchen to put together a cup of tea. "I hope it's all right. I rarely drink tea, can't remember the last time I did."

"It's perfect," Avalon said after taking several sips. It was over-steeped and bitter and slightly burned, but he honestly did not care right then. "I'm sorry, I only ever seem to bring trouble to your door. His Grace isn't wrong about that."

Midnight scoffed and sat on the bench opposite his, picking an apple from the bowl on the table and toying with it absently. "His Grace is wrong about a great many things."

"I'm also *right* about a great many things," Devlin said stiffly from the doorway, and when they both turned to look at him, added, "but I did not mean to assault you, Highness. I should not have done that."

"It's all right. You have every reason to think me an enemy." Especially if Devlin knew what he was and considered him a despicable hellspawn.

Devlin moved slowly across the kitchen, eyes on Midnight, and sat down at the opposite end of the table, looking very much like a boy still stinging from his mother's dressing down.

Midnight made a soft, impatient noise. "Stop sulking all the way over there, Heartbeat."

As easy as that, all of Devlin's tension and misery faded away, and he was back to his imperious, imposing self as he moved to sit right next to Midnight. "So I think it safe to assume that whoever is hunting you has gotten angrier and more desperate. Whatever it is they seek, they want it badly. I had hoped this would end with that imposter who stole the books from Brennus, but it would seem there is at least one more person in the mix. I would not be surprised if it was more than one." He set a small white card on the table, on which was written the name of a church

Avalon didn't know. "A location, but not a demand, which I take to mean you already know what they want and they're aware of that. What do they want?"

"My blood."

Devlin's eyes narrowed. "Your blood. Barra mentioned they wanted access to something. What?"

"Books so heavily protected nothing else they've tried has worked."

"Heavily protected by a demon, I'd wager, and they're using the demon's blood to try and break through. That's probably how they got through my wards," Devlin said sourly. "There was plenty of blood from Barra, Neirin, and myself for them to use, if they thought to reserve it from the different fights we've had. Bloody hell." He pressed a knuckle to his forehead and scowled at the table as his thoughts turned.

Avalon poured himself more tea.

"So you are the offspring, however that is possible, of a demon currently here on our plane," Devlin said, eyes resting heavy on Avalon, a blue more brilliant than any flash of lightning. "Storms heed your call, which narrows it down considerably. You're Cadfael's son."

"Yes," Avalon said quietly into his teacup. "How is anything impossible always accomplished? Ambition and magic." He finished the tea and set the cup aside. "Put those together and you can create anything, even me." *A despicable hellspawn.*

Didn't Devlin work for London's demon lord? Surely he'd have a higher opinion of demons. Never mind he was also in love with a draugr and would probably kill anyone who dared to call Barra a mongrel.

So what made a half-demon human so despicable?

Avalon banished the question. What good would it do him, or any of them, to hear the answer? He would help save Barra and Neirin as best he was able and then he'd return to his territory.

"If you want to interrogate me later, I will tolerate it," Avalon said, "but right now we should focus on rescuing our friends."

Devlin narrowed his eyes and opened his mouth—and swore at the hard kick Midnight gave him. Shifting his ire to Midnight, he said, "Yes, let's focus on rescue and address other matters later."

Midnight beamed. "So what's the plan?"

"Give them my blood," Avalon said. "I would imagine their plan is to trade my blood for our friends, and they can have it. Lord Sable assured me even that will not get them what they want. If we alert him to matters, he'll know they're coming and take care of the rest, I have every faith."

"You have faith, but I do not. Demons do as demons please, and they seldom care what happens to those around them. Word of my home burning to the ground surely has spread this far by now, but do you see anyone, anyone at all, coming to the townhouse to see if we might be here? No, the world is quietly grateful the Mad Duke might be dead and content to bury their heads and not poke around. Even the demon lord I have served practically all my life." For a moment it looked like Devlin might punch something, but then Midnight leaned against him, and the tension bled away, though plenty of hurt and bitterness remained.

Avalon regarded him pensively, mind whirring rapidly through possibilities. "Do you want to stay dead?"

Devlin opened his mouth, closed it again.

"I do not have much time left here, but I can send people to arrange and manage whatever you want," Avalon said. "This is my fault, I do not deny that. I only wanted help finding and saving the Holy Pendragon, I swear to you. I never meant for all this to happen, and had I known, I would have left you in peace. If you prefer to stay dead and build a new life from there, I can help with that. At the very least, you could be made honorary members of Clan Pendragon, which means you are bound to us but not held to all the same laws and requirements. More like a highly trusted friend and consultant. You can live wherever you want. We have holdings all over the world, to keep the clans funded."

Devlin stared at him, blue eyes like flames, then finally sighed and looked away. "An idea worth considering, Highness, though I have no love for your clans. Your offer is far kinder than we deserve after my terrible treatment of you. I do not think that is a decision that can be made right now, but I will consider your offer once everyone is safe. Do you really think Lord Brennus can be relied upon?"

"He despises the way humans mistreat demons and so many other nightwalkers," Avalon replied. "They violated him in the worst way possible to create me. He collects grimoires so no one else can use them. He will not let those men anywhere near the books they seek."

"That does sound like a demon," Devlin conceded. "Very well, make the arrangements. I have my own preparations to make if we are going to get rid of these bastards once and for all." He rose, kissed Midnight hard, and strode off.

Midnight smiled and tucked back the loose strands of his hair. "He'll probably accept your offer, you know. He spelled the townhouse to make it appear deserted to most everyone. He wanted to include you, but Neirin wasn't having it. No one at all has come by to see if maybe, just maybe, we're here. Devlin acts angry but..." Midnight shrugged. "So I think perhaps Pendragon will be stuck with us for at least a little while."

Avalon nodded. "I am sorry for your losses, that I am the reason you've lost so much."

"You're not to blame, only the bastards who hurt us." Midnight's eyes glowed softly with a hint of his draugr madness. "Bastards who will be made to pay." The glow faded. "Are you really the son of a demon?"

"I am a piece of him forced into a baby barely after it was conceived," Avalon said. "I gave the grimoire with the spell to Lord Brennus, but my father kept a journal where he recounts the event. Son does seem to be the closest term, though I think Lord Sable would prefer a different one."

Midnight's eyes narrowed. "Would you prefer a different one?"

"I can see why the most powerful witch alive does not dare cross you and apologizes quickly when he does." Avalon rose, carried his teacup over to the sink, and left it with the other dishes waiting to be cleaned. "Thank you for the tea."

"My pleasure, Highness." Midnight stood and motioned for him to follow. "That's the library, the green room you know. Barra and Neirin often use the gold room, though, if you'd like to make use of it while you're here. How long will it take you to contact Lord Sable?"

"Only a moment," Avalon said, and finally did so, cautiously casting out his thoughts along a thread of magic that felt as familiar as his own but infinitely more powerful. He'd always thought his own power so remarkable, but next to Sable he was a bumbling child.

Perhaps, but I do have countless years of experience and practice. My power did not come to me in a century, or even a millennia. What do you want?

Did you mean it, about our foes having your blood not being enough to get them past the protections you laid on your books?

Sable's cool, smug laughter rippled through his mind like fading thunder. *Give them blood and you'll give them just enough rope to hang themselves.*

They've kidnapped my... friends, the two you said made me less frayed, along with their dragon. I have to give them blood in exchange.

Then by all means, let them hang themselves. I'll be ready.

Thank you.

Sable faded off, and Avalon blinked, shook himself. He looked at Midnight. "Lord Sable's confirmed that if we give them my blood, the only thing they'll manage is their own demise."

Midnight grinned, sharp and toothy. "Excellent. Let's go see what Devlin is up to. I'm a touch worried he'll get carried away. We're both still furious about the house, but where I would be perfectly content simply to rip heads off, Devlin is intent upon something more lasting."

"He may not get the chance to do anything if Sable takes care of them first. Which he'll have to if we hope to convince them they've won and return Neirin, Barra, and Troyes after I've given them blood." He followed Midnight to the library, where Devlin was poring over books with a scowl on his face.

"What has you so upset?" Midnight asked. "Well, what's adding to the pile?"

Devlin cast him a look. "I want to know what they're after, what book could be worth all the trouble they have gone to. This was not a scheme they threw together in a matter of days, or even weeks. They probably spent months alone just trying to get to the books on their own. They must have failed miserably—painfully—when they tried to go directly at Lord Sable. But they could not have known about Prince Avalon; that is knowledge they came upon while working on a new way to circumvent Sable's wards. How did the clans come into all of this?"

"Our grimoires, likely," Avalon replied. "If they went looking hard enough for ways to break through wards of Lord Sable's formidability, it's probable they learned the books they wanted—or rather, full, complete versions of books they already had—were in Pendragon's possession. That would have taken them to Linden..."

"Linden knew you were half-demon?"

Avalon shook his head. "I never told him—I've never told anyone. You're the first to know since the last of my family died. But there is a journal which contains knowledge of my making, and he had permission to access that bookcase, though it was because of other books. I didn't know he'd ever touched my private journals." He'd made the infinitely stupid mistake of trusting Linden, but for so long Linden had seemed loyal, honest... Even after he'd grown mercurial and too ambitious for Avalon's tastes, he'd still seemed faithful to Avalon and the clans.

This whole mess really was entirely his fault.

No, it's Linden's fault, and the bastards who approached him, and those who attempted to commit murder. The only thing you're to blame for is throwing out the two men you wanted to keep close.

And if I had, they might not be in the hands of the enemy. No matter where I step, it's the wrong place.

Self-pity and self-recrimination will accomplish nothing, and do not suit you anyway. Fetch me and let us finally put all to rights.

I can't fetch you. I mean, I can, but I've barely an hour of freedom left. Which reminded him he needed still to *say* that.

"I wish we had given that bastard Linden a more miserable death," Devlin said. "Lightning seems entirely too kind in retrospect. I suppose I shall even it out by making the lingering bastards suffer his share in addition to their own."

Midnight gave him a look, shaking his head slightly. "I do not think that's how it works."

Devlin sniffed. "It works how I say it works."

"As you say, Heartbeat," Midnight replied softly.

Avalon smiled faintly. It was clear he was no longer in the room, and he was loathe to remind them that wasn't true, but matters were pressing. He coughed faintly, making them both startle. "My apologies, but I am running short on time. I only had a couple of hours left and one of them is now gone. I am afraid that I will have to give you my blood and leave the rest of the matter to you, much as it pains me to do so."

Though it was probably for the best. Much easier to walk away and return to his solitude if he did not have to see them. *Despicable hellspawn.*

You're not. I doubt he even knows he said that,

given how angry he was at the time. He is definitely the sort to go for blood the moment his is up. The family has a reputation for it, if I recall.

That was true, but it didn't lessen the sting of the words.

"Is there a way to give you more time?" Devlin asked. "How does it work, precisely? I assume it's because you're half-human that you can leave your territory at all?"

Avalon nodded. "Yes, though only for what equates to one day a decade. That time actually ran out a while ago. The time I'm using now was a gift from Barra, after he summoned me to your manor."

"Barra gifted you time." Devlin stared at him with narrowed eyes. "How? Barra doesn't have a scrap of magic within him. All his abilities are sensory, even the wind-feeling thing he uses so seldom I tend to forget about it."

"One day for one year, that is the bargain if I want to leave my territory beyond my own time. Someone must freely sacrifice a year of their life to give me one day."

A thunderous look overtook Devlin's face. "And you took it from Barra in a moment—"

"Don't you dare insinuate that," Avalon said levelly but coldly. "He was the one who summoned me, and you were all on the very precipice of death. It was not what I wanted to do, but if I was going to save you, I needed to be able to leave my territory and that was the only way."

Devlin turned away with an angry noise but lifted his hand to surrender the point. "Fair enough." He glared at his bookcases. "We do not have time to summon you up every time we need a chat, and it would be better to have you to hand, so I suppose it is my turn to offer up a year of life."

"You don't—" Avalon stopped as Devlin turned around.

"It seems the least I can do, all things considered," Devlin said.

Just behind him, Midnight smiled. "I think he's thawing. By the end of the year, we might even get him to admit Your Highness is not the enemy."

Devlin turned enough to cast Midnight a scathing look. "You are not going to enjoy the conversation we'll be having later."

"Neither are you," Midnight retorted.

Heaving a sigh, Devlin faced Avalon once more. "So what do I need to do? This is magic beyond my experience."

Avalon winced. "Declare it, that you give me one year of your life to give me one day of freedom."

Devlin eyed him warily, but then stood up straight, shoulders set, and said, "I grant to Prince Avalon, freely and with full understanding, one year of life that you may have one day of freedom."

Avalon was absolutely certain he was about to die. Stepping forward, moving as quickly as possible, he grasped Devlin's face, kissed each of his cheeks, and finally the softest, briefest kiss he could manage across his mouth. Stepping hastily away and bracing to be hit, he said, "The bargain is struck and sealed."

For a moment, Devlin just gaped, too taken aback to react. But before disbelief could turn to anger, the room filled with the sound of laughter. They turned to Midnight, who was laughing so hard he had to lean against a nearby chair to keep himself from falling over.

He looked up, saw them staring, and just laughed harder. "Your *faces*. I have never seen two people enjoy a kiss less, and it barely counts as a kiss. I—" He broke off, laughing too hard to speak. Devlin stormed past him, pausing just long enough to shove Midnight over, and left the room.

Midnight curled up in the seat he'd landed in, muffling his laughter in his arms as he folded them across one armrest.

A smile teased at Avalon's mouth and finally caught. "In my defense, I was certain his reaction would not be pleasant."

"I wish I had some way to freeze that moment so I could look at it whenever I was feeling gloomy," Midnight said between breaths as his laughter finally eased. "You looked like you were going to your execution and Devlin looked like someone had just told him he was really a cat." He dissolved into giggles again.

"I'm going to wait until you turn into a cat and then I'm going to lock you in a box and throw it in the Thames," Devlin replied as he returned dressed for going out. He yanked gloves on and rolled his shoulders to better settle his coat. "Are we going? I assume, Highness, that you did not come prepared for battle."

"You assume correctly. At the very least I would need Caliburn."

"Then let's be off," Devlin said, not quite meeting their eyes before storming off once more.

Midnight grinned at Avalon as he stood and smoothed out his rumpled clothes. "I think you flustered him. Make note of it, for it's rare indeed that anyone *flusters* His Most Unflappable Grace the Duke of—"

"Finish that sentence, Midnight, and I will not be held responsible for my actions," Devlin said from the hallway.

Still grinning, Midnight led the way out of the library and, in the hallway, threw himself into Devlin's arms and kissed him soundly. "Is that kiss more to your liking, Heartbeat?"

Devlin sighed, but a wisp of a smile curled the corners of his mouth as he drew away. "Time is ticking away, angel."

"Then let's go end this once and for all," Midnight said.

Avalon stepped forward, grasped both their arms, and they all vanished, bound for Clan Pendragon.

Blood

The church where the meeting was to occur was an abandoned, derelict building in the nightwalker parts of Bath, which Avalon hadn't seen in at least two hundred years. Two hundred fifty? A long time, at any rate. He'd been hunting down a traitor from Clan le Fay.

He could not wait to be done with this debacle and settle back into all the duties he'd been neglecting to rescue the Holy Pendragon. The castle and clan largely ran without him, but there were still things that required his attention.

And focusing on his duties would take his mind off the abysmal failure that was his attempt to convince Neirin and Barra to give him a chance. *Despicable hellspawn.*

I wish you would latch onto the good things people say about you as firmly as you've latched on to those two words, Caliburn said, nipping at his thigh as they walked along an old cobblestone road toward the church in the distance. Behind them was Bath proper, largely the domain of normals, oblivious to the secret spaces all around them where nightwalkers dwelt.

In many places, like London, no such divides existed. The larger cities were so busy and scattered it was easy for nightwalkers to live amongst normals with little to no trouble. Some places, like Amesbury, were entirely nightwalker, or near enough. And still others, increasingly few in numbers according to what he'd been told in meetings, reports, and passing conversation, were like Bath and Canterbury.

What would it be like to live alongside normals? They were a world wholly apart, something he saw only in books and art and music. His chambers were filled with miscellany normal and paranormal, and it was the former that puzzled him most. So much of what normals did seemed to be the most difficult way possible. But it was long established that normals— long ago called daywalkers, a term that had been lost around the time nightwalkers had been forced to go completely into hiding—could not handle the paranormal world. Bad things happened when the two crossed, save here and there where a presumed normal found their way into and inevitably made a home of the paranormal world.

"So what are the chances this will go smoothly?" Midnight asked.

Devlin snorted, and Caliburn growled with malice.

"Yes, that was what I feared." Midnight sighed. "I definitely will be glad to leave work behind for a goodly length of time once we're done."

Avalon stifled a wince. "I will make all the reparations I can."

"It's not your fault, though I will be happy to compose a list of suitable reparations all the same," Devlin said.

It was a pity Devlin hated him so much; Avalon quite liked him, even after the choking bit. He offered a smile, trying and failing not to be disappointed when Devlin did not return it.

Yes, it really had been stupid of him to think he could have ever had something with Neirin and Barra.

Even if they'd been willing, how could Avalon do something that would cause a rift in their family?

Caliburn's sigh rolled through his mind like a wave, heavy and cold. *If you don't stop moping, I am going to do something drastic.* More *drastic than pitching you off a roof.*

What could be more drastic than pitching me off a roof?

Quit moping and you won't have to find out.

Avalon shoved him into the grass.

Devlin quirked a brow at him.

"He's being difficult."

Caliburn chittered at him, tail lashing in the grass.

Midnight laughed. "I beg pardon, Highness, but I believe he just said that *you're* the one being difficult."

"You are quite mistaken, I assure you," Avalon replied, and gave Caliburn another shove when he laughed again.

"I see," Midnight said, grin widening.

Devlin eyed them both. "What are you being difficult about?"

"I shouldn't have involved any of you in this," Avalon said. "That's all."

Devlin looked far from convinced, but the conversation was forced to a halt as they reached the churchyard and magic washed over them, a minor spell to alert the people inside that they'd arrived. "Everyone ready?"

Midnight nodded. Caliburn growled. Avalon reached into his pocket and pulled out his gloves, flexing his fingers to settle the snug, butter soft leather in place.

Devlin's eyes landed on them, widening slightly. "What are those?"

"Sorcery gloves. Also known as—"

"Rune gloves," Devlin said, fingers twitching like he wanted to touch. "I've read about them. I have ten different books detailing every last failed attempt to make them. Do yours *work?*"

Midnight laughed, immune to the look Devlin cast him. "Are you envious? Maybe you should try being nice and make friends, Heartbeat."

"They take a long time to make. That's the problem with most of those experiments," Avalon said. "I can show you later, after everyone is safe and this matter is closed, if you want."

Devlin looked like he'd bitten into something bitter, but his eyes were sharp and hungry. "Perhaps." He turned away, and Midnight rolled his eyes, sharing an impish smile with Avalon.

"Come on," Devlin said, and reached into his jacket, pulling out runes that he kept cupped loosely in one hand. His power whirled around them like a winter wind. Avalon might be half-demon, but there were reasons even demons feared witches. He strode on, leading the way into the old church.

Two men, long and lean and so alike in appearance they must be brothers, sat in the front pews. They slowly unfolded themselves as they heard footsteps, baring their teeth in malicious smiles. "The Mad Duke himself, I'm almost honored," said the slightly taller of the two, displaying a broken tooth, and the others in such poor condition they'd probably rot out or be yanked out in another year. "Keeping fancy company these days, Your Grace?" He looked at Avalon. "Your Highness."

Thunder rolled above them, and the sound of pattering rain echoed through the church, making both men startle. So they weren't nearly as collected as they wanted to appear.

Lackeys, Caliburn said. *They smell of blood—Neirin, Troyes, and Barra.*

So they've probably hurt them. That is a mistake they won't live to regret.

Caliburn growled.

"I do not trade with lackeys," Avalon said. "I'll speak with your master or I'll leave."

"You won't leave, sweetheart," the other man said, tugging the cigarette out of his mouth and blowing smoke in their direction. "We got something you been wanting."

Bad Teeth strode off through the door at the back and returned dragging something.

Neirin. Battered and beaten to hell, one eye swollen shut, his mouth in even worse shape, dried blood covering most of his face and matted in his hair.

There was a collar around his throat made of thick, black-green leather with a silver buckle, etched heavily with runes that kept him asleep and weak.

Caliburn roared and tensed to crouch.

Steady, Avalon said.

I won't stay still forever.

Bad Teeth vanished again and after a moment returned with Troyes, who was in even worse shape than Neirin, and naked as well.

"There, half of what you're owed. All yours once we get the blood, and you'll get the other half once we get what we want."

Avalon stared at them coldly. "One last chance, gentlemen. Fetch your master or die for him, because *I do not trade with lackeys.*"

They laughed meanly, and Cigarette lit himself a

fresh one before saying, "You ain't got no choice, sweetheart. It's us or nothing."

"Have it your way, then." Avalon stepped forward past Midnight and Devlin and threw out his hands, fingers splayed. The spell poured into the gloves, the necessary runes flashing, connecting, spinning the spell out faster than chalking and more predictable than traditional runes.

Thunder cracked and boomed outside, shaking the old, crumbling church. Black-purple light flashed as the spell was cast.

The two men on the altar dropped without a sound, hearts stopped so suddenly they would have felt nothing.

"Now!" Avalon bellowed. "I've had enough. You want my blood, then stop hiding behind brainless thugs."

The sound of clapping echoed through the church as a man came from the door Bad Teeth had used when fetching Neirin and Troyes.

He was handsome in a pale, chilly way, small and thin, more bone than meat, with delicate features that tipped slightly toward childlike. "I never thought I would enjoy the dubious honor of meeting the mysterious Prince Avalon. I did not expect you to murder them."

Caliburn growled, the sound resonating throughout the church, and Avalon stopped banking the intimidation they naturally emanated as the two most powerful figures in the whole of the clans. "If they hadn't worn the blood of my friends on their hands and clothes, I might have let them live. I am quite finished suffering your insolence. Return the Holy Pendragon and my friends."

The man was gritting his teeth as he struggled uselessly against the force of Avalon's presence.

"Did you think I was to be trifled with?" Avalon demanded, walking toward him slowly, Caliburn at his side. "Did you think you could steal from me, hurt me, and get away with it? Did you think because you managed to squirm into the mind of my Steward and wreak havoc upon me that you were better than me? Did you honestly think any of you would get away with this?" He stopped a few paces away and met the man's eyes.

He looked away, but he trembled visibly and sweat dampened his hair and dripped down the sides of his face.

"I think you need to start showing me proper respect," Avalon said.

The man snarled but dropped to one knee and bowed his head. "A deal is a deal, Your Highness. When we have what we want, you will have what you want."

"The deal was that I give you my blood and you return what belongs to me," Avalon said. "What you do with the blood has nothing to do with me and does not factor into this bargain."

"We said only come. We left the details to be discussed here," the man replied to the floor. "Anyway, I cannot give you the mongrel and the Holy Pendragon even if I wanted. We knew you'd be displeased, so my companion took them and hid them without sharing the knowledge. I have no idea where they are, and no matter what I say or do, he will not surrender their location until we have the book we want. You'll not find him."

"Do not be too sure of that," Avalon replied,

although the bastard wasn't wrong, unfortunately. They could be in Bath, they could be in Germany, or even as far as China. Magic made it easy to go anywhere on a whim. "But a bargain is a bargain as you say, and holding up my end will see this matter concluded faster than killing you and looking for them myself." He banked his powers. "What's your name?"

"Reimer." He collapsed, landing on his ass on the grimy floor. He looked up, wiped away the blood dripping from his nose. "I thought you were a storm demon."

Avalon laughed. Peeling off one of his gloves, he dropped his hand to Caliburn. With a soft, rumbling growl, Caliburn bit into his palm just enough to draw blood with one of his sharp teeth. Avalon pulled a kerchief out of his pocket and dabbed it in the wound. He gave the handkerchief to Caliburn, who carried it over to the man. "That should be just enough blood for your purposes."

Reimer reached out one trembling hand to take it and stood slowly as he shoved the kerchief into a pocket of his poorly cut jacket. "You must be Cadfael's whelp, but a storm demon can't control people like that."

"It wasn't control, and it's nothing to do with my demonic nature," Avalon said. "You should have done more research on dragons and their knights. What you feel isn't me controlling you. It's fear." *Caliburn.*

In a flash of gold, Caliburn's tail struck, knocking Reimer out cold. Avalon pulled another kerchief from his pocket and crouched in front of Reimer to dab at his blood. Folding the kerchief neatly, he tucked it away in a small metal box and returned it to his pocket.

"I'm not remotely certain why we bothered to

come," Devlin drawled as he and Midnight came to join him.

Avalon ignored them in favor of going to Neirin and Troyes. Pulling his glove back on, he grabbed hold of the collars and cast a spell to break the magic on them. Thunder boomed and cracked, and with a smell of ozone, the collars fell to pieces.

Surging forward, Avalon pulled Neirin into his arms and lap and checked for his pulse. Caliburn shifted and examined Troyes, rumbling softly in relief. *They seem well, if in need of healing and rest.*

That's good to know, Avalon replied, frown deepening as he pushed back a blood-stiffened strand of hair to get a closer look at the cut on Neirin's forehead. His fault. Whatever anyone said, this was all his fault. He should never have bothered Neirin, should never have given in to that moment of weakness.

He rested his fingers against Neirin's cheek, a familiar ache stirring. Now that Sable had said it, he could see it was him recognizing his version of a consort. He'd thought he was just particularly attached, or making more of an attraction than was really there just because he was lonely and Neirin had always been so intriguing—compelling.

And all he seemed to do was get Neirin almost killed over and over, and now he was doing the same thing to Barra.

Avalon...

Even if they don't mind I'm half-demon, which is still quite likely, how could I ever ask them to subject themselves to a lifetime of this? Hard enough to ask people to serve as my Steward. He let his fingers linger a moment longer and then finally withdrew them. *I won't do it. I can't. You don't ask people you love to be a human shield.*

Caliburn growled softly and looked up, his eyes glowing more brilliantly than ever. *But I do. All dragons do exactly that. Ask you to be our shields because you love us and we love you and we strive to protect you just as much as you protect us.*

Avalon ignored him, mostly because he wasn't wrong, but it still felt different.

You're impossible.

Avalon shifted so he could lift Neirin, gently settling him over one shoulder, grunting at the weight. He turned—and drew up short to see Devlin watching him with a shuttered expression, his vivid blue eyes gone dark. "Is something wrong?"

"I'm undecided," Devlin replied. "Midnight dumped Reimer outside. I take you have a plan you did not share with us regarding that blood you took?"

"More like a precaution. I am hoping that finding Barra and the Holy Pendragon will be a simple matter, but on the chance it's not, his blood may be of use."

Devlin nodded, and once Caliburn hefted Troyes up, turned around and led the way out of the church. Outside, the rain had settled to a soft shower, the clouds slowly drifting away. "Shall we to your home or mine?"

Avalon's brows shot up. "I had not expected my home to be an option for you, Your Grace."

"I've not yet had a chance to repair my wards, and right now have not the time to rebuild them to the level required." He regarded Avalon thoughtfully for a bare moment. "Camelot will have to suffice for now, if you are amenable."

"Yes," Avalon said, dying inside. He didn't want

them on his land. He didn't want to have seen them in his home again knowing all the while he'd have to send them away—assuming they didn't choose to get as far from him as possible.

Midnight strode up to them, hair soaked, jacket sloughing water. "Shall we?"

He and Devlin held fast to Avalon's arms, Caliburn resting heavily against his legs, and he took them all back to Pendragon lands, arriving right in the middle of the ward. People came rushing out to assist them, taking away Neirin and Troyes, no doubt right back to the healing rooms they'd only just left.

A woman lingered, Amy, who managed the keep. Once there would have been a Seneschal over her, to manage the whole estate, but much like the position of Steward now, it had fallen to corruption and betrayal so many times Avalon had finally ceased to use it.

Would Barra take up such a post if offered, if...

But there was no point in getting his foolish hopes up yet again. *Despicable hellspawn.* He smiled as he approached Amy. "Impeccable as always, my lady. Thank you for taking on so much while I am busy with our stolen Holy Pendragon. Can you see rooms are prepared for His Grace and Lord Midnight?"

"Of course, Highness."

He kissed her cheek and glanced back at Devlin and Midnight. "I will see you shortly, after I've cleaned up and put away the kerchief." He walked off, shoulders set, head high, smiling politely at the people he passed, but not pausing in his stride.

Safely in his own rooms again, he sank to the floor and sprawled out with his back against the door. The knot he'd wound his hair into came loose and flopped to rest on his shoulder. Avalon reached up absently to comb it out.

Caliburn sprawled across the floor with his head in Avalon's lap. *You aren't going to go see him?*

Oh, I'm sure I'll give in eventually. But I'm exhausted from all the magic and traveling, and tired of feeling cut open. He stroked Caliburn's head, rubbed the spot behind his left ear, smiling softly as that got him a happy rumble. *I can endure Lord Devlin hating me, but I need a break.*

He doesn't hate you, I think he wishes he could hate you. Certainly you frustrate him, but that's not remotely the same thing.

Yes, I suppose you're right. But hate or frustration, it was easy enough to see that Devlin was counting the hours until they never had to see Avalon again.

He stared across the room where he'd discarded his suit on his way to his changing room. It had been a brand new one, black with fine gold stripes to match his eyes, lined in the same, and beautiful gold and pink roses embroidered on the waistcoat. He couldn't recall the last time he had dressed to impress anyone, it had been so long.

It was probably all to the good he'd never gotten a chance to make a fool of himself. And once everyone was safe again, and the Holy Pendragon back where he belonged, Avalon would be absurdly busy tending him and catching up on neglected duties.

So yes, all for the best, though he wished it was not the brutal kidnapping and beating of his... friends that had saved him from himself.

Caliburn sighed, audibly and in Avalon's mind. *Humans are quite ridiculous.*

Mmm, says the dragon who has been secretly fond

of Troyes all these years. Don't think I haven't noticed despite your efforts to keep mum.

Caliburn lazy nibbled on his arm. *Yes, but I'm peculiar for a dragon. We don't do that. I would never presume. I'll be content if they all show good sense and choose to stay here.*

Avalon petted Caliburn a few more times, then moved his head and stood. Shaking his hair completely loose, he started stripping as he headed for his washing room and was naked by the time he turned on the shower.

It had been designed by a clansman who loved to tinker about with such things, an amalgamation of things he'd read in books and such published by normals, installed roughly fifty years ago and improved upon many times since. Avalon was fond of it, especially when he had to wash his hair.

He stepped into the hot water and simply stood, happy to be surrounded by all the wonderful heat.

But there were matters to attend, and it would likely be only a matter of hours before those bastards tried for their damned book and Sable took care of them once and for all.

He dealt with his hair first, because if he didn't, he wouldn't bother to do it at all. When that was accomplished, he pinned it up and finished the rest of his shower. Caliburn appeared as he was finishing, and slid right into the hot water as Avalon stepped out.

In his dressing room, Avalon pulled on an old, favorite pair of black breeches with a line of shiny gold buttons up the side just below the knee. He pulled on a shirt, gray waistcoat with a silver paisley pattern, and a jacket that matched the breeches, the ensemble modified so he didn't need one of those throttling scraps of silk around his throat.

He twisted his hair into a loose knot at the back of his neck and went to clean up the mess he'd made with his other clothes. He'd just finished when Caliburn appeared, back in dragon form, his wings and scales gleaming in the lamplight flickering about the room—gaslights, all of them, which was a change he'd been most pleased with. No magic or servant required. He could just flick a switch.

Stalled enough? You'd be a good deal less anxious if you did not always insist on stalling and stalling before finally addressing matters.

Probably, but when in six hundred odd years has that logic ever penetrated?

I think it happened twice back in the 1600s, and once last century.

Avalon cast him an unamused look. Caliburn's eyes shimmered. *I don't know why I have put up with you all these years.*

Would you like a list?

Avalon knelt as Caliburn reached him, grabbed his head behind his fanned ears, and kissed him between his eyes. "My heart of gold, it would have to be several books."

Caliburn preened and nuzzled against his throat, tongue flicking out to taste and tease.

Avalon shivered, but then laughed and pushed him away. "None of that now, dragon. I believe I was told that I've stalled long enough. Let's go see our poor fellows. You can have your wicked dragon way with me later."

They made it to the room where Neirin and Troyes rested without interruption, though Avalon's steps slowed the closer they got. Caliburn huffed and finally shoved him forward. Avalon cast him a quelling look, but quickly closed the remaining distance and pushed the door open.

No healers or guards were present, but if Neirin and Troyes were merely resting, there was no need of them.

The room was dark when they stepped inside, save for a single lamp by the bed, its stained glass shade throwing small bursts of color around the room. His stupid heart kicked up as he approached the bed, like he hadn't checked on them multiple times when they'd been here only a day ago. Avalon stifled a sigh.

He pressed against the side of the bed, curling his fingers into the blanket to keep from touching; it wasn't his place to touch, and he'd been able to ignore that back in the church when he was frazzled and Neirin was still and covered in blood. Not so easy to ignore now, especially when all of Neirin's most egregious suffering had been Avalon's fault—the whippings, the sorcerers and werewolves, and now this.

Caliburn rumbled softly, lifting up to rest his front legs on the bed. Troyes rumbled in answer, though he was still fast asleep, and Caliburn settled into the draconic equivalent of a purr. Troyes smiled in his sleep and curled even closer to Neirin, who shifted and turned in his sleep to better hold Troyes close.

And they would look all the better and sweeter once they had their wolf-elf back, a lovely, happy trio only a fool would dare interfere with.

Ava…

It's all right, Cali. I'll be fine. I have you.

But he couldn't deny that he'd enjoyed those few, fleeting hours where he'd stupidly believed there might be room for him.

Caliburn rubbed his head against Avalon's arm, whining softly.

It's not your fault.

You said not to get your hopes up and I did. I still think you give up too easily.

Why risk it? Maybe this is what I deserve for dragging them into this mess and nearly getting them killed more than once—three times now, for poor Barra, assuming he's still alive. Let's go.

He headed for the door and slipped out into the hall, frowning when Caliburn did not appear right behind him. *What are you doing? Get out here.*

Caliburn's soft growl carried out into the hall, but just as Avalon was about to go in and drag him out, Caliburn appeared.

"What were you up to?"

Nothing. Are we going to look for the pretty wolf now?

"A witch would be better suited to that, but I'd rather wait and see what happens with Sable. I do not think they'll kill Barra or the Holy Pendragon; if that was their inclination, they would have already done it."

It would be exceedingly stupid of them to go that far. Though they have already proven they're not the wisest. The most powerful are often intelligent but seldom wise.

"Says the most powerful dragon in the world."

Caliburn chittered. *Seldom, my paradise, I said seldom.*

"You're ridiculous."

They'd just returned to their rooms, and he was about to call for a servant to summon Devlin and

Midnight, when Sable's presence rolled through his mind. *The good news is one of them is dead, and for what it's worth, he died neither quickly nor pleasantly. The bad news is that there was only one.*

Damn. The other stayed back. He must be the one really in charge.

No, I think he is the man who works for the man behind it all, and was in charge of the men hired to steal a very particular book from my collection. Not the one I expected.

Avalon didn't like the troubled tone to Sable's thoughts. *What book did he want?*

A set of books, actually, though they're often lumped together under the title The Book of Worlds. *I've heard rumors, here and there, of someone trying to access all the planes. I've ignored it because, frankly, I am busy enough with my territory and do not care what the rest of the world gets up to until they bring their idiocy to my door. Still, that is troubling knowledge for a human to have.*

Avalon gnawed on his bottom lip. Yes, that was exceedingly troubling knowledge for a human to have. Humans could do many things, up to and including the impossible, but they were a race meant to stay on their plane. A human seeking to learn more about the planes was a human planning to travel to them, or worse, bring something from them. They did enough damage with the planes they currently had access to.

It's rather charming you do not consider yourself human.

I'm not. Only half, and amongst nightwalkers, half may as well be not, especially when my father is the Prince of Storms.

Sable laughed. *Prince of Storms. I prefer Lord Sable*

Brennus. Have you further need of me?

I don't think so, unless you happened to learn where they've hidden Barra and the Holy Pendragon.

No, but I'll send you all his belongings. Maybe there is something useful in the pile. Farewell.

There was a sharp tug as Sable felt out where to send the belongings, which almost immediately thereafter appeared at Avalon's feet: bloody clothes, a few banknotes, a pocket watch, and a folded slip of paper.

The connection with Sable broke, and the link Sable had stirred faded back into practically nothing.

That seemed to be all the help they were getting from him. But they didn't really need him further, that was true. Avalon shook himself and went to ring the bell pull, sending the servant who came to bring Midnight and Devlin to him.

Too restless to stand still, he discarded his jacket on one of his tables. Picking up the items, grimacing at the still-wet blood soaked into the clothes, he laid everything carefully out on a mostly-empty table in the center of the room. Next, he summoned his reading glasses. Climbing the stairs to his most prized bookshelves, he went to the case that held all of the clan's plane-related books. He possessed one volume of *The Book of Worlds,* but it was a copy of a copy of a copy, and incomplete at that. It held information pertaining to hell and the dream plane, which was all he really needed.

He slid his spectacles on and started looking, his fingers landing upon it right as the door opened.

"This is marvelous!"

Avalon turned, removed his spectacles, and watched as Midnight roamed excitedly around his study. Most of the clan referred to it as his laboratory, but it had begun life as a library and study. He smiled as Midnight explored every nook and cranny like a child in a toyshop—well, as Avalon assumed a child would behave given free rein in a shop full of toys—oblivious to or ignoring Devlin's admonitions not to pry. "It's all right," Avalon called down.

Midnight halted, his fingers on one of the music boxes Avalon was taking apart in the hopes of using parts from it and several others for a present he was making for Caliburn. He smiled sheepishly up at Avalon. "Apologies. Your room is wondrous! There's so much to look at, I don't even know what all of it is, and you make Devlin's library look like a pale imitation."

"I beg your pardon," Devlin said icily. "The quality of my library certainly makes up for its lack of quantity."

"Yes, Heartbeat," Midnight replied, and grinned when Devlin's glare just darkened.

Avalon smothered a laugh. "You are welcome to look around, though I'd be careful touching. I have a terrible of habit of wandering from one project to another and leaving each in a precarious state. I've heard from Lord Sable, that's why I called for you. One moment." He tucked his spectacles away and carried the book with him as he returned to the ground level.

As he reached them, he related all Sable had told him.

"So where are the belongings?" Devlin asked when he'd finished.

"Right behind you. I haven't gone through them yet. It seemed simplest to wait until the two of you had arrived."

Devlin turned and strode over to them and

immediately began picking through the sparse pile. His shoulders slumped slightly as he finished. "Not much to work with." He reached into an inner pocket of his midnight blue jacket and pulled out his bag of runes. Setting them on the table, he pulled out a chalk case and drew a casting circle. When that was set, he fell into a light trance as he focused on what he wanted to know, and formed a question for the runes to answer. It was a tricky art, reading runes, and more often than not the reader got them wrong.

After a few minutes had passed, Devlin reached into his bag and cast five runes. *Water. Wind. Life. Illusion. Earth.*

Devlin frowned as he studied them.

Avalon studied them as well, but rune casting was not something he'd ever mastered. He didn't need it, between his human sorcery and demonic powers. Once he'd managed to make the gloves, they'd allowed him to blend the two seamlessly—and more importantly, disguise his demon magic as sorcery.

"Barra's been hidden on an island, and his presence is masked by way of illusion or similar such deception," Devlin said at last.

"How did you extrapolate that?" Avalon asked, staring at the runes again.

Devlin pointed to the water, wind, and life runes. "See how they're all clustered together and touching each other? That is frequently a representation of the ocean. In that context, earth could mean the continent but more likely means island since additional runes are needed to mark out a particular continent, or place on a continent. It could mean England, I suppose, or the British Isles, but again, different runes come into play. Which means an ordinary, run of the mill island, likely one not too far away. Illusion means simply that in this case, something about the island is illusory, and my educated guess is that our foe is using magic to hide Barra, and perhaps himself, on that island."

"Well, then, I believe it is Caliburn's turn." Avalon strode over to his writing desk in the corner and penned a quick note. Caliburn stirred from where he'd stretched out by the fireplace and prowled toward them. Returning to the group, Avalon offered the note for Midnight and Devlin to read. He then carefully removed a page from his own copy of *The Book of Worlds* and gave it to Devlin to put with the note. Taking the bloody shirt from the pile of the dead man's belongings, Avalon held it out. "Do you need a fresh whiff?"

Caliburn scoffed at him. *His blood is sunk into my nostrils, along with the smell of the harm they caused Neirin and Barra and Troyes. I'll find the last one, and possibly bring his corpse back.*

Do not do anything reckless. You know what happened last time.

It was worth it to break every bone in that coward's body.

Avalon threw the shirt back on the table, sank to his knees, and held Caliburn close. Drawing back, he rubbed Caliburn's ears right where he liked best and kissed him between his eyes. "Go find him, my heart of gold, and deliver our message." He secured it in a special leather case and fastened that to Caliburn's right front leg.

Caliburn growled, nuzzled, and licked him, then turned and headed through the garden doors. Avalon didn't bother to follow, well familiar with the way he'd scale the wall, climb onto the roof of the neighboring armory, and launch into the sky from there.

"He won't be seen?" Midnight asked.

Avalon shook his head. "Not while it's still dark, not by anybody who would be believed. If he cannot find them before sunrise, he'll return and I can enchant him."

"Do you really think the bastard will believe your note?"

"I believe their actions speak of fanatical determination or desperation," Avalon replied. "I also think that if we had not made the offer, he would have made the demand. If he cannot use my blood to get to the book, then he'll use me, thinking I can get past wards that defeated everyone else. This way, he'll think I'm so desperate and scared to save Barra and the Holy Pendragon that I already took the book."

Midnight laughed.

"Nicely done, Your Highness." Devlin's mouth curved in the first smile he'd ever given Avalon. It was full of teeth, and his eyes gleamed with anticipation of retribution, but it was a smile all the same.

Avalon smiled tentatively back.

Confrontation

Shortly after Caliburn left, they scattered about his chambers to each pass the wait in their own way. Midnight lost himself in the various tables that took up the bulk of the main chamber, moving from one to another, the smile never leaving his face.

Devlin availed himself of Avalon's books, though he spent most of his time surreptitiously watching Midnight with his heart in his eyes. Avalon had a sneaking suspicion Midnight would soon have a similar laboratory in the near future.

Avalon left to take care of a few matters, starting with going to the far northwest corner of the property to look over the house there. Like the rest of the grounds, it was a combination of centuries, though most resembled its rebuilding in the mid-fifteen hundreds. Unlike everything else, it didn't have much in the way of modern touches as the house was so apart from the rest of the village that no one wanted to live in it, though it was one of the largest houses available.

It didn't compare to Devlin's townhouse, and certainly was nothing like his manor, but it was nothing to scoff at either. Six bedrooms, a private courtyard, the surrounding land walled off as well... It wouldn't take long for the groundskeeper and her people to get the grounds in tiptop shape, and Amy would see to the house itself.

Not that he thought Devlin or the others would want to live on Pendragon lands if they accepted his offer, but it couldn't hurt to be prepared, or to have something to offer. At the very least they'd realize he was sincere in offering them a new home, and wherever they went, he could rest easy knowing they'd have the protection of the clans.

Returning to the castle, he found Amy and made the arrangements, then dutifully went off to his public office to attend some of the work waiting there for him. He spent most of his time talking to various people who'd been waiting to see him, sorting out problems in the village and surrounding farmland, and a problem with the guards that had gotten thorny enough they needed him to attend the matter.

And still he was painfully aware of every minute that passed. Not just because of waiting to know if Barra and the Holy Pendragon were well. He *hated* the rare occasions when Caliburn traveled so far from him they could no longer mentally speak. Right then he could only just barely still feel Caliburn, and he fervently hoped Caliburn did not have to go so far Avalon stopped feeling him entirely.

Caliburn had once gotten so mad at him he had accidentally wandered off that far, and it had been so brutally unpleasant he hadn't left Avalon's sight for a full month.

He'd only just sat down to address the paperwork when a familiar rapping came at the door. "Yes?"

Amy dipped her head. "Beg pardon, Your Highness, but I thought you'd like to know Sir Neirin and Troyes are awake and asking after you. I sent them on to your chambers, figured they'd like to see their friends and you'd prefer to speak with them there."

"Yes, thank you. I guess I will have to do this another day, I'm sorry."

She waved it off. "It will keep. Bring our Holy Pendragon home, Your Highness. That's the truly important bit."

"I will." He kissed her cheek and headed back to his chambers, where Neirin was speaking with the guards. Avalon's heart sped up, nerves fluttering, mouth gone dry. He tamped it all down, determined to act like the six-hundred-year-old prince he was. "Sir Neirin."

Neirin turned around, a tired smile overtaking his face. At his side, Troyes rumbled softly. "Highness."

"How are you feeling?" Avalon asked, keeping his hands firmly at his sides, though he ached to brush back Neirin's hair, kiss him softly, and see for himself that Neirin was truly doing better.

"I'm fine. Thank you for rescuing us." His face clouded. "They left Barra behind, I think. And he was not in any of the other rooms, so I assume he hasn't been rescued, yet?"

"Not yet, but we are working on it. Come, we'll tell you all you've missed. Could you send for tea, please?" he asked one of the guards before leading Neirin into his chambers.

Neirin laughed softly as he stepped inside and looked around. "Not much has changed, though I think some of the items on the tables have, and you have more books."

Avalon shrugged, ignoring the heat that overtook his face. "I like having things to do. Come sit down. You do not want to overexert yourself before we go to rescue Barra." He moved away as Devlin and Midnight approached to fuss over Neirin, gut clenching at the way they could so easily touch him and show how much they cared.

Not that he'd hidden his feelings terribly much when he'd first gone to Neirin for help, and certainly he'd tried to be as open as he could with Barra... But that had been foolish and selfishly indulgent. He needed to act like what he was, not what he wished he could be.

Turning away, he went to clear off the large table set in a half-circle nook lined with panels of stained glass depicting the four seasons and a built-in padded bench.

A sharp, slicing pain cut through his chest, and the surprise of it knocked Avalon to one knee. Damn it. Roaring cut through the room and then suddenly Troyes was there pushing and nuzzling, growling and whining.

"I'm fine," Avalon said, and with Troyes's assistance pushed to his feet just as the others reached him. "Caliburn went so far afield our bond severed. It was a surprise; we haven't done that in a long time." A knock came at the door, and then swung open, servants coming in bearing a teacart. "Food has arrived, excellent." He strode over to the table and quickly cleared it, dumping the diagrams and blueprints and books scattered across it onto the nearest work table.

His hands trembled. Avalon scowled and balled them into fists until it stopped. He and Caliburn had been separated before and everything had been fine. All would be well this time, too.

The servants arranged everything on the table, bowed, and departed. Avalon motioned the others to sit but was too restless to sit himself. Instead he fetched his sorcery gloves and took them to the cleaning table.

"How did you get your gloves to work?" Devlin asked. "By all accounts—reliable, trustworthy accounts—run gloves are impossible."

"Not impossible. It merely takes patience, which I have in spades," Avalon replied. "It took me a good century to figure out how to make them work, and ten years to make a usable pair." He put the gloves down and went over to one of his bookcases, this one filled with the red leather bound books that were his personal journals and grimoires. He ran his fingers over them, looking... Aha, there it was. He pulled the volume out and crossed the room to hand it to Devlin—and belatedly removed his spectacles when he realized why his vision was off and they were all staring at him oddly. "I believe this is the one that details the process. But if I'm mistaken, simply let me know and I will find the correct one."

Devlin stared at him, brow furrowed as he slowly reached out to accept the journal. "Thank you, Highness."

Avalon smiled briefly and returned to cleaning his gloves.

"Someone tell me what has happened," Neirin said. "The last thing I remember is going to bed, then I woke up to the sound of Troyes roaring. We did our best to get free, but you don't need me to tell you how well that worked."

Midnight scowled. "We did not even know you were gone, that's how well they snuck in."

Devlin did not speak, but the expression on his face said more than enough.

"I'm not sure how much longer it would have taken us to notice if I hadn't gone to tell you that His

Highness had come to call."

Avalon didn't look up to see Neirin's reaction to those words, only kept his expression neutral and his attention on the gloves.

"Once I realized you were gone, Devlin threw a particularly vehement fit and tried to throttle His Highness—"

"You did what!" Neirin roared, dishes clattering, something falling to the floor. "Winterbourne—"

"Sit down!" Midnight said.

Avalon's head snapped up and he stared to see Neirin had reached across the table and yanked Devlin out of his seat. He moved around the table and helped Midnight pry them apart. "It's all right, Sir Neirin. He had every reason to be angry, and I am to blame for everything that has befallen you."

Neirin muttered something Avalon didn't catch, though by the look on Devlin's face he'd caught it just fine.

"I do not bear him a grudge," Avalon said. "There is no reason for you to do it on my behalf. Please, the matter is closed. I would not have you and your dearest friend angry with one another because of me." His hand fell from Neirin's shoulder when it seemed he would stay put, and he stepped back from the table—

Only to be grabbed about the wrist, reeled in, and yanked down to sit beside Neirin on the bench. "Join us, Highness."

Avalon's brows rose slightly. "That did not sound like a request."

"It wasn't," Neirin said, still glaring at Devlin. "Give me one good reason I shouldn't break your nose."

"You don't throw a punch worth a damn and would cause more harm to your hand than my nose?" Devlin said in the snottiest tone Avalon could recall hearing.

Avalon almost laughed because that was such a ridiculous lie. If there was anyone at the table who couldn't punch well, it was Devlin. Neirin, however, looked far from amused. Avalon barely kept him from launching himself across the table.

Midnight did something that made Devlin jerk and swear loudly enough it echoed.

"What in the bloody hell—"

"Stop being such an unbearable bastard," Midnight said, staring into Devlin's eyes. "That conversation we're going to have is looking worse and worse for you, Heartbeat."

"I said I was sorry. I took his offer to give us a home seriously. I know I overreacted. I don't need to be dragged across the scones and threatened with a broken nose."

Neirin pinched the bridge of his nose. "Enough. I shouldn't have said it. I'm exhausted and bloody fed up with this case. I do not think we've faced anything this infuriating since those djinn last century."

"We could all use proper rest," Midnight agreed. "Let us finish telling you what you missed."

"And you should explain all this about His Highness offering you a home. Was it in a cell? With bars? In the basement? I know how much you love basements, Winterbourne." Neirin bared his teeth.

Devlin returned the wolfish smile with a look haughty enough to outdo the rest of the aristocracy combined. "Says the man who lost a fight to a wine cellar."

Neirin's face flushed. "I've told you twenty—"

Midnight's laughter drowned him out. He cast a sly, playful look at Avalon. "I hope you do not mind their childish antics, Your Highness, because they seldom cease so long as they are in the same room."

"I assure you that everyone in Clan Pendragon can relate to you every last one of my childish antics," Avalon replied. "Caliburn and I can get rather absurd when we are on the outs. He once grew so exasperated he pitched me off the roof of the armory."

Troyes rumbled at their feet, and a scowl fell over Neirin's face. "Try it and see what happens to you, lizard." Neirin smiled and shook his head faintly. "Let's get back to what happened."

Midnight resumed the tale, which didn't take long to recount, though he did go on and on when he related Avalon's theatrics with killing the men.

If only there was an unobtrusive way to retreat. Why had Neirin made him sit?

Avalon didn't startle when Neirin turned to look at him, but only because he had a lot of practice.

"So you really are part demon?" Neirin asked. "Devlin posed the theory, but he was still doing research to confirm it since he didn't think you would admit it."

"I would have preferred not to admit it," Avalon said. "No one else has ever known, not since the last of my family died. Now five of you do, which is disconcerting. That doesn't include the people harassing us who figured it out, and there's no telling who else my late Steward or the rest of them told. If it becomes more common knowledge, I worry about the trouble it will cause the clans."

It also wasn't outside the realm of possibility that the clans would turn against him. Many already disliked that he could not leave Pendragon lands. It was spun as a protective measure to most people, but there were a precious few who knew he *couldn't* leave, and how much would their opinions change to learn he was half-demon and Pendragon lands his territory?

He simply did not know, but he had enough experience to suspect the reaction would not be positive.

At least Neirin did not seem upset, but then, he did not seem enthused either, merely curious. How would he feel about it after he'd had time to stew over the matter?

Warmth rushed over him and heat burned in his chest. Avalon shuddered with relief. "Caliburn has come close enough to reinstate our bond. Another hour should bring him back into telepathic range."

"Telepathic?" Devlin asked. "Neirin and Troyes aren't linked in such fashion."

"We are, just not as deeply. Our connection is too low level and subconscious for me to do more than always understand what Troyes means even when he can't speak as we can. Only the Holy Pendragons have so strong and vivid a connection as to share explicit thought."

"Fascinating."

Midnight's playful grin returned as he met Avalon's gaze. "I hope you are aware he is going to pester you with questions incessantly."

"And you will tag along oh, so casually to avail yourself of his workshop while I ask questions," Devlin retorted. He grasped Midnight's chin in one hand. "Your mouth is going to get you into trouble you will not be able to charm or pout your way out of."

Midnight's eyes gleamed like moonlight on water. "My mouth has other ways of getting me out of trouble."

"Says you." Devlin kissed him hard and roughly let him go.

Avalon rose. "I am going to rest for a couple of hours because I am already running on very little sleep and it is likely going to be a long night. You are free to remain here and do as you like. Though this entire debacle has given me a hard reminder in being more cautious in whom I trust, I do trust all of you. Excuse me." He rose and headed for his room, forcing himself to keep an even pace.

In the cool dark of his bedroom, he stripped down to just his breeches and padded across the room to the enormous tester bed that he'd owned for roughly four hundred years, though the mattress was less than ten years old and infinitely better than those used when he first obtained the bed.

Though he missed Caliburn, and was anxious about the coming confrontation, the exhaustion of waiting and pretending he wasn't being consumed by worry and heartache pulled him almost immediately under.

He woke to Caliburn's nudging thoughts and smiled. *Almost home?*

About an hour away. You were sleeping deeply. I hated to wake you.

No, I've slept too long. Thank you, Cali. It seems like you've had great luck.

Home soon, paradise. The affection that filled Avalon's mind then was better than any kiss, and he returned it full measure.

Climbing out of bed, he pulled his clothes back on, silently swearing at himself for not taking the time to braid his hair before falling asleep. And he'd left his comb in the dressing room. He could just call it to him;

his spectacles weren't the only object he'd charmed, but he needed sturdy boots so he may as well just grab the comb at the same time.

Leaving his room, he went to speak with the guards to have Midnight and Devlin summoned before he headed into the dressing room, found his comb and tucked it into a pocket, and fetched the boots he'd wanted. Returning to the main chamber, he set to the arduous process of fixing his hair. He swore softly as he caught the comb on a particularly stubborn snarl.

"Would you like some help, Highness?"

Avalon didn't jump, but only barely. He turned and saw Neirin sitting on the blue velvet sofa where he had clearly taken a nap. His clothes were rumpled, his hair a mess, and that shouldn't make him look so kissable but it most certainly did. "There are at least a hundred empty beds in this place. Why in the world were you sleeping there?"

"Caliburn wasn't here; it didn't seem right to leave you alone." Troyes rumbled sleepily from across the room, where he was sprawled in Caliburn's usual spot in front of the fireplace. Neirin stood and combed his fingers through his hair, frowning briefly as he glanced around for his lost ribbon. Giving up, he turned back to Avalon. "Would you like assistance?"

Avalon hesitated, but it was true his hair was a pain, and when would he ever again get to feel Neirin's fingers in his hair? "That would be appreciated. Caliburn usually does it for me and I've grown spoiled."

Neirin smiled, soft and sweet, eyes skittering to Troyes before turning back to share a look with Avalon. Reaching him, looking even more kissable with the firelight bathing his sleep-rumpled form, Neirin plucked the comb from Avalon's lax fingers and turned him around.

His movements were deft, careful, and patient as he tackled one knot after another, then set to combing the whole mass. Avalon closed his eyes and let himself enjoy it, a pleasure to tuck away and treasure. There were days his hair drove him mad and he wanted it gone more than he wanted anything else in the world.

But moments like this, when he could let down his guard and simply savor while someone else stood close and fussed over him... Oh, those moments were infinitely precious and worth the never ending hassle.

"I'm afraid I'm not much hand at braiding and the like, Highness, but I believe you're set." The comb clicked as Neirin set it on a nearby table. "Anything else?"

Kiss me. Touch me. Undo all your hard work so well neither of us minds it will have to be redone. Avalon shook his head, swallowed, and finally found his voice. "No, thank you." He stepped away and swiftly braided and bound his hair, painfully aware that Neirin lingered, eyes ever watching. When his hair was finally dealt with, he headed for the table where he'd left his gloves.

"Avalon."

He jerked back around, too startled to hear Neirin use his name to contain his surprise.

Neirin shoved him against the table, practically pushed him down on top of it, one thigh resting heavily between Avalon's. He pinned Avalon's arms to the table, and before Avalon could do more than draw breath to speak, dropped a kiss on his mouth. It was quick and hard, full of bite and determination.

Avalon shuddered, but before he could react—could decide *how* to react—Neirin let him go and stepped back. He licked his lips, which wasn't helping Avalon repair his shattered thoughts. "What..."

"I'm not certain why you came to talk to us at the townhouse, but I can surmise. I certainly remember what you told Barra." He stepped in close again. Avalon gripped the edge of the table and fought to hold still, not certain if he wanted to draw back or lean in closer. "I also am extremely familiar with the look of a man trying to do what he thinks is best for everyone else. I get in trouble for it all the time. Do not think we're letting you get rid of us a third time."

"Neirin—"

That made Neirin's eyes flash, and then Avalon was being kissed again, hands cupping his head, Neirin's lips moving against his, tongue pushing deep, taking Avalon's mouth like it was Neirin's to use whenever he wanted.

It wasn't a claim Avalon would deny, but it was a claim he couldn't quite believe Neirin wanted to make.

"Did you really think we were going to let you stand quietly by and fade off?" Neirin asked against his lips.

"I—"

Knocking came at the door. Avalon didn't know if he was annoyed or relieved. He pushed Neirin away and went to get his sorcery gloves.

The door opened, and Midnight and Devlin stepped inside.

I already liked Neirin immensely, but I think right now he is my favorite.

I thought I was your favorite.

You are my eternal paradise, Caliburn said, and Avalon could hear the rush of his wings and the rustling of leaves as he landed in the garden. *He is my current favorite.*

Cruel betrayer. Avalon smiled as he strode across the room to the garden doors and threw them open. He stepped back and knelt as Caliburn prowled inside. He rested his cold head on Avalon's shoulder and rumbled in approval when Avalon kissed the scales behind his ear and the spot on his throat he particularly liked. "You're ice cold, my heart of gold. Come on, rest by the fire while you tell us everything."

Caliburn rumbled in agreement, nuzzled against Avalon a moment longer, and withdrew. He didn't head for the fireplace, however, but walked over to Neirin.

Neirin's brows rose. "Am I in trouble?"

Gold flashed as Caliburn moved, and with a startled yelp, Neirin toppled to the ground. Caliburn settled over him, nuzzled against one cheek and then the other, rumbling softly throughout.

Then he moved away and headed for the fireplace, where he stretched out between Troyes and the fire, exchanging growls and rumbles. Avalon swallowed as their tails wrapped around each other and Caliburn spread one golden wing to rest over Troyes like a blanket.

Neirin was propped on his elbows, flushed and mussed and wide-eyed. "What was that about?"

"I'm sure I couldn't say," Avalon said.

Devlin snorted as he and Midnight walked across the room to finally join them. "I'm sure you could very well say that Caliburn approves of something, but then you'd have to admit to that something."

Midnight opened his mouth.

"One word out of you," Devlin said. "One word."

Midnight grinned. "You're just bitter because my

mouth *did* get me out of trouble."

Neirin laughed.

"Can we please learn what Caliburn has to say?" Devlin asked, pinching the bridge of his nose.

Avalon nodded, and as Caliburn shared his thoughts, he recounted everything to the others. "Kippering is the man's name, and he would give nothing away about his employer, but he slipped away to speak with the man and Caliburn overheard the name Howler. He could learn nothing more on that front, though it did seem that Kippering was frightened—likely about failing so many times. Caliburn was going to try and end the matter himself, but Kippering has chained Barra to him. If we hurt Kippering, we hurt Barra."

"Damn it," Neirin said.

"Quite," Avalon agreed. "He has agreed to meet us for an exchange at..." He paused, turned to Caliburn. "Are you serious?" Caliburn growled. Shaking his head, Avalon said, "The village that first brought you to our doorstep. The beach beyond it, technically, but all the same." He frowned at the last bit Caliburn had to relay. "Kippering has said I am to come alone."

"Of course," Devlin said, and he and Neirin both sighed. "What is our plan? Or are you simply going to slay him as you did the other one?"

"I think this Kippering will be craftier, but we will see," Avalon said. He pulled his gloves on and summoned his sword charm. "Shall we? Dawn is only a few hours away and we do not want to endanger Midnight. I will take all of you somewhere close by, and leave you to approach in your own way."

"It's going to be extremely cloudy, and I've extended his ability to stay awake by a few hours, so

Midnight will be fine" Devlin said, picking up the book they were using as bait. "But yes, let us get this over with." They gathered around Avalon and with a thought and rush of magic, they vanished.

They appeared a short distance from the beach, just far enough away Kippering was highly unlikely to sense their presence. "Be careful," Avalon said, and knelt to kiss Caliburn farewell before striding off.

The beach was dark, windy, and bracingly cold. Caliburn growled unhappily. Avalon wished he'd brought his greatcoat, but hopefully they would not be there long.

A short distance down the beach he could see fire, and the taste of magic was sharp on the air. He walked toward it, unsurprised as he drew close to see Barra and the Holy Pendragon in the center of a circle of fire that lined a spell cage. Both were unconscious, the baby gently cradled in Barra's arms.

Kippering stood on the far side of the fire, looking exactly as Avalon had expected—neither young nor old in appearance, probably somewhere between fifty and a hundred years of age. Respectable, even impressive, for normals. But amongst nightwalkers he was still very much a piddling child.

His magic was remarkable, and Avalon wouldn't be surprised to learn that he'd encountered the man's bloodline before. He was spindly, with muddy brown hair and eyes, slightly crooked spectacles on his face, and clothes that had been fashionable once but now looked only sad and faded.

"So you are the pathetic fool behind all this nonsense," Avalon said. "To be frank, I am underwhelmed."

"Watch your words and tone, Highness," Kippering

snarled. "You may be the lofty prince and demon's whelp, but I am the one who will leave your precious mongrel and baby dead should you cross me."

Avalon examined the spell cage more closely, then Barra, where he could now just see the runes around his neck, glowing faintly here and there as the firelight caught them. A chaining spell, precisely as Caliburn had said. A mean and nasty variation on the bonding magic that was so vital to countless corners of the nightwalker world, the most well-known version of it the consort bond.

The bastardization around Barra's throat meant that if Barra died, Kippering would be fine. If Kippering was harmed or killed, however, Barra would suffer the same. Chaining spells took hours to build and cast, and it was not something Avalon could simply break apart right there. The only one who could easily break it was Kippering, and he wasn't going to do so lightly.

But now that he'd stepped out of the shadows, Kippering was nothing Avalon had not seen a thousand times before.

Thunder rolled, and far out over the ocean, lightning flashed.

Avalon shifted his gaze back to Kippering. "Let them go or I am going to cease being nice."

"Nice? Is that how you're trying to pretend to yourself that I have bested and outsmarted you at every turn?"

"You've proven to be quite the challenge," Avalon said. Thunder rolled again, slightly louder—loud enough to cover the sound of flapping wings as a raven alighted on the branch of a tree several paces behind Kippering. "I am not so weak I need to lie to myself about being bested. It's a waste of time and energy.

You, however, have much to learn about arrogance and decision making."

Kippering sneered, though his eyes were not filled with nearly as much bravado as he thought. "Give me the bloody books and we can go our separate ways."

Avalon laughed, the sound as chilly as the wind slicing down the beach, the sound of a demon who'd finally tired of playing by human rules. "Do you think so? You act this way—desperate and malicious and murderous—because you are greedy and ambitious, but also because you realized too late your employer is a man you would have been better off refusing. You're afraid of him, and what he will do to you should you return to him empty-handed."

Kippering's face flushed. "How dare—" He stopped as thunder cracked-boomed, momentarily muting the rest of the world.

"You will have more to fear from me, whatever you do this night, unless you somehow manage to mollify me," Avalon said. "You know what I am, but maybe you should have put more thought into what it means to tangle with the Prince of Dragons who is also the son of a demon. Not only have you stolen away a Holy Pendragon, an innocent child who did you no wrong, a dragon infinitely precious to us and worth killing for. In addition to that crime, the men you kidnapped are my consorts, though I've not yet had time to bond them. So go ahead and kill him, run away and try to hide. How well do you think you'll succeed knowing you murdered a demon's consort and that demon has the power to leave his territory?"

All the color drained from Kippering's already pale skin, and he seemed to sway ever so slightly.

"Release them right now and I'll let you live. You

can run and hide from your angry employer, hope he is more interested in the books than in revenge. Or you can continue to haggle for the books, and whether you let Barra and the Holy Pendragon go or not, your life will be counted in hours if you're lucky, minutes if you're not."

Kippering's face filled with hate, for which Avalon could not blame him—but that did not mean he particularly cared.

Finally Kippering collapsed. "You'll let me live?"

"Yes."

Kippering nodded, and with a flick of his wrist, banished the flames around the spell cage. He stepped past it, knelt, and with a few muttered words, broke the chain.

Avalon threw out his hands and cast the spell he'd used to kill the men in the church. Off in the distance, Caliburn and Troyes roared.

Midnight cawed and flew over to him, shifting as he landed in the sand. He tossed his hair over his shoulder and laughed. "You really are a demon. That was remarkable."

Shoving Kippering's body out of the way, Avalon crouched and went to work on the manacles at Barra's ankles and wrists. "Despicable hellspawn, that's me," he agreed.

Midnight flinched. "I should have made Devlin apologize for that. I completely forgot about it after his assault."

Avalon didn't reply, more interested in making certain Barra was really and truly well. Minus some bruises, a black eye, and bloody lip, he seemed well. He carefully extracted the Holy Pendragon, tears stinging his eyes as the baby cooed and nuzzled closer.

Thank the heavens. Finally, *finally* everyone was safe.

And he would never be stupid enough to put them all in danger ever again, and neither would he be creating a new Steward. Duties would have to be shifted, even if that meant he would have to take them up again himself. Trusting them to someone else clearly had not been the right idea, anyway.

Or you could make your consorts your Steward and Seneschal. Barra would be good at it, and we already know Neirin was all but born for the role of Steward.

Avalon ignored that, too, slowly standing as the others reached him.

"You have a flare for the dramatic, Highness, that pales the rest of ours combined," Devlin drawled.

"I wouldn't go that far, Heartbeat. You can be delightfully melodramatic when you're in a snit," Midnight said as he hefted Kippering's body and waded into the water to consign it to the sea.

Caliburn rumbled and came to sit next to Avalon, resting heavily against his legs. *Time to go home and put all to rights.*

"Yes," Avalon said, and when the others looked at him said, "Caliburn says it's time to go home and put all to rights. Shall we?"

Neirin's eyes were dark and pensive as he stared at Avalon, Barra cradled in his arms. Troyes growled softly beside him.

When they'd all gathered in and were ready, Avalon took them to their townhouse. Before any of them could realize or protest, not that he thought they would, he vanished again to finally take the Holy Pendragon home.

Consorts

The people milling in the ward cried out as they realized Avalon and Caliburn had returned with the Holy Pendragon. They clustered around him, laughing and cheering and crying, hugging him and kissing the baby, clamoring loudly as they demanded to know how in the world it had been done.

Avalon had told his council what Linden and his conspirators had managed, and the news had trickled through all the clan, but knowing and seeing were different.

"Move, move, move," Amy grumbled as she shoved her way through the crowd. She bowed her head. "Highness. Took you long enough."

Avalon laughed. "Yes, indeed. Drag the council out of bed, see the primary candidates are summoned. Let's see if we can't get our poor boy to where he belongs. I'll be in the den." He disentangled himself from the crowd after a last few hugs, kissing several cheeks on his way, promising to relate the whole tale at dinner in a week or two.

After he'd had time to put together a version of events he felt comfortable sharing.

The den was a large room immediately behind the great hall, laid heavily with wards and kept always at temperatures comfortable for dragons and utterly miserable for most humans. There were currently three nests, the dragons who'd laid the eggs sleeping in the middle of the room, twined together and rumbling at each other in their sleep.

Assistant dragons were all around, watching over the eggs while the mothers rested, along with knights to keep them in food and water and company. There was no proper furniture, minus tables to work on when managing the food, merely a few piles of cushions and pillows in sunken nooks.

Avalon headed for the largest of these nooks and set the baby down in a pile of cushions. Then he stripped out of everything save his breeches and shirt, already sweaty from the damp heat.

One of the mothers stirred—Magdalena, thirty years old, large and hale, and of a demeanor that left her unimpressed with the glory of the Holy Pendragon who'd mated her, which made Caliburn all the more fond of her.

She had not, however, been above preening loud and long about the Holy Pendragon egg she'd laid, and they'd had to put her to sleep for a time after she'd realized the egg had been stolen.

Growling inquisitively, she padded up to the baby and sniffed it over thoroughly—then whined happily and burrowed into the cushions to wrap around him. Caliburn rumbled and stretched out so he lay in a half circle around her and Avalon.

Avalon reached out to pet Magdalena's head, and she lifted it just enough to nuzzle and lick before going back to the baby. Smiling, Avalon rested back against Caliburn and closed his eyes. It would take a few hours for everyone to arrive from the other clans, and there was no telling how long it would take to see if there might be a worthy match amongst the first round of candidates.

Gentle shaking stirred him awake some hours later, and he dragged his eyes reluctantly open. "Yes?"

Amy smiled. "The candidates are gathered, Highness."

"Thank you. Send them in, but keep it small, groups of four. I do not want Magdalena or the Pendragon stressed further."

"Yes, Highness." She bowed her head and strode off.

Avalon hefted himself up to sit on the floor, legs hanging over the edge into the nook. He unwound his mussed hair and rebraided and bound it. There was nothing to be done with his clothes, but the situation was hardly the normal affair with all the ceremony and trimmings.

The first three groups, twelve candidates total, were all from le Fay. None of them matched, and only one of them met his eyes at all, clearly feeling ashamed that some of their own had been party to such a deep betrayal.

It was the seventh group where they found success. As the latest batch entered the room, the baby shrieked and a young man of fifteen, part of the ruling family of Clan von Blumenthal, cried out in surprise. His eyes turned dragon gold, and he nearly toppled to the floor as the power rushed through him. His father caught him up and helped him finish walking across the room.

Avalon inclined his head to Chief Blumenthal, then to the boy. "Congratulations, Prince Redford."

The boy flushed and sputtered an answer to the floor—and jerked when his father gave him a hard nudge. "Thank you, Your Highness, for giving me a chance. I am most honored to be considered worthy by a Holy Pendragon. I will take care of him, should doing so cost me my life."

"I have every faith," Avalon said softly. "Come and greet your dragon."

The baby whined and cried, wriggling helplessly. Redford knelt in the mass of pillows, smiled at Magdalena, and gingerly took the baby—which immediately turned back into a dragon.

Avalon rose. He motioned for the other candidates to go, and Amy bustled them out, leaving only Redford, his parents, and their dragons. "Do please stay and get acquainted. There will be a banquet in celebration in a few days. If it's no trouble, I would like for Prince Redford at least to remain for several months to train—and so Magdalena can spend more time with her kit before he is taken to von Blumenthal."

"Of course, Your Highness. We'll make the arrangements at once."

"Then if you will excuse me, I would like to find my bed and rest properly. I will see you at the banquet." He embraced them all, kissed their cheeks, and took his leave.

Caliburn caught up to him in the great hall, and they walked in silence back to their chambers.

"Your Highness," one of the guards greeted. "We went ahead and let your guests inside to wait for you. I know it's against protocol, but it seemed appropriate in this case."

Anxiety and anticipation drove away Avalon's exhaustion. "You were correct, thank you. If anyone else comes by, I am not to be disturbed until further notice, save for an emergency."

Caliburn rumbled happily and led the way inside.

The door closed behind them, and Avalon stayed close to it, staring across the room at the men sitting in the nook where earlier they'd waited for Caliburn's return.

Troyes was already by the fire, resting there like he'd done it a hundred times. Caliburn prodded Avalon forward then went to join Troyes, rumbling in greeting as he joined him, the two dragons happy to rest together and leave the humans to sort themselves out.

Neirin stood first. He and Barra had both washed and dressed in fresh clothes, looking far too handsome and refreshed, leaving Avalon feeling at a messy, sweaty, exhausted disadvantage.

Barra rose and fell into step just behind Neirin as they crossed the room.

Neirin's eyes held Avalon's as they drew to a halt in front of him. "I believe there was a discussion you wanted to have, Highness, and now there is plenty of time to have it."

"Shouldn't you be at the townhouse resting still?"

"We are doing well, thanks to you," Neirin said. "If you think avoiding the matter will get you anywhere, you are mistaken." He stepped in closer, the scent of his soap, like a forest and fresh fallen snow, wafting over Avalon. He braced one hand on the door next to Avalon's head. "You must know by now we're untroubled by the fact you're half-demon. I am more intrigued to know if what Midnight told us is true."

Damn it, he'd been so focused on Kippering he'd forgotten Midnight would have been able to hear everything he said. "I have no idea—"

Neirin kissed him, his other hand coming up to curl into Avalon's hair to force him to hold still. It was a hard kiss, stinging and punishing, and left Avalon's lips sore when he finally drew away. "I do not know why you're trying to push us away, but it's not going to work."

"So you want to be chained again?" Avalon asked bitterly and shoved him hard, sending Neirin stumbling into Barra. "I remember when you were a little boy, you know. Sweet and happy and open. Bit by bit your family smothered you, until you never smiled unless it was with Troyes and you thought no one else could see. Midnight was right: you are my consorts, because I am demon enough to have such a thing. But I saw how you withered here, and how you flourished out there, and I know how wolves and elves feel when they are caged. I'll not chain anyone to my side, no matter how much they think they want to be there. Everyone changes their mind eventually, and affection always turns to hate. How much worse would that be when you're so bound to me you can't even leave me without breaking the bond and hurting or even killing all of us? I won't do it." He pushed past them and vanished into his washroom, where he closed and locked the door.

Though he was tempted to linger he showered quickly and stepped out—and realized only then that he hadn't thought to grab a dressing robe first. He was too used to being alone. More than once he'd thought of having the rooms connected, but he hated having people in his space and it had never really mattered since he was always alone.

Caliburn.

Already doing it.

Thank you.

He unlocked the door, and a moment later it opened just enough for Caliburn to slip inside. He held out one of Avalon's dressing robes, emerald green with paler leaves and gold roses, lined in matching gold. Helping Avalon into it, he then pulled him in close and kissed him, petting and soothing.

Did they leave? Avalon asked, resting heavily against Caliburn's chest.

No. They look sad, but sad for you. If a consort is supposed to be someone who can out-stubborn you, then I think you definitely have found yours. And I certainly think two is perfect.

Until they turn to hating me.

You have given people far less worthy a chance. Why give less of a chance to men who have already proven they are worthy of you?

Avalon smiled against Caliburn's chest. *Approval of the Holy Pendragon, that is a rarity.* He looked up, met Caliburn halfway, and kissed him softly.

Caliburn withdrew and shifted. He pulled the door open and returned to his place by the fire. Avalon hurried into his dressing room, feeling eyes on him but unable to look their way.

There seemed little point in fully dressing, whatever happened. He pulled on trousers, socks, and an old, worn and faded shirt, only pulling the laces loosely closed, too restless and tired to bother with more. He brushed out his hair, which he'd been too tired to wash this time, and wrapped it into a loose knot.

Seemed he'd run out of ways to avoid and stall.

Taking a deep breath, he rose from his dressing table and left the safety of his dressing room.

And nearly walked right into them. He tried to back pedal but reacted too late. Instead of safely at a distance, he was pulled right into them, one arm wrapping around Barra's shoulders for balance, his other hand held firmly by Neirin's, who was pressed against his other side. "What are you doing?"

"What I always have to do when you suffer-alone types get unbearable," Barra replied, and leaned up to kiss him.

He was as sweet as Avalon remembered, but there was a toothiness to it this time, a stubbornness that would be necessary in the company he kept. Avalon tried to pull back, but all he got for his efforts was a hand in his hair holding him firmly in place.

Barra drew back, looking flushed and decidedly pleased with himself. Avalon's head was turned and then it was Neirin's mouth taking his. This kiss was worse than the last three he'd stolen because it was slow and savoring. Oh, he'd missed this more than he'd ever wanted to admit to himself. He'd always been happiest when he'd had two lovers rather than one.

You knew what you needed the whole time; you just had to wait for them to be born, Caliburn said, voice heavy and slow, and in the next moment, he was fast asleep.

Reluctantly breaking the kiss, Avalon said, "Ignoring all the other reasons you're making a mistake, you do realize I am over six hundred years old?"

"And yet still too stubborn for your own good," Neirin replied. "We're a century old, and I have you to thank for that. At some point, it stops mattering. Now cease arguing with us." He kissed Avalon again, one hand slipping beneath his loose shirt to skate across his skin.

Another hand slid across his stomach, hot where

Neirin's hand was almost cool against his back. Avalon shivered and kissed Neirin harder, until he was abruptly torn away and kissing Barra once more.

Neirin slid away and Avalon twined around Barra, consigning good sense to the wind as he kissed him thoroughly, sucking and nibbling at those full lips, dragging his tongue across them before pushing in deep. The more he kissed, the sweeter Barra became, with that undercurrent of wolf adding a fine bite.

There was nothing sweet, and everything deliciously wicked, about the hands that skimmed his body and rested firmly on his backside. Avalon drew back and licked Barra's lips again. "Something more you want, pretty wolf?"

"No one ever uses my name," Barra complained with a smile. "You get a name. Neirin gets a name. I just get wolf-elf or pretty wolf or—"

"Sweet wolf," Avalon cut in and kissed him again, cupping Barra's face, fingers just barely dusting the beautiful red curls. "You're too pretty not to use endearments."

Barra huffed. "That's what Neirin always says." His eyes flicked past Avalon, hot approval filling them.

Turning around, Avalon had to agree completely—until Neirin turned to set his shirt with the rest of his already discarded clothes, and his horribly scarred back was visible. Avalon's ardor cooled, but as much as he wanted to retreat, that wouldn't do.

Instead he walked over to Neirin and rested his palms right in the center of his back, where the scars were most severe.

Neirin twisted sharply around and caught his wrist. "None of that. I can see it in your face and I'm telling you we're not having that discussion. It was more than seventy years ago, and I remember every word of protest that the council ignored." He cut Avalon's words off with a kiss then pulled away and deftly yanked Avalon's shirt off, skimming a hand down Avalon's chest. His eyes were hot and bright with approval as he teased his thumbs over the silver and emerald hoops in Avalon's nipples. "I used to hear rumors of these. I thought the guards were having a laugh at my expense."

"Rumors of what?" Barra asked as he came to join them. His mouth dropped, face going brilliant red as he saw the rings. "Caliburn has them. I assumed it must be a dragon thing. I thought when I glimpsed them before I must have imagined..." He trailed off, face flushing even further as Neirin and Avalon both laughed. "Oh, be quiet."

Neirin kissed him, pulling Barra close and holding him with the grace of a man who'd done that very thing more times than could be counted. And oh, wasn't that the loveliest sight in the world, Neirin and Barra tangled together, kissing and touching like there was nothing else they'd rather do.

Before Avalon could decide whether he was content watching or wanted to try touching, they drew apart and Neirin made quick work of his remaining clothes and all of Barra's.

Then they turned to Avalon, and in short order he was naked as well.

Neirin's fingers went to his hair. "You'll tangle it hopelessly," Avalon protested, but let Neirin pull his fingers away before he finished the job, the loose knot coming free easily.

The looks they gave him then were worth the tangles he'd spend forever combing out.

"I'll fix it later," Barra said. "I'm good at it."

Avalon kissed him instead of replying. Barra's hard cock rubbed against his skin, leaving wet trails. Neirin pushed up behind him, teeth and mouth working on Avalon's throat, sending shivers down his spine. Barra broke away from the kiss and put his mouth other places, starting with Avalon's collarbone and working down to his nipples. His movements were hesitant at first, like he was afraid of causing harm, but when he tugged one more firmly than he'd clearly meant and got a very telling reaction, he grinned and worked them in earnest.

Caught between them, unable to escape, Avalon moaned and whimpered and held on for dear life. "We—we should move to the bedroom, unless you really want to risk my rugs."

Neirin chuckled and withdrew. "I think bed sounds like a fine idea."

His bedroom was dimly lit, only two old, flickering lamps casting any light on the tester bed and other rich green and gold furnishings. Avalon climbed into his bed and dragged them with him, laughing as he was toppled over and straddled by Barra.

Leaning down, Barra braced his hands on either side of Avalon's head and kissed him breathless, not stopping until Avalon's chest ached and his lips throbbed. Neirin slid a hand into Barra's curls and drew him into a kiss, and Avalon was more than happy to enjoy the view—but this time he touched, teasing along Neirin's thigh, wrapping his other hand around Barra's cock and stroking, savoring the full-body shudder that elicited.

"I could spend hours simply watching the two of you," Avalon murmured as they drew apart. "I would check on you from time to time in my mirror, make certain you were well. Nothing untoward, and I never watched something I shouldn't, but I always wished I could."

Neirin leaned down to kiss him, hard and hungry, dragging his teeth along Avalon's jaw and down his throat to bite at the mark he'd left earlier. He nipped Avalon's earlobe. "Watch all you like." Drawing back, he dragged Barra off Avalon and toward the foot of the bed, put him on his knees and elbows. Settling behind him, Neirin folded himself against Barra and slowly kissed his way down Barra's spine, fingers teasing along his skin all the while. The flush on Barra's face spread down his neck and across his shoulders, making his freckles stand out sharply.

"Do you have something to ease the way?" Neirin asked.

It took Avalon a moment to tear his eyes from Barra's face and comprehend the words, but when he did, he twisted and crawled over to the little set of drawers on the far side of the bed and pulled out one of his jars—this particular lubricant faintly gold in color and scented of honeysuckle.

Crawling back over to them he held the jar out to Neirin—and nearly dropped it as Barra's mouth sucked at the tip of his cock. He dropped his free hand to Barra's hair, twining his fingers through those soft curls and groaning as Barra took more of him.

Barra moaned around Avalon's cock as Neirin's fingers worked him open. Avalon gripped his curls tighter, using his free hand to stroke Barra's cheek, tracing the edge of his mouth where it was stretched around Avalon's cock, then back to scrape nails along his neck and trace the line of his spine. He kept his hips to small, gentle thrusts, savoring Barra's wet, hot mouth, the feel of his tongue and the way his throat worked. Barra knew what he was about, and Avalon had no trouble imagining all the ways he'd acquired such skill.

He watched avidly as Neirin slicked his cock and slowly slid into Barra's body, admiring the heavy, scarred hands that gripped Barra's hips. Neirin met Avalon's gaze and loosed one hand to drag him over far enough to kiss him hard and wet and messy. Then he pulled back, a hot glint in his eyes. "Still watching, Highness?"

"Don't call me that," Avalon replied, but forgot what else he'd wanted to say as Neirin laughed and started moving, fucking Barra with long, deep strokes that pushed him further onto Avalon's cock, making both of them moan and Neirin laugh even more.

The laughter soon faded, however, as Neirin focused on fucking, driving into Barra harder and faster. Avalon shuddered with every thrust, every taunting pull of that too-talented mouth. It took everything he had to hold on, but it was worth it as Neirin sank in deep one last time and came with a hoarse cry.

Neirin withdrew and Avalon pulled out as well, flipping Barra onto his back and bending to swallow his cock. Barra screamed, hands flailing, finally finding purchase in Avalon's soft sheets, and he thrust gracelessly, desperately, into Avalon's mouth.

Heat pressed up behind Avalon, a slick finger gently pushing into him, a rough, calloused hand wrapping around his cock and stroking him off while the first finger stroked inside him. It was all Avalon could take, and he moaned his release even as Barra cried out and spilled down his throat.

It took a bit of effort and coordination, but eventually they all settled comfortably in the large bed—though Avalon couldn't say how he'd wound up in the middle when he was certain Barra and Neirin would prefer to be next to each other.

But he couldn't muster the strength to protest, especially when it felt so nice. With his face resting against Barra's shoulder, and Neirin's arm heavy around his waist, Avalon fell asleep smiling.

He woke gasping, hard and aching, writhing in the sheets as sleepiness warred with the images flooding his mind and the sensations being shared. "Caliburn—" He broke off moaning, clinging to his pillow and rutting against the sheets. *I'm going to kill you.*

"What..." Neirin sat up, messy hair in his face, eyes fogged with sleep, blinking in confusion as he stared at Avalon. "What's wrong?"

"Our dragons—" Avalon turned, wrapped a hand around his cock. "Our dragons are having fun with Barra and Caliburn thought it would be amusing to share with me."

The sleepiness vanished from Neirin's face. He sat up and moved to settle between Avalon's thighs. "And what are they doing with our pretty wolf?" He leaned over and snatched up something out of Avalon's sight—but it became pretty clear what it was when slick fingers teased at Avalon's hole. Neirin knocked Avalon's hand away and replaced it with his own. "Give me details."

Avalon groaned, dizzy and hot and frustrated, caught between too many sensations. "Settee. The settee," he gasped out. "They bent him over the arm of the settee and are having fun taking turns."

"There's a lovely idea," Neirin replied, and stopped tormenting him to slick his cock and nudge at Avalon's hole. He pushed in slightly and resumed stroking, going a little deeper with every thrust. By the time he was fully inside, Avalon wasn't certain which he'd do first: come or pass out. He moaned at the onslaught of images and sensations and the feel of Neirin fucking and stroking him. "I never thought I'd get to see you like this, and what a tragedy that would have been."

Avalon didn't even bother trying to muster a reply, just reached up to cling to Neirin's shoulders as Neirin let go of Avalon's cock to grab his hips and fuck him in earnest.

Overwhelmed with it all, Avalon lasted only moments and screamed as he came, nails biting into Neirin's shoulders.

Neirin kept going, fucking steadily into Avalon's spent, pliant body, sweat dripping from his brow, gleaming on his skin in the light of the remaining lamp. Finally he gave a few last, hard, jerking thrusts and sank in deep, leaning down to kiss Avalon hard as his release washed over him.

They lay there panting for several minutes, Avalon occasionally whimpering as Caliburn tortured him for a few more minutes. "I'm going to go kill him." He sat up with a wince at sore muscles, swung out of bed, and shrugged into one of the dressing robes hanging nearby before heading out to the main chamber.

Where Caliburn and Troyes were sitting on the floor, backs against the edge of the settee, looking extremely pleased with themselves. Behind them, draped on an abandoned dressing robe on the settee, was Barra. He was sweaty and messy, and looked equal parts dazed and exhausted.

"You're incorrigible," Avalon said.

"Pretty wolf, wanted to play," Caliburn said with a shrug. Beside him, Troyes gave a toothy smile.

Kissed him yet?

Caliburn scowled at him.

Oh, and who was lecturing me on stalling?

I'm not stalling. I'm taking my time. There's a difference.

Avalon laughed out loud, drawing confused looks from all of them, save Caliburn, whose look promised revenge. "Some brave and mighty Holy Pendragon."

Caliburn growled but conceded defeat. He turned to Troyes, who was watching him with confusion, and kissed him. Troyes jerked in surprise, but Caliburn chased him, kissed him more firmly, and after a moment, Troyes rumbled softly and returned it.

Barra shook his head in confusion and went back to dozing.

Neirin, however, was watching with mouth open. "Dragons don't do that."

"How many six-hundred-year-old dragons have you met?" Avalon asked. "Caliburn gets as lonely as me; most dragons are too intimidated and in awe."

"Troyes used to be," Neirin replied with a soft smile. "I don't know when he got over that."

Drawing back, cheeks flushed pink, Troyes looked at Neirin and growled softly.

"Go back to kissing your pretty new friend and stop being a brat," Neirin said.

Troyes growled louder at that but didn't protest when Caliburn abruptly knocked him over and went about some much more thorough kisses.

Avalon stepped carefully around them and scooped up Barra. His head lolled against Avalon's shoulder, and he smiled as Avalon kissed his temple. He settled Barra in a large reading chair in a small seating area often overlooked and forgotten as it was hidden by bookcases, plants, and various contraptions hanging from the ceiling. The walls were entirely glass from about the height of the sofa all the way up to the ceiling, which was also glass. It had been a greenhouse at one point and overlooked his mess of a garden on one side, but he was terrible with plants and had finally given up ages ago minus the few on one of his work tables.

Going to his dressing room, he fetched a new robe for Barra, pausing on the way to ring for tea. After handing off the robe, he went over to a section of wall between two bookcases that contained a safe and various locked drawers and cupboards of various sizes. He unlocked one, opened one of the many little drawers it contained, and pulled out the two rings there—one only recently replaced after he'd taken it from Linden's fingers.

Both were made of gold, but the Steward ring was set with a square cut emerald, the Seneschal's ring set with a sapphire. Both were heavily spelled.

With a thought, he summoned his sword as well, still in its charm shape, dangling from a gold chain.

Barra was still more asleep than awake when he returned, but Neirin's expression was sharp and knowing. "So may I now assume that you are going to give us a chance and not get rid of us for our own good? Binding ourselves to you isn't the same as chaining."

"I know," Avalon said quietly. "At least, I am willing to trust you and work on really believing it. I do not think I can bind you the way Sable will someday bind his consort. It's strange what he and I have in common, and where my human elements change things. But if you are willing, I will make you my Steward again." He offered the emerald ring to Neirin, who accepted it, then took hold of his fingers and kissed them, smiling when Avalon frowned at him.

Turning to Barra, Avalon offered the sapphire ring. "We've not had a Seneschal for a long time, but I think it's a position that would suit you. Do not feel obliged; if you'd rather stay with Devlin and Midnight, I understand."

Barra smiled shyly and reached out to take the ring. "They'll learn to get on without me. Before we came here, we took them to the new house Mistress Amy said you'd had prepared. They seemed quite pleased with their new home. It will take time, but I think they'll settle into their new life just fine. So will we. Seneschal sounds a bit much for me, but I'm willing to learn."

Neirin snorted. "It's like taking care of Devlin but a bigger house and a larger number of arrogant, insufferable prats."

Barra laughed and, after looking at Neirin, slid it onto the middle finger of his left hand. He jerked slightly as the magic worked to fit it to his finger—and seal it so that it could not be removed by anyone else save Avalon.

Finally Avalon held out the sword charm. "You're my Steward, and you've always been better with a sword than me, so I entrust this to your keeping."

Neirin nodded and took it, pulling it over his head to rest around his neck, the gold gleaming against his light skin. He reached out and pulled Avalon down to sit next to him, stretching out his legs to sprawl more comfortably on the large, deep sofa. "How long do you think until Devlin shows up?"

"Oh, I think he's rather more enamored of that house than he wanted to admit to anyone," Barra said. "It was kind of you to give it to them."

"No one else was using it, and honestly, it seemed to suit." Avalon shrugged one shoulder. "I admit I was also hoping it might mean you were close by, even if I never saw you."

"I think you're going to see all of us more than you wanted," Neirin said with a smile.

"Not possible," Avalon said softly, going easily when Neirin drew him into a kiss.

A moment later Barra joined them. Avalon yawned and succumbed to the urge to simply stay right where he was pressed up against Neirin, soaking in his warmth with Barra resting heavily against his other side. He closed his eyes, content to bask in the fingers combing gently through his hair, Caliburn's happy thoughts at the back of his mind, and the anticipation that he wouldn't wake up alone.

Fin

New Beginnings
Bonus Short

Devlin stared through the window down at the garden. Well, what had once been a garden. Currently it was a mix of weeds grown wild, dead flowers, and a few scraggly trees that should be put out of their misery. But that was good, because he could simply have the dead garden torn out and start fresh. He would pay whomever he needed in the clan to create a night garden that would make Midnight smile for days.

The clan...

How had he gone from consultant to London's demon lord and the last remaining White to... well, a ghost. There'd been an announcement in the papers, and he'd managed to learn that a funeral of sorts had been arranged.

The attendance had not been small, and it had been gratifying that the demon he'd helped for so many years had said exceedingly kind things... But overall, Devlin was left with an impression of relief. People were sad, but not unhappy, that the Mad Duke and his odd family had been laid to rest.

Had he become so unpleasant?

But even his ego wasn't so fragile. He'd become that powerful, and this abrupt upheaval in his life was due to powerful people. All of them human. Even demons did not care for humans who lived long enough to grow as powerful as Devlin was coming to be—especially with the strange effects caused by his bond with Midnight.

He could handle most of the world being relieved he was dead. The hardest part was his house being so empty. Smaller, not as grand, those were trivial things. But it was only him and Midnight, and his closest friends living in the castle as consorts to a half-demon prince.

It suited them, though he'd be damned if he said it aloud. Neirin would be so unbearably smug there'd be no living with him.

As lonely as the house felt without the noise of a family going about their day, it wasn't all bad. He was, at heart, an eminently selfish man, and now he had Midnight wholly to himself. Barra and Neirin were close by, and Avalon...

Well, he wasn't anywhere near as odious as Devlin had wanted him to be, but so it went. Hard to hate a man after witnessing twice the way he looked at Neirin when he forgot there were other people around, as he had in the church, or when he thought he was alone, as he had in the room where Neirin had been recovering from his kidnapping.

And there was the delightful book detailing how to make himself sorcery gloves. They'd never replace proper rune casting, but they would be fun.

Perhaps it was time for change. He'd never cared much, but mostly because he'd never thought he would live long. Witches in general had a relatively short life expectancy, given the dangerous lives they generally led, and the Whites especially were known for getting themselves killed at a brisk pace.

So, yes, it was long past time to try something new. Being a ghost wasn't all bad so far. The clan element he was less enthusiastic about, but he'd adjust. Even if His Highness insisted on paying his witch consultant a stipend and the others had finally made Devlin accept it.

"Brooding, Heartbeat?"

"I never brood," Devlin replied, turning away from the window, clasping his hands behind his back. "I was pondering the finer points of the night garden I plan to have installed."

Midnight's face brightened, boyishly open in happiness in a way even time could not to diminish. "Really?"

"What else would I do with all that space?"

Midnight laughed, tossed his long, loose wavy hair over one shoulder as he crossed the empty room to join Devlin at the window. Most of the downstairs rooms had been properly furnished, but with only the two of them, there was plenty of space left over and he was in no hurry to decide what to do with it. Other than combine two or three of them into one large room so Midnight could have his own version of Avalon's laboratory. Devlin was ashamed he'd never thought of such a thing before.

"You're brooding again."

"I am not."

Midnight draped an arm behind his neck and dragged Devlin down to brush a soft kiss across his mouth. Devlin chased him when he tried to pull away, because he damn well wanted more of a kiss than that. Midnight laughed against his lips and complied, slow and sweet and deliciously thorough.

He'd come a long way from the little brat who'd once lied about his amorous skills in the hopes of finally getting Devlin to see him as more than a ward. *Dark. Love. Lies.*

It had worked, in a strange and needlessly difficult away, but Devlin would go to his *actual* grave before admitting that. Especially as he knew full well he'd been the difficult part.

He rested a hand lightly against the small of Midnight's back and drew back just enough to say, "You're being awfully sweet this evening. Are you distracting me, trying to soothe me before I get angry about something, or in want of something?"

"So suspicious. Maybe I just woke up needing you and the bed was empty." He draped his other arm around Devlin's neck and drew him into another kiss.

Devlin savored it for several minutes but eventually drew back again and reached up to remove Midnight's arms. "You're only sweet and pliant when something is afoot. If you simply wanted a fuck, you would have come in here naked, my shameless dark angel."

Midnight sighed, resting his hands on Devlin's biceps. "I was walking about the village last night while you were with Avalon. There was a woman complaining to a friend that her cat had recently had kittens and they were big enough to start getting into trouble, and she was glad they all had places to go, minus one."

"You want a cat? You want a *pet*?"

Midnight's shoulders sagged. "Do you hate the idea that much?"

"Why on earth would you want some yowling, flea-bitten menace prowling about leaving dead mice and fur everywhere?"

The smile on Midnight's face flickered, faded, came back distinctly forced. "It was only an idea. Cats aren't scared of me the way most animals are, and we've always been too busy and gone for anything but the horses, and even those we had to stable elsewhere most of the time..." He leaned up and kissed Devlin again. "Stop brooding and come have dinner while it's still hot." He stepped away and turned to go.

Devlin knew there had been days when he could refuse such a request without a second thought. When he had been the lofty lord of the manor everyone obeyed. He knew those days had existed, but he couldn't remember them and honestly didn't want to.

"Just because I don't understand the appeal doesn't mean I'm forbidding it," Devlin said, and sighed. "It's not like you need my permission, anyway. As you oft remind me, you're my lover, not my ward. Although, in all things, you remain a spoiled brat."

"You have no one but yourself to blame for that," Midnight replied—then launched himself across the room and into Devlin's arms, sending him slamming into the windows, cracking his head against the frames. "Sorry."

Devlin's mouth tipped in a half-smile. "I'm long used to being shoved into things, for one reason or another. At least I tend to enjoy your reasons."

"I still hate when I accidentally hurt you." Midnight drew back, a cloud falling over him that only ever came when he hated or feared his own nature. He was as beautiful as his namesake and as compelling as the stars, but a lifetime was not enough, it seemed, to make him stop seeing himself as a monster.

"It's called exuberance," Devlin replied, grabbing

hold of his wrist and reeling him back in. "Stop fussing over my hard head knocking against a bit of wood, and let's return to the part where you were seducing me into letting you have a kitten."

Midnight smiled, braced his hands on Devlin's chest, and leaned up to kiss him. He was always slightly cooler than Devlin, but by no means cold or less alive. Whatever crass remarks and taunts had been made over the years about Devlin fucking a corpse—and on a few charming occasions, a child's corpse—Midnight was vibrantly, beautifully alive.

He was so intent on the sweet, bratty mouth, he nearly missed the fingers working deftly at his clothes. But there was no missing when they wrapped around his cock and pulled it free of his trousers.

Midnight drew away from the kiss, and Devlin protested briefly, but words and thoughts were gladly forgotten as Midnight sank to his knees and swallowed Devlin's cock.

His head thunked against the window again, but Devlin barely noticed, far more interested in burying a hand in Midnight's untamable hair and thrusting over and over into that wicked mouth that drove him mad in too many ways to count, left him infuriated one moment, awed speechless the next, and on the verge of begging the moment after that.

Midnight looked up at Devlin through his long lashes, which he knew drove Devlin positively mad, added some last note of obscenity to the whole thing that sent him over the edge every time.

When Devlin had finished coming, Midnight licked his lips and wiped his chin on the handkerchief he pulled from a pocket of his trousers. Devin grabbed the front of his shirt and yanked him to his feet, kissed him hard and deep, spent cock twitching as he tasted himself in Midnight's mouth.

He reached down with his free hand and got Midnight's trousers opened, shoved a hand inside and fisted Midnight's cock, stroked it hard and fast, swallowing every moan and whimper and breathless plea. Turning around, he shoved Midnight up against the glass and moved even faster, tearing a ragged groan that sounded like his name.

But when he finally came a short time later, it was *Heartbeat* that spilled across the room.

Midnight clung to him as he slowly calmed, his hair even more of a mess than when they'd started. Devlin brushed it out of his face and gently kissed his swollen lips. When Midnight finally looked at him, Devlin lifted his other hand and thoroughly enjoyed watching Midnight lick it clean.

"Send a note to have your kitten delivered," Devlin said. "Bring dinner up to bed."

"Yes, Heartbeat," Midnight murmured, and kissed him one last time before sliding away to do as bid.

Devlin cast one last look out the window, mentally refining his garden plans to accommodate a damned cat, then headed off back to bed.

About the Author

Megan is a long time resident of queer romance, and keeps herself busy reading, writing, and publishing it. She is often accused of fluff and nonsense. When she's not involved in writing, she likes to cook, harass her wife and cats, or watch movies. She loves to hear from readers, and can be found all over the internet.

meganderr.com
patreon.com/meganderr
pillowfort.io/maderr
meganderr.blogspot.com
facebook.com/meganaprilderr
meganaderr@gmail.com
@meganaderr

Made in United States
North Haven, CT
03 June 2022

19806752R00182